VAMPIRE WARS

THIS BOOK CONTAINS EXTREME VIOLENCE AND GRAPHIC SENSUAL AND EROTIC BEHAVIOR. THERE IS ADULT LANGUAGE AND SITUATION NOT FIT FOR CHILDREN.

WITH THAT SAID PLEASE ENJOY THIS BOOK TO IT'S FULLEST.

MY BOOK COLLECTION:
VAMPIRE HERO SERIES;
BLOOD BY DAY
SHADOW'S REVENGE
SHADOW GUARD
GUARDIAN SERIES:
ENTER THE GUARDIANS: KYL
LOST ON GROT
THE ASHAN CHRONICALS:
BLACK WINGS
THE ELEMENTAL KIDS SERIES: (kids –young adult)
WORLD OF ICE
WAR FOR ICE
THE DRAGON AND FIRE SERIES (PG)
BREATH OF MAGIK
INFERNO IN TIME
RYAN THE WILDFIRE/ ALBERT YETI: (young adults)
RYAN OF THE WILDFIRE
CHARITY
ADULT VAMPIRE SERIES: (Adult)
VAMPIRE WARS: BEGINNING
THE LORDS OF ORDER SERIES: (PG)
DESTINY'S KEY
LITTLE MONSTERS (Kids) book one
THE SPRITE ADVENTURE BOOK 2 RONAN'S BOOK
GAVIN THE GNOME BOOK 3
COWARD SERIES:
TAD'S TALE
AN ASSASSIN'S TALE
ONE DARK NIGHT (VAMPIRES) EROTIC
A VILLAIN STORY?
HERO'S BLOOD
HIDDEN

VAMPIRE WARS

Distributed through LULU.com
First printing: 2009
Book Printed in America (via digital printer)
ISBN: 978-0-578-01639-9

All characters in this book are fictitious; any resemblance to an actual person is living or dead is coincidental.

COVER ART BY SCOTT BREITENSTEIN

I DEDICATE THIS BOOK TO MY FAMILY.

MAY MY STORIES ALWAYS BRING YOU WONDER AND JOY.

EVERY CHARACTER IN THE BOOK WAS INSPIRED BY AN ACTUAL PERSON, BUT THE CHARACTER ARE ALL MAKE BELIEVE AND DO NOT SADLY REFLECT ANYONE IN THE REAL WORLD.

TO ALL OF THE BEAUTIFUL WOMEN WHO INSPIRE ME TO WRITE SUCH AN EROTIC BOOK. I LOVE YOU ALL.

TO THE STRONG MEN WHO I WROTE INTO THIS BOOK MAY WE ALL LIVE UP TO THE VALOR I HAVE GIVEN US, AND MAY WE BRING A WORLD OF PLEASURE TO OUR MATES.

THE VAMPIRE WARS

THE BEGINNING

BY

W. SHANE WILSON

VAMPIRE WARS

SHANE

INDEX

VAMPIRE WARS

SHANE

VAMPIRE WARS

In the year 952BC a regal lord by the name of Brian Garrett ruled the land then called Eire, now called Ireland. He was unique in the entire world, because he was the first vampire lord who was loved and cherished by the people, not because of fear, but because he used his power to protect them. When all those years ago the land was invaded by a superior force, Brian came out of nowhere and asked the people if they would stand and fight if they thought they could win? They were afraid because they were farmers and peasants. Brian walked over and lifted a horse above his head with his bare hands. The crowd was enchanted and scared, but they watched and listened carefully to his every word. He set the animal down and strolled to the well, which he jumped up onto.

"I am a vampire, but I am not the kind to prey on the weak. I give you my solemn promise, to never taste a countryman, or allow any of my knights or myself taste innocent blood, and my blood line after me also will hold this vow precious and sacred for all time" Brian explained.

Aye, the crowd yelled back to Brian.

"So be it then, I will offer the vampire's kiss to only men and women who have already had babies, if you have not had offspring to continue your blood line, then do so now. I will offer a word of caution, you will lead a very different life and I am the absolute law, if you break my law; I will kill you dead" Brian told the people.

It was four days later and the fourteen vampire knights stood in well made armor, from the forge and hand of the lord Garrett himself. They were all so beautiful; the rest of the town's people could hardly recognize them. What the people did not know the excruciating pain they all endured during the passing as Brian called it. They all were armed with a single sword and no helmet. All of the fourteen sets of eyes were super light blue. Only Brian's eyes were a crimson-orange shade. Brian noticed the people looking at the eyes and spoke as word of warning.

"If you see their eyes go black run for your bloody lives, if you see mine go clear steer away from me, it is a bad time for us; at that time and you may be in peril if you come to near" Brian explained. "They are here to defend you, so as long as you can see next to no eye color you are safe from any enemy when they are with you".

"What about helmets, if they don't cover their heads an arrow or sword will take it off" the black smith said?

"No, they can't be killed that way, and the enemy must see our faces and eyes and know despair at their foolish decision to invade out land" Brian said.

Out of the fourteen knights only ten went to fight the invaders the other four stayed and guarded the people in the valley just above the moors. The people followed the lord Garrett and his undead knights to the battle. The Viking invaders were in the hundreds and they saw the lord and his men coming they were confused. They sent scouts around the countryside to ascertain where the ambush was going to be. The scout reported there was none, just the eleven knights walking down to meet them on the field.

"Hail, Viking horde" Brian yelled.

"Where is your army man" The big Viking in charge said.

"We are all that is required, no army is coming, and you will face only me and these good knights. We are willing at this time to accept your surrender" Brian said with a smile and a flat serious tone.

"You jest man" The Viking asked?

VAMPIRE WARS

In answer to the question, Brian's eyes turn completely white and his teeth and claws came out as did all of the knights. The peasant started down the hill, but the vampire guards stopped them. "Just watch and learn the cost of crossing the lord of these lands". The peasants were shaking from fear at the brutal ferocity their lord and his knights displayed. The Viking horde was destroyed before morning and all of the vampires gorged themselves on the enemy's blood. Brian called the guard down and he replaced them as guardian over the people. He stood there like a god covered in blood. A little boy brought him a bucket of warm water. Brian handed the boy a Viking dagger and smiled "thanks son". He poured the water slowly over his head and armor, until the bucket was empty and he was clear of blood and gore.

Strangely, the people were not afraid of the Vampire knights or the lord that ruled them. The people wanted to build a castle for Brian, he just laughed and said they were going to build a Keep to protect the people, he would live in a house like other men, and the knights would do the building because of the weight of the stones he would put in place.

True to his word the Keep was built in the months than passed calmly. Farmers still lived on and worked their land, however, if there was any trouble or another invasion, war whatever the people could go to the fully stocked Keep and survive unharmed.

Brian was a great Lord, he asked for, well nothing actually. No scarifies, or tribute of any kind. The people worried about him, to them it seemed that the lord was lonely. Brian traveled the borders of their lands to make sure the people were safe. The people offered him a fine horse, which he accepted barely ever took on patrol with him. Brian could move faster than any animal and completely quiet, so a horse was a hindrance to him if a fight broke out.

VAMPIRE WARS

One fine spring day, the glorious sun was on the fields and the people were happy and joyful. That all changed when forty knights rode over the hills and down on to the potato fields. The people ran for the keep. Five vampire knights were on the field in a heart beat. They stood like statues barring the intruder's way.

"Step aside infants; or I will be forced to punish you" A handsome man with flowing black hair said.

"NO".

"Do you really think that you can stand us off with only five knights" The man asked amused?

"Yes, and we will. We gave our oath" The knight answered calmly.

"What oath is worth your lives" He said lunging at the knights.

It all happened so fast, to fast for a human to watch. The black haired man came off his horse sword drawn, which he slashed at the knight. Only the knight was not there. When the man turned the five knight's eyes were black as onyx and their teeth were white and sharply pointed as were their finger nails, which were more like claws. Completely undaunted the man smile and went after them. All five knights pulled their swords and it sounded like thunder as the sword play rang. The man to the knight's surprise was as fast as they, and just as strong. The man was in fact beating them; they were not worried until two of their heads hit the ground free of their bodies,

"Not as good as you thought" The man said bringing his sword down in a killing blow at the nearest knight.

All time stopped as a bare hand, reach out and stopped the sword dead in the air next to the knight's throat. The man looked at the hand and traced it down the arm to the burning red eyes of Brian Garrett, both Brian and the man heard his heart stumble and skip some beats.

"Garrett" the man whispered and let go of the sword and stepped back bowing his head.

"What a mess, Val. (Brian swept the area with his eyes and then looked back at the man). You could not just send a Page and announce a visit" Brian said calmly?

"Lord he killed our brothers" A Knight said in anger!

"Val fix it" Brian ordered.

The beautiful man with long black hair and a crooked smile, walked passed the knights to the two dead ones on the ground. Val placed a head on a body, when one of the knights stopped him.

"That head goes with that body" The knight said pointing.

"My Pardon" Val answered.

The man lined up the correct head to the right body and then he did something that shocked the knights. He cut his wrist and let the blood flow into the dead knight's mouth. Suddenly the knight sat up and looked into Val's eyes and smiled. Val repeated this process and the other knight did exactly the same thing.

"You would have thought they would be angry" One knight said out loud?

(Brian and Val both smiled).

"Not at all, in Val's blood is the knowledge of what he just did, it is very unlikely that they will ever want to fight Val again, they are blood you see, as all of you and I are blood, kin if you will my knights" Brian told them. "We are hard to kill".

The army and the knights went to the Keep. Brian asked the people if they could cook some food for the visitors, but Val said no. He brought along a cook and supplies and he wanted to make amends for his little game. So it was that Val cooked for his host.

(Later near the fire place, they gathered to talk).

"Let me introduce Valor, also called Prince Valiant. He was one of my first knights. Yes, the terms valor and valiant came from this man. So is his nature that others measure themselves by his standard. Moreover, except for myself, there is no living person who could hope to take Val in combat, he is the finest swordsman in the world and a vampire lord himself" Brian said placing a hand on his friends shoulder with a smile.

"Too kind as always my lord" Val said with a smile. "I ask your pardon, I would not have harmed you if you were human, when I realized you were vampires, I decided to test your steel. You are all fine warriors, a credit to your lord. I could smell animal blood on you all and knew you to be friends of humanity when you came to the farmers aid without being called" Val said and then Bowed to the knights.

The shock on their faces was refreshing to Valor, it meant that they were young vampires and had not acquired the senses of a full vampire yet. Val could tell your clan, your race, your origin and your food source by smell. It was one of the many things Garrett had taught him in the thousand years of friendship.

"Now, has good king Brian told you about himself children" Val asked?

The knights and humans in the room all looked at Brian who sat on the only gift he ever accepted and used all the time. It was a God blessed hand carved art work of a chair, finer than any earthly king had ever sat upon. Brian smiled and said nothing.

"May I tell a little Brian" Valor asked with a serious face.

It was obvious Valor was afraid of Brian deep down and because of that he was not going to cross his Lord and Sire. Brian smile and wave a hand to go on; then made a pinch motion with his fingers, meaning only a little though. A human child toddled over to Brian, he place the child on his lap and rocked the tiny babe.

"First let me start with education, Brian wear a cross around his neck, that does not mean anything to you now, but he has fore seen the Son of GOD coming and it is his symbol that Brian wears. If a vampire had this symbol on his armor, sword, or person they are knights and a force for the balance of good, if not they serve dark agendas and are your enemy. Brian is the oldest most powerful of all of us, none know of his origin, he is unique even among us. He can not be killed" Valor said.

There were a few low gasps at that little factoid. The knights all seemed to beam with pride that they served the best of the best in their lord Brian. Valor decided to continue.

"Brian Garret found me on the shores of Sweden, I was an ill baby and dying of a fear, so my kin set me floating into the sea to meet our gods. Brian found me and healed my illness, I still know not how. He raised me as a son, taught me the blade and the written word alike. When I was a man he gave me a choice stay his human son or accept the vampires kiss and take the vow for all eternity to serve and protect humanity from us, other monsters. I could not in truth decide. My answer came a year later when my son was born and bandits attacked my home when I was working in the field. My son was injured, and my wife (Valor's eyes were glowing in the dark and the strain on his face was amazing and terrifying to see) they had their way with her then cut her throat. She did not die right away, my father, Brian tried to save her but in the end she was lost after she told me who to look for. I begged for the embrace at that time, my mind was made up. Brian later decided that all his knights must be able to have a family before the embrace. I hunted down the bandits alone and dealt with them harshly, they lived for weeks until they finally died" Val said as his eyes faded from the stars they had been.

"A ruff time for all of us when Gwen was lost" Brian said.

VAMPIRE WARS

CHAPTER 1: W.T.F.

Today was like most days for the happy little blue marble in space. There was war, poverty, stupidity and want. Despite all of those regular things, today was literally the last day of the world's old life. A new dark life came today.

A shiny bronze ball landed on the grass in the front of the White House. Out of it came three very odd looking creatures, they ran right up to the secret service and began trying different languages until they got to English.

"We come in peace, and your world in grave danger. We have to warn and help you if we can. There is no time for foolish waiting, we must speak to the authority on this world immediately" The slight grey alien with big black eyes said in perfect English.

The marines and the secret service looked at them and the sheer determination and fear that was written all over them and decided to help, odd but true. They took the aliens by van to a small private, easy to guard conference room. The president, vice president and the two joint chiefs that were available came in and sat down grave faced.

The three tiny grey aliens stood up and each of them took some object out and put them on the table the secret service tensed.

"No, not weapons or anything like that, information devices to help you understand the threat to your planet" The middle alien said.

It took only seventeen minutes for everyone in the room to be scared to death. The aliens called themselves Tiguns. Their planet had a defense barrier to keep out the Reptilian Korv. They watch the Korv always and try to protect the weaker races from becoming a Korv food source. The Korv had amazing technology but they preferred hand to hand, blade to blade warfare, very old school, and deadly efficient. Tiguns were not fighters, they were thinkers and in the three thousand years they had opposed the Korv, they had found no equal in combat to the mighty Korv. The Korv decide Earth was a good source of food and resources, so they began their journey toward that goal.

"We are sorry; we can not do much more than aid you. The Korv are ruthless and twenty times stronger than your race, you're lost as a people" The Tigun said sadly.

"The UN must meet two days from now, and the entire world must get ready to defend the planet" The President of the United States said as his face darkened "I guess I will be making history more than once in my presidency".

The UN met and they would not have believed a word of it if not for the aliens in the assembly. Many countries tried to say this was a ruse, but when the Tiguns showed the real enemy to life, all opposition evaporated and fear set in. The delegate argued about how to fight and defend their counties. Obama had enough, he told them if they did not pull together as one common human race they were all lost. Then hope came in the form of an intruder and his friends.

"Ladies and Gentlemen sit down please and do be quiet" The red haired man said in an odd voice.

The security ran forward and shot the man and tried to subdue him. The man just knockout the guards and looked at the hole in his suit. Then he addressed the assembly.

"What a waste of a good suit. I am Brian Garrett, I was born before Jesus Christ was, and I am here to save your lives" He said to dead silence. "I know it is hard to accept, it has been so long since I have meddled in human affairs, but since the Tiguns have come to help so must we. You can not hope to defend or defeat those Korv, but I can, with the rest of my kind behind me".

To illustrate his point he walked over to a marble ball on the edge of the dais and crushed it softly in his hand with no effort. He turned and pointed to the rafters and five new vampires dropped from the roof to the floor landing with no sound at all.

"Greetings" Said a black haired god of a man.

"This is Valor, yes he is where the term came from, he is over two thousand years old and the finest swordsman the world has ever known. These three are they are the vampire knight brothers, they are loyal to me alone. The last member is Lady Victoria leader of her clan. We offer you this hope, we will defend and train you and you will leave the defense of the Earth in my hands alone" Brian said.

"Why should we trust you, you're a monster as well, a blood drinker" the Iran representative said?

(Brian chuckled amused, Valor did not).

"Unless you are a strict vegetarian so are all of you" Brian chuckled.

"Enough of this mindless banter, we are strong enough to defend the planet and you are not. Your foolish myths about our kind are insulting and laughable, we do not need your permission to do what must be done, know this if you interfere we will destroy you to save our world, so you are literally with us or against us" Valor said white eyed and teeth bared. He was simply beautiful.

"America pledges its support and cooperation to your efforts Mr. Garrett" President Obama said loudly to the shock of all the assembly.

"Very good; Brothers three take knights to America and find my blood heir Will Garrett and his family, then call for me. I must embrace him myself" Brian said.

"Excuse me, embrace" The tiny little old lady from Africa asked?

"Yes, I am going to bite him and make him a vampire like me, he has a choice though. It is my law that no human is turned against his will, and none of us are allowed to taste the blood of an innocent. I am the absolute law in my world. I will ask of each of you for volunteers to be granted the Kiss of the vampire. They will take an oath to never attack humanity on penalty of death, and they will serve their clan with Valor" Brian said smiling at his adopted son of the same name.

"How do you decide who is innocent" the lady asked Brian?

"If we are not at war, and you do not attack me or my charges, if you don't sell drugs to kids or prey of the weak or poor, if you don't pedal death, than loosely speaking you're an innocent" Brian answered her.

"How is it that we have never seen you before Sir" The African lady asked.

"It is simple, you have. We are always among you, the best doctors, extreme rescue teams, sometimes athletes as well. We don't meddle in government; it is your own choice to self destruct. I have been reading for the last two hundred years, and training my Knights. My human subjects have been as well educated as I could manage, the have been to the best university's around the planet and home again, to use those stills to help our people and others around the globe who needed us" Brian explained.

The woman and all that were carefully listening to Brian speak looked a little nervous at my subject comment; that is until the Japanese ambassador came over and practically tackled Brian and Valor.

"Ho my friends; I am so glad you decided to help us" He blurted as he hugged both Lords equally in turn. "I wanted to thank you again for the help after the flood; we are finally all okay and back to normal life, without your help many would have died" Isha Zu said.

"You know them" The lady asked Isha Zu?

"Yes, they are my oldest friends, quite literally" He chuckled. "My father had me study the sword with master Valor, and later tactics with Lord Garrett, on how to lead a people with intelligence and strength and not be a tyrant. They are the strongest of all the Vampire lords and they are (He chuckled) unusual, they enjoy human food, bread especially as I remember" Isha Zu said.

"Yes, I adore bread, fresh baked dark Rye is my favorite with real butter freshly churned" Brian made a happy face. Val could not help smiling at his adopted father and Lord.

"Gentlemen and ladies as well, I would love to run down memory lane with you, but we are about trying to save the planet from invaders as silly as that sounds" Valor said in his harmonious voice. "I suggest we place our collective head together and figure out how we can manage that task."

"Quite right." The African woman said.

(In America)

The three vampire knights had removed their armor so they could move around easier without drawing to much attention. They used their heightened sense of smell to probe for the essence of Garrett in the blood of a human. They traveled at a crazy pace all over major cities, but notta. Finally in Washington States Aaron noticed that the wind smelled a lot like Garrett, too much actually. The brothers followed the scent easily, to easily. These were warriors, born in blood; they felt a trap coming on. However, the truth amused them more than they would have thought.

There was a group of young human men playing basketball, they were pretty good, but the pace of the game was so slow by vampire standards, but fast by human standards. A small white male was slashing to the hole and his black team mate was shadowing him, at the last possible instant the smaller man dished the ball for an easy lay in.

Great coordination and timing Ian thought.

"Which one of them is the Garrett" Evan asked to nobody in particular?

"Red head middle of the court, 6 foot 200 pounds" Ian said.

"No, it is the small guy who can dish at the last minute to the black guy, he is our man" Aaron explained.

The other two brothers bowed to Aaron's superior sense of smell. Each brother had a pronounced gift, and they always worked together as a well oiled team. This was a modified snatch and grab mission for the Lord Garrett, so it will be done. They were not as prepared as they thought, for Will.

Two hours after the game was over and Will was at home showering before dinner with Tana and the kids, when he got out and dressed. Tana told him to chop the salad. Will being fond of blades took the biggest knife to chop the salad out and went to it. The door bell rang and he went to get it. When Will opened the door three young men rushed through the door, Will managed to cut everyone of them on the neck, in the same spot, right across the jugular. The brothers just looked at each other in surprise and awe. A mere human wounded all of them in an instant even as fast as they were. Still, they had orders, so they went about trying to capture Will.

"Oh, Shit" Aaron heard behind him just as a baseball bat bounced off his head.

"Get off my dad" A teenage boy said as he went on the attack. Evan jumped to intervene, but the boy switch tactics in mid-movement from a swing to a stabbing motion and hit Evan in the left eye.

"Stop" a commanding voice sounded!

Will was covered in blood, his and some of the attackers. He was not about to let his guard down. He had never seen such good fighters, they worked flawlessly together, if they had not been caught be surprise by his skills he would already be dead and sadly, so would his boy. Will was scared because these guys were too good for Navar and him to beat.

"Out" the voice said calmly.

All three attackers walked right passed Will and looked him in the eye with no malice at all. They all had strangely light blue eyes.

VAMPIRE WARS

CHAPTER 2: HERITAGE

Will and Tana looked at the man who had ordered the other three out, he was younger than Will and almost too beautiful to be a man, yet he carried himself like royalty. He has medium length red hair and a killer smile, he was five foot eight and maybe one hundred seventy pounds, all muscle likely by the graceful way he walked. All of that would have marked him as special, without his eyes. They were the tip off. They were red, not dry and itchy red but true deep red and they were exquisite. The man closed the door after telling the other three to guard and patrol the area.

Will never let go of the knife. The man smiled but made no move to attack Will. Instead he walked over and grabbed a clean towel out of the basket of laundry the daughter was sorting and handed it to Will.

"You must be my blood relative, no other could stand toe to toe with the brothers and stay upright long enough to tell the tale. Anyway, I am Brian Garrett and it is my blood that flows in your veins" Brian stated.

Lee came in and sat on the couch and started folding the clothes. She really just wanted to listen. Brian could tell, so could Tana and Will. Navar stood like a statue with his bat ready. Brian sighed and walked over and then indicated he wished to sit, and was that ok?

"Be my guest Brian." Will said. "Here Tana put this in the sink, he could take it away from me anyway anytime he wanted" as he handed her the knife handle first.

"I am not here to fight and I apologize for the brothers over dedication to the task" Brian said. "However, you needed to be found and turned as soon as possible; there is no time for subtle".

"Fine Brian, you talk, I will listen to you" Will said.

What Brian told Will and his family was incredible, yet they sat as a group and did not utter a syllable for three full hours as Brian told the story of Will's family until Will was born. Then Brian explained the matter of saving the planet, he took out a memory device and showed Will and family the speech the Tiguns gave to the UN. Incredible turned too probable in that instant.

"Here is the plan, you're my blood and so are your children, you are more special than you could know. It is once again time for our blood line to save the world, I need you to be king Will and go face the Korv menace before they reach our world, however you have to be embraced before you go" Brian explained.

"What if I don't want to be embraced, what if I just want to live a normal life" Will asked?

Faster than a heartbeat Brian was across the living room and had Tana by the throat off the ground. Brian's eyes were light red now and his fangs were extended as he turned his vampire glare on Will.

"There is no more normal Will, either serve of prepare to have the Korv come here and kill everyone you ever knew or ever will know. (He put Tana down softly on the couch beside Will and Lee), as a vampire lord you can't be killed and you will have the power to defend them all, but you alone can choose" Brian said as he placed a hand on Will's shoulder and looked at him with sympathy.

Brian bowed and apologized to Tana and turned to leave when Navar grabbed his arm, looking back at his dad.

"I will serve and fight grandfather. Embrace me" Navar said in earnest.

"One day perhaps son, but it is against my on law to embrace a child, you're almost a man, as soon as you have a son or daughter of your own, then you can become a knight as your father will be king, you will be a prince of the Garrett clan" Brian said with pride in his voice.

Will looked at Brian and said nothing. There was a passion in his eyes that Brian could feel; Will hated him for making him have to decide this. What was he to do with his family? Will's whole life was his family. Brian left.

"What are we going to do, run for it" Tana asked, though she knew the answer already. Will was going to fight!

The next day Will met with his friend Jay Har, a big black man he played ball with, his best-friend. Will had slept very little and he was exhausted. He sat with Jay and told his boy everything, leaving nothing out. Jay looked into Will's eyes and said something that made tear spring to his eyes.

"You're a fighter, so fight. I remember when the gang bangers cut me up, I just about died. They tore you to pieces, way worse than me. You carried me to the ER, and then you went back and put every one of those bastards on their back, none of them ever walked again. You bled nearly to death before Ruby found you. The police disregarded the claim that you bust those guys up because the Doctor said you were near death and it was impossible for you to do it. Ruby and I knew better. Only death would keep you from killing someone who hurt your family, you the bravest man I have ever known, and I love you for being my brother man" Jay told him. "If you were willing to trade your life for mine, are you really struggling with saving the world and your girl, mini you and the man child, fuck no your not". Jay gave Will a twisted smile.

They sat there and talked about life's odd twists for an hour, then Will went home. Brian and the brothers were there, only this time they were in their jet-black armor and they had very serious faces.

"Damn, you fought those guys" Jay asked?

"Yes, he did and he did quite well for a human" Ian said with a toothy smile.

Brian was sitting with Lee and they were playing cards, she was giggling. Brian looked into Will's eyes, but he did not have to ask, he knew. Brian hugged Lee and promised to return for a rematch at cards. She sighed and then stood and walked away.

"Let us go blood of my blood" Brian said to Will.

Brian looked at Jay and felt his arm, and walked around him. Jay did not move, he was far too terrified. Brian's red eyes usually scared everyone to the bone; even the other vampires obeyed him instantly no matter how powerful.

"You should recruit that man as your first knight" Brian told Will as they left. Will just looked at his best friend and wondered.

CHAPTER 3: REBIRTH

Brian took Will to an old factory in the country that was abandon and remote enough not to bring unwanted witnesses to the birth of a Vampire king. Brian had the brothers bring the biggest chain Will had ever seen and locks that were as big as soccer balls. Will was going to ask about them but Brian waved all of his questions away with a smile. It was finally time to be turned. The brothers came and stripped Will of all of his clothing and chained him up. It was so heavy the weight was literally crushing him already.

"Please my tiny lord don't fight it; the pain will only be worse" Evan said with sad eyes, his face next to Will's.

Brian came and knelt down by Will; he hugged him and then said a single word.

"Ready"?

It was not what Will thought it would be like. He thought that there would be pain from the bite, but the initial pain of the bite on the back of his shoulder was not really that bad. Will was almost relieved once Brian nailed him. It was the, I kid you not; worst pain in all creation, being burned alive would have been less painful once Will began to die from the embrace. You see that is what you do, you die, the human that you were is no longer there, in his place is a mass of wreathing misery and gut wrenching screams that are not human or beast.

For three days Brian sat with or held Will and though Brian had turned many people before, none were like Will.

Will was of his own blood line and had the mark of the King on him, so the pain was a thousand times worse for him than any mere soldier or knight before him. Brian cried quietly twice for this was hard for the first time ever for him, he had never brought suffering to anyone like this before. It was literally like the world was dying with Will.

"Wake up little king" Brian said softly while he cradled his heir in his arms.

On the second day of the ordeal Evan and Ian removed the heavy chains since Will no longer moved at all, and stopped screaming a day ago when his vocal cords exploded. Brian gave his permission, so there after Brian himself held his heir Will and waited for his blood family son to wake from his dark sleep. The brothers thought that Will had not survived the ordeal, never in their three centuries have they ever seen such suffering before. Yes, the embrace was painful, but it usually was but a single night's pain, not three miserable days and nights. Will was so small and broken looking.

"You no good son of bitch" Will said as he opened his eyes.

"Oh thank God Will you finally woke up" Brian said.

"What...how long has it been out granddad" Will asked confused?

"It nears a fourth day of your ordeal, you are done though, come with me and have a hot shower" Brian said

Will followed Brian to a man made waterfall in the back of the foundry where he died to be reborn as a king. The water was rushing and it was indeed hot, Will was not sure how they did this but he did not care at this moment. His own smell was rank and he was so ravenous he could eat a moose whole, hypothetically. Will slipped into the water and it fell over him like spring after a long winter. His body never felt so alive as it did now. He could feel every drop of water individually and that was without concentration, if he thought about it he could have counted the drops, which ranged into the millions. Will was not sure if he was supposed to be able to do that, but he smile to himself because he could. Brian held out a towel to Will thirty minutes later, and a white silk shirt, solid silver cross on a silver and gold twined chain, linen pants, and white satin socks, and light tan leather shoes. Will put them all on, and was surprised that they all fit perfectly. He gave a quizzical look at Brian, who just smiled and gave Will an exquisite ring with a family crest on it. Brian explained this however.

"You are king, that ring marks you as the King of clan Garrett, who rules all clans of vampires" Brian said with pride.

"I don't understand Granddad, you're my king right" Will said as his new crimson eyes focused on Brian?

"No, I rule the vampire world, I am the law, the overlord if you want for an explanation. I am not your ruler though, you are my kin and my clan king, I stand with you not above you Will. Though we can never be equals, you're as close as it gets to being my true equal" Brian explained. "Come my son".

   The vampire knight brothers were startled by the change in Will. Gone was tiny human fighter, come now the king, there was no physical size change, Will had not grown. Will was different, focused and perfect in every way, his hair was long and red, his eyes were sharper at the edges and crimson. His body looked as if drawn, it was hard and lean. Will's smile made your heart jump with joy.

   Will got into the tan T-top mustang GT500 with red racing stripes and dropped the hammer. If felt so good to just drive, Will loved to drive.

Brian apparently loved to go fast because the 600Hp engine was screaming at the top of the rev limiter, the speedometer said 197MPH and climbing. They blew passed a motorcycle cop; the police jumped out behind them, but gave up the chase pretty fast, since he had no hope of catching them.

"Do you like the car" Brian asked?

"Yes very much sire" Will said.

"Brian, pop, granddad, but not sire please" Brian answered.

"Sorry Grandfather. I meant no disrespect" Will said. "Could you kill me if you wanted to, and I did not want to die"?

"Yes, I can beat any of our kind; you are not a fight I would want, it would be like fighting myself. You are stronger, faster and smarter than any other clan, because of my blood in your veins, it would be hard to kill you for even me, no other vampire or being short of God could likely kill you Will. There are a few things I want to talk about while we drive. The rules, you can not drink the blood of an innocent, ever. You can not turn anyone against their will, they must agree to the embrace. You must always protect humanity at all costs and our world as well. The penalty for violations is death son. Do you understand" Brian asked seriously?

"I don't like bloody stuff, I am a gentleman, always have been, and I have the gene to protect, I was born with it as a human. Now about blood, how do I get it if I can't bite people" Will asked?

"You can eat anything you want it is a gift of our family blood line and it will nourish you as it did as a human. Blood will make you strong, but any blood will do, human is the best but not necessary to survive" Brian explained to Will.

"If I am going to be fighting a war, who will be going with me, where to I find other vampires to take with me" Will inquired?

(Brian smiled),

"First choose and turn your person knights, no more than five. I will arrange knights from the many clan and human soldiers to fight along with you" Brian said. "I am going to defend the home world, so Valor stays with me, I need him to watch my back and train half the world's fighters while I run the show. I give you the brother knights as a gift, they must always stay and fight together, they already love you as their friend and lord, and they will never let you down or turn on you. They will kill anybody that turns traitor to you automatically, they have super senses by the way, and each one has a different one" Brian said.

The tan mustang was a blur and the wind whistle for hours while the Lords of our future drove like mortals, neither spoke. Words would ruin the blissfulness of the open road. Will thought of only one thing. Tana. Would she still want him, was he a monster to her now? He never dreamed of a life that Tana was not the driver in, his life was Tana. Will knew Navar and Lee would like the improvements to his look, but would his tiny dancer?

(In the home of Will and Tana Garrett)

The news had been on for three day without ever going off the air, it was all just the way Lord Garrett had said, we were one people now, fighting not for independence but for the chance to survive at all. Tana cried herself to sleep every night in her empty bed. Where had her partner gone? Did that no good son of a bitch Brian sneak her man away for the war before she could say her final good bye. Lee watched the news and saw aliens building ships with her Grandfather's crest on them. Vampires were coming out of the wood-work and volunteering to defend the planet, since they are born to fight; and the chance to freely drink the blood of war was a big ass plus, believe me.

(There was a super loud knock on the front door).

Lee went and looked out the window, she saw her vampire bodyguards that Brian left to look after her and her family, and they would not beat on the door though. She opened the door and the prettiest man she ever seen was standing there smiling as her. She was floor by him as he grabbed her and held her close to him.

"OH...OH, DADDY" Lee screamed as she started crying!

"What"?

"I love you, dad" Lee croaked,

"I love ya too sweaty baby" Will said in a new satin voice.

Navar came into the room and was about to toss the guy touching her sissy a beating, when he stopped and stared. He blink and turned his head at different angles, move his glasses up and down to see if that was the trouble, but it changed nothing. His father left a man and came back a demigod, red eyes and all.

"Dad" Navar asked unsure?

"Yes son" Will answer?

Will could hear Tana's weak voice in the background, she seemed upset. Will gave Brian a sour look; he put Lee down and went to his mate. She was having a nightmare. He put his arms around her and held her. Will began rocking his tiny bride back and forth. When her eyes suddenly fluttered opened, she was shocked at first. Tana did not know Will anymore. It took her a second then she saw it in his lovely glowing red ember eyes, the deep love he had for her. You can't fake that, not true love.

"Will, please baby be really here" Tana cried her little eyes out?

"Yes, I am right here sugar-baby. What do you think of me now" Will said in a shaky voice?

Tana wiggled out of Will's iron new grip and turned on her bedroom lights and turned on him. She looked him over very thoroughly; she ran her hands over his body and smiled a great deal.

"You're hot" she said and she jumped on him.

He let her knock him over on to the bed. They kissed and then somehow she got all of his new clothes off without ripping them. She was a clever girl; he chose his bride well. After careful lovemaking for two hours and Tana's pleasurable reunion was satisfied; Will let her sleep exhausted in his arms.

Tana woke up and looked at her man; he looked like a god, perfect in everyway, young powerful immortal. Oh, he is not going to want me anymore, I am forty one now, I have some fine laugh lines, and stretch marks from childbirth. My impossibly beautiful man will leave me soon.

"Not a chance of that shit Tana" Will said.

"What" Tana said.

"I am going the embrace you wife, I will be damned if I am going to live forever without your sexy wee arse" Will said in a slight Irish accent.

"So will I be as beautiful as your Will" Tana asked?

"More, much more beautiful, you had better materials to start with. I will turn you after diner tonight okay, you will wake up a Goddess my one true love" Will said as he pulled her under the covers and nuzzled her until she went to sleep.

Will was worried because he had suffered more than even his wild imagination could have done justice, how could he do that to his wife, she was so tiny and fragile. Will never noticed before just how small and helpless she seemed. Nevertheless, he would not go an eternity without her and that was final. If she died then Navar would have to take the forces to the war, he would have Brian kill him, so he could rest with Tana.

Later that day Will took Tana out for a wonderful diner and dancing. She wore her sexy little black mini dress and knee high leather boots that matched. They danced and ate and played like children. Tana who rarely drinks decided to have one because it was a special occasion. The female bartender drooled over Will and gave him all he could drink for free. Will kissed her hand and accepted of-course. Tana drank happily as they danced. She got sleepy and tired faster than normal; she chalked it up to the stress of the last week. What the tiny dancer did not know was all the girls in the club glared at her in jealous ways and that Will put liquid morphine in her drink.

Tana who just turned forty one looked like a twenty five year old, she had great genetics. Even so when she went to use the rest room a tall model looking girl locked her in, and then went to make a pass at Will.

One thing about being a vampire is your senses become very very tuned. Will heard Tana's small inebriated voice calling for help. Will walked right by the tall model girl, without a second look. He reached down and ripped the door handle off the door and held Tana's wobbly body close to his. He smiled into her little face and picked her up and cradled her to his chest and walked out of the club, right up the tan Mustang where some punks were trying to break into it.

"Gentlemen don't bother my car please I am in a hurry, so have a good night" Will said.

"Just give me the keys and I won't have to hurt you and bone your girl" The big red neck one said.

Will placed Tana on the side walk softly and then turned to the idiot mugger and snarled at him as he held the man by his throat. The muggers never even seen Will move. Will bared his teeth and his eyes became amber flashlights pointed in the mugger's faces.

"I said GOOD NIGHT" Will growled low and dangerous.

One of the four men was armed with a pistol. He reached into his coat and pulled it out just before a hand grabbed him by the neck and threw him into a building wall fifty yards away, the man was almost killed by the impact. Will was looking in Ian's eyes; his brothers had the other men on their knees.

"Not the blood of the innocent my lord" Evan said pointedly.

"Break their legs, but don't take their lives. Go see to the one near the wall, don't let him die" Will said.

The brothers smiled and bowed slightly, and went to tossing the muggers a good old fashion beaten. Evan took the injury ping pong ball mugger to the ER as was suggested by Will.

Will smiled as he drove 150MPH all the way home in the dark with no lights on. He didn't need them; vampires have perfect vision in the dark. So, Brian set guards to protect me, the new clan chief, nice.

"Where are we" Tana said with her head on Will's lap.

He smiled down at his lover and mate, ruffled her hair gently and spoke softly to her.

"Soon we will be home my tiny dancer" Will whispered with a nervous smile.

It was 3:45Am when Will embraced Tana. Even with the Micky Finn, she was in horrible pain. She bravely uttered very little sound; she was able to grunt out only one set of words a single time.

"Anything to be with you, anything" Tana gargled out, and then collapsed.

8:23Am two days later Tana opened her eyes, they were deep rich amber. Her body was changed slightly. Her skin had no marks, no scars, no stretch marks, nothing, just silky smooth. Her tiny breasts were closer to medium sized now and hard as rocks. She still had her islander skin tone. It was then that both Tana and Will realized what the embrace did to you. It made you the ultimate you, the best possible version of the person you had been. Will was speechless; Tana was so amazing to look at all covered in a fine mist of sweat as she ran her hands over her hard naked body. The animal in Will came out suddenly and violently.

Two days ago when Will took Tana to bed he had to be so careful not to kill her by accident; that was no longer a problem. Tana was a vampire lady now and her body and physical strength were more than enough to handle Will's sudden rise in desire. It was Tana who attacked and ripped Will's clothes to shreds. The made love on the floor so intensely that the house shook and so did the ground on the entire city block they lived on. Tana sank her teeth into Will's chest and tasted his blood, while he held her firmly on to her back and loved her like a tidal wave. Tana was not prepared for her incredible hunger for Will. She had thought she loved him before but her attraction and lust for his body and touch was near insanity, with his blood on her tongue when she finally reached a point of pure ecstasy and orgasm, she felt sheepish about her loony behavior. Will did not seem to mind at all.

Will and family went out for a late Breakfast. Tana could have been in a parka and got a ton of attention, but she wore tight black slacks and with a linen shirt with no bra. Her vampire body was amazing to look at, and her natural exotic look only made it even more charming and alluring. With Will sitting touching her, it caused quite a stir. People could not seem to look away from them; they were daydreaming about being with one or both of them. Will smiled graciously, Tana made kissy faces at a few pretty girls to send them giggling away. Nobody was more impressed than Lee at her tiny mother's sudden Goddess transformation. Tana was a gorgeous woman as she had been; now she was perfection in every detail. Lee looked at her father, and his natural playfulness was still in his eyes. That was it, her parent new hot bodies was not what made them so appealing it was their eyes, they were simply magnetic and they seemed to be trained on each other like always.

In the afternoon of the same day Brian and Val showed up with the US army with them at Will's home. Brian did the introductions. Will shook hands and greeted each of them in stride. It was then that Will and family met the Tigun. He truddled into Will's living room with his huge black eyes and looked around. Then he spoke.

"Your ship will be ready to leave in the morning Lord Will Garrett" The Tigun said in a jolly little voice. "I will be your science and engineering officer; since it is a Tigun ship you will be taking the meet the Korv".

"Well, nice to know we will have an expert along to nurse us through the trip, so we don't space ourselves" Will answered. "What are you called my friend"?

"I am without a designation in your tongue" The Tigun said.

"Very well, how about Tiger, it sounds like your people, but is referring to you only" Will said.

The Tigun looked at Lee who winked at him and made up his mind.

"Yes, I will answer to this name Lord" Tiger said.

"Hey none of that your lord stuff you may call me Will" Will added quickly.

"Or King Will" Val said sternly looking at the soldiers gathered, both human and vampire alike. His stern gaze was not lost on them at all, a clear warning.

"What is this about leaving in the morning" Will asked.

"I am Sorry Son; but the Korv have put down on a planet they want to raze before ours, so you have to catch them on the ground and stop them from leaving" Brian said.

The look Will gave him made everyone step away from the Garrett's; they thought that Will was going to refuse. Brian however, knew the look had little to do with that, and more about the time table and things left undone. Will looked at his family and suddenly spoke in an authoritative voice.

"See to it my family are securely on board the ship and properly quartered as due their rank as the royal family. Aaron, Evan, Ian see to their safety and needs. Brian...my father, my friend, I have had so little time to train for this; I hope I don't disgrace the family name. (Will and Brian smiled at each other). I have a few people to see before morning, and they will need arms and quarters, see to it knights, and if I am able; two of the three I am bringing are big so their arms will have to be made for them" Will said.

"You plan to take you family to war" An Army general asked.

"Yes he does." Tana said as she held Will's hand.

Every man in the room felt their heart jump at the sight of her, even Brian was surprised.

"A damn fine mixing of our blood Tana, you're unlike any embraced female I have known. Welcome to the clan darling" Brian kissed her hand as he spoke.

(In the hood behind the college in the Couve).

   Jay opened the door and near died of fright. In front of him was a perfect version of the best friend he grew up with, red eyes and all. Jay reached out and touched Will on the chest.

"Your warm, I thought your kind were cold" Jay asked.

"Myth. Jay, I need you boy, I can't stand and fight if my strong right arm is not with me. You want to live forever and be young and hot the whole time, never get sick again" Will asked?

"Is it going to hurt" Jay inquired?

"Yes".

   One hour later in a tiny book store downtown Rudy turned and pulled her knife in one fluid motion to stop slack-jawed at her friend. Rudy was a fighter and she could sense danger as a 6th sense, she was fearless and merciless in combat. She was also one of Tana and Will's closest friends.

"It is time to step up love, are you ready" Will asked.

Ruby was both shocked and amazed by her long time friend, he was more than a man now and yet, still he was her Will, her blood brother. Ruby put up her blade and hugged Will.

"You know it baby" Ruby answered with a smile.

Lastly before sunset Will went to the county jail to see a friend that no one could figure out why they got along. Ogre was a giant, in the exact meaning, 500lbs and 7'5. He was covered in scars, Ogre was a mean bastard, there was no nice way to put it. A few of his worst injuries were compliments of Will. They over time had found a respect for each other and friendship blossomed.

"You have a visitor" The guard said.

Ogre did not even act as if he heard anything at all. Will knew better, despite his great size this man was fast as a jungle cat and as strong as a bear, and a natural born killer to boot.

"Want to get out of this shit hole Ogre" Will said.

The giant stood up and then leaned all the way down to look at Will with his only good eye. He was lost for a moment, the voice was sweater and the face was super handsome, but he knew this man.

"Will" Ogre grunted?

"Yes, I have had some changes old friend. I want to offer you some changes as well. I need your strength and skills, and I will drop your leash and let you fight and kill as you see fit. I can provided you with even more power than you have now, and as a bonus your left eye will see again. Interested" Will asked?

"Done, get me out of here" Ogre said smiling.

"Wait, there are a few rules I feel compelled to mention at this time. First, you can kill only enemies, no comrades no matter how stupid they are. You cannot drink or taste the blood of an innocent ever, and no human is ever to be attacked. The penalty is death" Will said. "Lastly, Steven, Ogre, you must swear an oath of loyalty to me and serve as my knight and protect the clan".

Ogre looked at Will for a second, and then he went and sat down. He looked at his own monster hands. Finally he spoke.

"Will, I swear to follow you into hell's fire if you're for going, I will kill your enemies and protect your family, I swear to never betray your trust, because...you're my only friend in this world and I will not let anything change that, not even my death" Ogre said.

Will smile and ripped the door off the cell like it was made of paper. He walked out and grabbed the nearest guard.

"Take me to the Sheriff immediately" Will said.

One half hour later, Will and Ogre were standing in a court room with the district Judge, Sheriff and so on.

"By order of the President of the United Sates of America, Steven Ogre is granted a full pardon and it commissions into the Vampire knights under the command of Myself King Will Garrett" Will explained.

"It is not that simple your lordship, we have to verify the order" The judge started to say. Will stopped him.

"You miss understand me sir, I am not asking you for permission to take Ogre, I am taking him, here and now. I have absolute authority over the entire world at this moment or are you so under educated that you don't you this. It matters not, in the morning the Tigun ship and crew and the knights will be going to face the Korv at my back, and Ogre will be at my left elbow. Now we are leaving. If you value your lives and welfare do not interfere with me" Will said as his eyes paled and his teeth bared.

Ogre tasted absolute freedom for the first time since his fifteenth birthday and he liked it.

CHAPTER 4: SPACE

The morning of the take off, Tana was hurrying to get the kids ready and the gathered delegates from many countries were there. They pledged support to Will and his army, saying they would fill other ships and send them to join the fight.

Brian was with Will, they looked like two gods in their red form fitting armor. They both wore red Wolf head daggers, but Will had two short swords to Brian's single two handed sword. Brian made the armor for Will himself and the arms as well. Brian was incredible; Will often thought to himself, he wished Brian could go so he could learn from him.

Jay woke up chained to a wall, next to him was ruby, they were both naked. Jay always liked Ruby and she liked him as well. Jay snapped his chains and went over and grabbed Ruby up off the floor, she seemed to want to be held so they filled heir common need...together. When Will came in they were still locked in passion, he cleared his throat and they looked up and started laughing.

"I see you found out how powerful your senses have become and you sex drive will be off the hook as well. A word of caution both of you, be careful if you take a human lover on this tub, you might kill them during sex, so another vampire is a much better plan. Now stand up let me look at you both" Will said.

"Hey Man, we aren't done yet" Jay said and Ruby giggled. Will smiled walked back out of the bay. "Top or bottom Ruby"?

Ogre woke up alone, if Ruby or any woman would have been in the same room with him when his hunger and desire were upon him, he might have killed them by accident. Will did not know how much a female vampire could take but Ogre was a big undertaking for anyone. Chained to the wall with huge chains, the giant took it in stride and just tossed them off like they were not there. He turned around a suddenly realized he could see out of both eyes, in his excitement he yelled. It brought the three Vampire knight brothers, and they were confused, they thought he was angry and dangerous so they moved to attack him and end the contest early when four strong hands stop them.

"No, I would not try that on Ogre boys" Jay said.

"He would have ripped you apart, he is much faster than you could imagine, and he is Will's friend" Ruby said with a smile.

The brothers looked at Ogre and bowed to Ruby and walked away. Ruby walked into the bay right up to the new vampire, a naked Ogre. She taped his manhood with her fingertips. Ogre was scar free and actually very attractive. His hair that was black, he hints of red in it and his eyes were a light amber color. Ruby was wearing only what looked like a black scarf. Her long shiny black hair and bright blue eyes that were now red was so amazing to look at. Her hard muscular body seemed to glide around with no effort. Ogre reached down and pulled the scarf off of her body and smiled as he picked her up. Ogre kissed her cheek and ran his bear paw over her back and bottom.

"You are so temping right now little Rudy, the change in you has made you a Goddess, I can't believe I would say this out loud but would you consider me as a lover" Ogre asked in earnest?

"I am not sure what this new body can do yet, but I have always wondered what it would be like to be with you, when you're not trying to kill me that is. So yes, come with me to my quarters and let both us see what we can do" Ruby said in a sultry tone.

Ogre looked at Jay, he could smell Jay on Ruby, so he stopped for a moment. Ogre took what he wanted, now was different a new start, so he was not sure what to do, because he wanted Ruby in the worst way.

"Hey big man, it is all good, we are all just friends, you do what you like, Ruby is a big girl, if she wants you then so be it" Jay said to Ogre's relief.

Ruby did not rewrap her body as she led Ogre to her quarters. Jay heard her say in passing "You should see Tana Ogre she will blow your mind".

Hours later Will was still touring the ship, it was huge. The human Army, Marine, and Seal captains were happy that Will had served in the Army. The troops were from many countries, all could converse in English passably. The vampire clan leaders were less happy about Will's leadership. He met with them as a group and read them the law. It started like this.

"I am in absolute command, you may lead your clan as you see fit unless it runs counter to my commands, and in that case it is forbidden. I have no mercy; please test me if you think otherwise. It is Brian Garrett's blood that runs in my veins, only he is capable of killing me. I want your full support and demand your loyalty" Will commanded.

"Brian is not here now to command us to follow you" Lady Deathkill said.

"Come, I wear no armor and try to slay me, as you say my grandfather is not here" Will said.

Lady Deathkill lunged at Will and was about to reach him curved blade extended, when a thin hard fist caught her square on the jaw. The blow sent Lady Deathkill spiraling into the bay bulkhead.

"Fool, I just saved your life" Lady Victoria said as she whipped her black hair over her shoulder. "Look upon him, his beauty is flawless, and the tell-tell sign red eyes of the Garrett clan. He is posturing not, there is none among us that can slay him, we are not strong enough, and he meets us without armor or knights. Do any of you question his courage or resolve? I Lady Victoria and my clan follow him as king, my clan is old and powerful, we are willing to fight if we must for our king" Victoria said.

It was common knowledge that Victoria was the black mistress, or vampire queen. Thousands of years ago she ruled a kingdom, and was a tyrant. Brian Garrett had come to her, he judged her and her people to be evil and unworthy. It is said that her one act of kindness for her people was done that day, when she begged him on her knees to spare them. Brian found he believed her so he granted her request. It should be noted as well that only Lady Victoria knows what Brian Garrett true wrath looks like. She watched him destroy her entire civilization is a single day. She has never spoke of it, but trembles when it is discussed. Terrible is her vengeance though, it is said that only Val is her better with a blade.

Will stood there bemused by her cold intervention. Also he was curious as well, why should she bother if she actually thought him so formidable? Her action baffled him somewhat, had Brian ordered her to protect him. No, that was ridiculous, Jay, and Ogre were more than enough, and Tana can protect my kids, so then why?

"Dine with me Victoria" Will asked?

"My pleasure" Victoria said with a smile.

That evening Ogre with Ruby holding his hand walked into the King's private dining area. They were followed by Jay and Navar who were immersed in a debate about something, Jay stop long enough to kiss Ruby passionately and punch Ogre in the arm, seems those three found balance as vampires. Lady Victoria came with the three brothers, she entered they did not. Victoria was a tall beautiful woman, with high cheek bones and red pouting lips. She was not in her armor but a sheer white gown that showed off her sleek form. Jay and Ogre knew she was some sort of royalty so they tried not to notice her naked body in the lovely gown. Victoria's breasts were full and they had powerful strawberry red nipples that demanded attention. She knew that they were young and it is common for vampires to engage in adult play often and vigorously, therefore it is an insult to a Lady if you do not desire them and drool a little.

"Boys, please feel free to enjoy my company freely, if I did not want you to look at me, I would not wear a dress that is see through. I am not aloof when it comes to play only politics. I will enjoy your company fully" she smiled sweetly.

"You are a vision my lady, I must admit you warm my blood. Can I introduce my wife Tana" Will said.

Tana sat down beside Victoria and touched her hand. The sudden change in Victoria was startling; her breasts heavy as if her heart would comes out through her sternum. Tana was dress in a short sheer black dress that was as see through as Victoria's was. Tana was bare foot, with a gold ankle bracelet on. Victoria leaned over and kissed Tana passionately on the lips while fondling her breasts gently. Tana did not resist although she had never let anyone touch her but Will before this, if it were a man she would have hurt them for this insult. Tana and Victoria embraced for a long time while Will watched in wonder. He had never known Tana to let anyone touch her body; she was violently opposed to being touched. It was not unpleasant to see his mate and the lovely Victoria, vampire queen embrace; it caused a new stirring in Will that he had never felt before. It was not jealousy, although Will was pretty territorial about Tana. Finally, the girls let go. Victoria was gasping like she was drowning; Tana was smiling in a curious way.

"What brought that own Victoria" Will asked?

Lady Victoria looked at him as if she forgot there was anyone in the room but Tana.

"Her visage coupled with her scent over came my natural barriers, she is intoxicating" Victoria said breathlessly, then added "It is the same with you the attraction is overwhelming".

"You hardly lost control before Tana sat down" Will said.

"You are across the table from me, she was leaning on me. I lost myself in the sudden violent burst of desire" Victoria said innocently.

Will got up and walked around the table to Victoria and sat down next to her, he let his hand trail down her spine to her bottom. Victoria gasped and her eyes changed from the rare violet to a pale lilac, and her heart nearly came thru her lovely breasts from the way it was machine gunning inside of her. Victoria tackled Will to the floor and kissed him hungrily, her hand ripped his shirt open and her hands were groping him all over, when they reached for his pants Tana stopped it.

"Well that answered that question" Tana said with a smile. "Come you two I think we need some privacy".

Tana grabbed both by their wrist and literally ran down to her quarters towing Will and Lady Victoria in her wasp-like wake. Will was unsure why Tana was acting like this, he was so far passed turned on there was no name for what he felt like at the moment.

Will did not know where they were until her heard Tana slam the door-hatch closed. The three of them just looked at each other and smiled. Tana stepped up to Victoria and undid the clasp that held her dress up over her lovely breasts, as the dress fell over Victoria's strawberry colored nipples, Tana already had one of them in her mouth and was biting and sucking at the same time. The look on Victoria face was pure raw desire. Will undress Tana and himself and carried the girls, who were tied in a little knot to his big soft bed.

"Wait, I want to say something before we loose what is left of our sense" Victoria gushed out.

"Yes".

"I have not had a lover of any sort in over a thousand years and I am not use to restraint, if there is any rules to our coupling please say them now so I don't insult or anger either of you" Victoria explained.

Tana smiled at Will and reached out to pull Victoria to her, and Will as well.

"I have never had any thought of sharing my bed and my man with another woman before, and I am sure Will felt the same, we have been madly in love for more than twenty years, however you make my breath come in gasps when you touch even my hand. Since Will turned me I have felt the desires of others pointed at me and was in no way tempted by any of them, or I would have told Will so we could face it together. You on the other hand Vicky make the woman in me come right to surface, and I was not angry when you attacked Will, It turned me on. I was surprised by that, I will not put restrictions on our affair if you both agreed to do the same, because I don't think I can resist either Will or your desires much longer" Tana told them with a wide bright smile.

"I have never wanted another woman, I was satisfied with Tana in everyway, and she is my perfect match. I am confused why only you seem to have the same effect on me as Tana does, where I can't resist you. Is this a vampire thing, if so why am I not lusty after all of the vampire females" Will asked?

"We are special, I do not have the desire for another either, that is why a thousand years have gone by and I have not had a lover. I want both of you in the worse way, I have not been like this since..."Vicky said.

"Since Brian, isn't that right Vicky" Will asked?

"Vicky"?

"Yes, I shortened your long name to that, because I want you to be my pet" Tana said as she pushed Vicky on her back and went to suckling her breast again.

Will kissed all the way gently up Tana's back from the crack of her hard golden skinned ass to her neck. She moaned softly. Will dropped his mouth over Vicky's mouth, he lay down beside her and ran his hands over Tana's naked form and Vicky's equally, both women were appreciative of his efforts. Tana was kissing down Vicky's firm abdominal muscles until she came to Vicky's thighs, Tana decide to pleasure her orally, something Tana had never done or dreamed of doing before, it just seemed so natural at the moment. Will looked down at Tana in surprise and she winked. Vicky was lost in the passion of the moment, their effect on her was even more toxic than her's on them, Will thought. He got up and made love to Tana from behind while she was continuing her Victoria tasting. Vicky's whole body was shaking. Victoria opened eyes and there was tears in them and a smile on her lips.

"My turn to give" Vicky said with a girlish giggle, "Trade places with me Tana".

Tana laid down where Vicky had just been, Victoria got up and turned her back to Will, she wiggled her butt and rubbed her body against him teasingly. She bent slightly forward, Will's powerful hands were on her hips and he was slowly, gently entering Victoria's body for the first time. She gasped at the sensation and lean back into Will so he was fully inside of her. Victoria was struggling to control her passion. She closed her eyes and kissed Tana's inner thighs on both sides, then went to work returning Tana's excellent efforts to make her reach orgasm. Tana had never had a woman's tender lips and silky smooth face between her legs, she could not believe how fast she came and often, Victoria may have been lover less for a great length of time but she knew how to pleasure Tana like an expert.

Will wanted to be more aggressive with Victoria body, but this was the first time they were coupling, so he was not going to over do it.

"Oh my God Vicky, I think I am in love with you, we have to do this everyday" Tana said breathlessly.

"Will lie on the bed and let us pleasure you" Tana said.

"A moment Tana, I am nearly there" Victoria choked out as she convulsed and went limp in Will's waiting arms.

Will laid on the bed, Tana was about to put his manhood in her mouth when Will stiffened, the thought of his junk in a mouth with deadly teeth gave him a brief pause.

"We would never ruin you precious tool Will, we both need you fully functional to service our needs and your desires" Vicky said.

Victoria leaned down and slid her satin lips and tongue down and around Will's manhood until her soft lips were touching the belly of his whale. Then she sucked and nibble gently on it in a most pleasurable way. Tana was never one to be left out so she crawled up and straddled Will face; his hand went to her tiny hips as he tasted his lovers tender parts. After a short time the girls switched places and Will tasted his new lover's goodies, she had a very pleasant taste. Tana was sucking and fondling his tool like a mad woman.

"I wish to ride you now my lord and master" Victoria said with a grin.

Victoria slid back and place herself where she wanted to be, she placed Will within herself and her hips began to move and twist at an incredible rate. Will sat up and sucked on Victoria's breast while Tana Sucked the other one. Will came very hard, so did Vicky. Will rolled Tana on her back and loved her vigorously while Vicky kissed her until his tiny bride came violently.

"Magnificent, truly" Victoria said exhausted.

"You are welcome" Will said.

"You know you should rape Lady Deathkill, you will get more support out of her if you bed her, instead of fighting her. If you dominate her in her own bed, she will be loyal to you unconditionally" Victoria stated as a matter of fact.

"Why should he bother" Tana asked, not liking the idea?

Victoria smiles and held Tana close to her.

"I like it not either Little Tana, but we vampires decided long ago that there are only three things we like to do, drink blood, fight and enjoy sexual pursuits. We decide in order to keep the peace we would lean more toward sexual pleasures. Therefore, if Will dominates Deathkill in her own bed, he will gain her respect and obedience. It is like that with all female clan leaders, yet, you only need bed myself and Lady Deathkill, we are the most powerful, all the other minor clans are loyal to one of the male clan leaders, who are in turn loyal to the Garrett clan. So take her for the political gain if not for pleasure" Victoria said.

"So are you to be my advisor, first we make love then we chat during the afterglow about matters of state" Will said teasingly?

"Yes, can you think of a better way to decide something than after your mind has been cleared of all clouding thoughts. Sex is useful in that way" Victoria said.

The hatch opened and Rudy came in and walked up to the bed. She smiled because Rudy was always a Manx, she loves to flirt and fool around and she was partial to both men and women equally. She went to sit on the bed near Will and both Tana and Victoria snarled at the same instant. They looked at each other in surprise. Tana was shocked at her reaction because Ruby was her close friend, and she just spent hours enjoying a near complete stranger sexually? Victoria was embarrassed because it was not her place to decide Will's lovers; that was between Tana and Will, yet she did not want Ruby or any woman to touch him or Tana for that matter. My God Victoria realized I am already hopelessly bonded to them, I hope they feel the same.

"So don't share, no need to get mad" Rudy chuckled. "I came because Lee was looking for you. By the way you are three sexy bitches, wow, hot. Think about sharing with your friend hey". She turned still smiling and left.

"I am sorry, I should not have snarled at your friend, she is very beautiful, and maybe you would like to enjoy her company" Victoria said?

Will and Tana looked at each other and smiled.

"No, not really. Besides she has her hands full with Jay and Steven Ogre, and I would guess even more. She does not need to play with us. Besides we have found the friend we want in you" Tana said.

Later Will was making the rounds, attending meetings with the Human military and overseeing relations between the vampire clan knights and the regular soldiers. There was not much strife, since the clans were more interested in playful pursuits than fighting. It is hard to be afraid of a beautiful person trying to gently seduce you all the time. When the human population on the ship realized just how much fun the vampires were and well mannered, the coupling began at an alarming rate.

Will found Jay trying to get the knights to practice fighting, but they protested because they said they were experts and did not need to train. Will was amused but his face said anger instead.

"Is it a fact that you are experts" Will said stripping her armor off.

Will removed his garments, armor to the waist and pulled his twin short swords and move around a little to stretch out. Then he turned on the clans in the huge bay.

"Any four of you attack me all at once" Will said.

Lady Deathkill was standing there with her knights and she gave them a nod to attack. Four of her personal guard went after Will' however his twin swords countered or parried every slash or strike. Will was not really trying, he was genuinely surprised at how easy he was blocking the attacks, they seemed slow to him and un-timed. He had enough of playing footsy so went low with the flats of his blade and knocked all four attackers off their feet at once in a whirlwind of motion.

"If your not going to seriously attack me, then what do you intend to do with the Korv. Jay come attack me like you mean it" Will said gruffly.

Jay pulled his three and a half hand sword out and saluted Will then came at him with blows so powerful that a normal human made sword would have been shattered to sand at the impact. Will block and traded shots. Will and Jay were locked in a tornado of spinning blades; it was the most amazing dance of death anyone had ever seen. Jay was bleeding from a few strikes but he did not slow at all, until Will stepped back and lunged forward suddenly trapping Jay's blade.

"Well done my friend, that is enough" Will said.

Jay only smiled and stepped back bowed a little and took his place at Will's back as all good knights do. Ogre stood in the corner silently watching with his piercing orange eyes.

"You fight well King" Lady Deathkill said.

"Care to try your blade against mine" Will said.

All at once Deathkill's knights attacked Will at once. (SLAM) They never even got close, Ogre's four hand sword still in the sheath hit them all at once like a baseball bat, vampire knights flew every which way. Ogre stood up to his full height and pulled his sword, Jay was beside him sword drawn, eyes like dirty liquid ice, only clan Garrett had the amber or orange tint to their eyes, and both meant business. Lady Deathkill jumped forward and held up her hands.

"STOP. I do not desire this. My knight's are trained to spring to me defense at any threat, I ask your pardon" The lady said swiftly.

"I am told your private name is Salen, I am not offended, but I think your going to have to learn your place, before you cause a war among our kind" Will said.

Will stepped forward and placed a hand on each of his knight's shoulder, so they would stand down, only Ogre was not for putting his sword away.

"I don't think I trust them to be honorable Will, the moment we stand down what is to keep them from attacking" Ogre said in his baritone voice, his eyes unblinking?

"How dare you question my honor" Salen screamed!

"I do question it, what are you going to do" Ogre said in a growl.

"Do you challenge me knight" Salen asked?

"With or with out armor" Ogre asked?

　　In answer to his question she dropped her dress to the floor, beneath it she had on a curious set of sexy armor. She had black armor that went from her ankle to her sleek hips, and metal thong for under wear. Her arms were armor to her shoulder, she wore a metal bra, her back and abdominal area was completely bare. Salen's body was a work of art, she was long and lean and finely muscled. The only thing that ruined her perfection was the perpetual scowl she wore. She pulled a sword and a dagger and advanced on Ogre.

"You're a fool girl, I have no equal in a melee" Ogre said as he placed his sword over his shoulder.

"Then this should be easy for you" Salen said.

"Wait". Ogre dropped his chest armor and back armor on the floor, the floor shook at the impact. "Now, at you leisure baby" Ogre said.

　　Salen moved like a snake, she coiled and struck, she was amazing with her blades, she was so far superior to her own knights. Her attacks were measured and thought out and recalculated instantly. Victoria was right he must dominate her, her worth to him as a general was limitless, and her body held a certain minor appeal, the coupling would not be unpleasant since it was necessary to keep the greater peace.

Ogre laughed at Salen as she zipped around and tried to kill him. She nailed him twice in close succession but it did not good, he blocked everything else and she had to do amazing acrobatics to keep his sword from cutting her in two at the waist. To Salen's chagrin Ogre was as fast as her and ten times stronger, he did not move like a giant, he moved like a tiger ready to pounce at all times. Moreover, his ambivalence at being wounded was unnerving to her, she had never met a foe she could not beat, and she understood he was not going to be beaten. Therefore, she stopped just inside of his guard and dropped her blades and looked at him defiantly. He surprised her then by reaching out and cupping her butt and lifting her up to his handsome face where he kissed her on the lips, she did not resist, even if she wanted to she could not, he was too strong.

"You are a great fighter my lady, and a good looking gal as well" Ogre said, as he put her down.

"You are not the mindless brute I took you for and your kiss was not unpleasant" Salen said smiling at Ogre. "I say that my clan must train harder so that our swords are second to none, and if Jay and the mighty Giant don't mind sharing the training, then they should join in" Salen offered

"Wait till these boys cross blades with Ruby" Ogre said. "She is faster than I am".

"What" Said Salen shocked.

"Hell, pretty baby, my boy there was practically walking while he spared, you are lucky he decide to keep it in granny gear or your knights would be dead" Ogre said pointing at Will.

Salen looked at Will with a distinct appraisal. She was looking at him as a foe and more likely a lover, she had a reputation for sampling as many lovers as she could, Nympho was a gross understatement.

(Later in the Galley)

Lee and Tana were eating lunch with Victoria. Tana talked Victoria into wearing clothes so they could eat in peace, not that she did not like the attention that the two got in their usual attire. Victoria wore only one of Will's sleeveless tee-shirts, her strawberry nipples were pushing hard against the material. Tana wore linen pants and a cute blue top. From the way they were being looked at, they might as well been nude. Lee and Tana order some steak and chicken with bread and corn.

"I don't see how you can eat that tasteless fodder Tana" Vicky said?

"Here try it with this hot sauce" Tana said as she poured hot sauce over a beef chuck and stuffed into Vicky's lovely mouth.

"Dear God, that is great, it is burning my tongue" Vicky said with a laugh.

"Yes, we love spicy things" Lee said sweetly.

"I think I will have meat and hot sauce for a meal when you eat, I find it enjoyable" Vicky gushed.

"Momma, I want to talk too you about a boy I met. I think he is the one for me, my heart pounds at thought of just being with him" Lee said.

Lee was fifteen and nearing her sixteenth birthday, she was a full grown woman in everyway. Boys and men alike gave her a lot of attention but she only flirted with them nobody ever got to score, she truly wanted to find what her parents had, true love. Lee had brown-red hair and tan skin, she was soft in the right places and fit from being a tomboy. Tana knew soon a man would claim her heart and her baby would become an independent adult.

"Does the boy feel the same way" Vicky asked "He is not a vampire is he"?

"Yes, he feels like I do, and no Victoria he is not a clan knight, they are honestly too afraid of mother and father to approach me" Lee said.

"When can I meet him" Tana asked?

"Now if you want, no grilling or biting Victoria" Lee said sternly.

Lee turned and scanned the milling crowd and her eyes had no trouble finding her boy. He was 6 foot 175lbs, blond hair, and pale blue eyes. Victoria smiled because the young man was as beautiful as any vampire could hope to be. He wore the symbol of an Army Ranger LT.

"Mother, Victoria this is Chad Sorren my guy" Lee said. "Do you know how hard it is to get Ogre not to kill every cute boy that comes up to me, only Chad had the balls to stare Ogre down" Lee finished.

"A pleasure to meet you ladies" Chad said honestly.

Victoria moved like a blur to put her face into Chad's and her hand on his neck. Chad looked at her and did not flinch, he smiled.

"Your very fast Lady Victoria, but look down" Chad said.

Tana busted out laughing; Chad had his pistol under Victoria's breasts. Chad obviously was very fast as well, for a human. Victoria kissed Chad on the cheek and smiled.

"He will do nicely as a mate Lee. He is brave, strong and handsome. If he was not yours I would take him as a plaything" Vicky said.

Chad's face clouded over, but he wisely held his tongue. Brave not stupid was he. Tana only smiled since she knew how choosy Vicky was about lovers, Chad would never have found his way into her bed, it was a test for Chad, and he passed it seemed. Victoria pulled Lee in and hugged them both; she kissed both Chad and Lee on the lips gently. It had the effect of making both of their blood boil with desire. When Victoria let go and stepped back Lee turn to Chad and pulled his face to her and kissed him long and deeply. This was the final test, when aroused it was each other they reached for even with a goddess like her right there.

"They pass the test." Victoria said.

Both Lee and Chad's heads turned suddenly, although their arms were still tightly around the back of their true love.

"What test"?

"I set both you senses off, you felt it didn't you, and your first instinct was to reach for each-other not me. Not to brag but if you were not deeply in love you would have jumped right on me" Vicky said slyly.

"Oh we felt it, but all I want is Lee at any cost" Chad said firmly.

"They are meant for each other Tana" Vicky said, "They passed my test easily".

(Elsewhere on the ship)

Mya and Navar walked up to Will holding hands, Will looked at her and knew she was Salen's knight, she even had the same body frame, very attractive and she was radiating affection for his son. Will at first wondered if this was Salen's order but he discounted that when Mya spoke to Navar.

"I will leave you alone to speak with your father loved one" Mya said with such loving in her voice, as if parting even briefly was painful to her.

Will brought all of his sense to bear on the girl, her heart was pounding and her throat was dry and she was on the verge of emotional. Mya noticed the King's scrutiny and blanched.

"Dad, we need to talk alone" Navar stated in a serious voice.

The son was bigger by a few inches of height and twenty pounds of muscle. He was eighteen going onto nineteen, he was already his father's son, he was proud head strong and loyal and way to fearless for his own good; a few trips to the ER could attest to that. Yet, other than his close friends Will could not think of a more fierce opponent in a fight than his son. He taught Navar to win by out thinking your foe, but if all else fail just go after them as if you lost your mind.

"What is up boy" Will said

"Can we talk dad alone" Navar said.

"Sure let's go sit on the stairs, they are huge and we can chat uninterrupted" Will answered.

When they were sitting on the stairs, Will looked at his son and waited for the young man to come to what ever was on his mind. Will was a cool father, he never bullied his kids, he let them be themselves and grow into adulthood strong and self reliant.

"Dad I have three girlfriends, two are pregnant. All three are friends so that is not a problem. Now that my girls are having babies, when do I get turned" Navar asked?

"The moment your babies are born Buddy" Will said.

"Yah, about that, it seems that the Tiguns have a birth enhancement technology that speeds up the pregnancy from months to weeks" Navar answered.

"Wow, that is cool, so when are you girlfriends due son" Will asked?

"Any time now actually, once I am embrace, I want to turn the girls dad, I want to turn them too. Damned if I know how but I found three women I can't live without, greedy huh" Navar said with a sheepish grin?

Will and his son went down to see the mother's of his grandchildren to be. Both of them were very lovely girls. One had dark skin and pale green eyes, the other was a petite red haired girl also with green eyes, and they were both very pregnant.

"Hello I am Will Navar's father" Will said.

"You look like his brother not his dad" The red head said, in a soft little voice that sounded Australian.

"You are a fine looking man, I see the son in you easily Will" The dark skinned girl said in a sultry voice.

"Welcome to the family ladies. So, how did the Tiguns speed up a pregnancy" Will asked?

A short Tigun walked up and touched Will's hand and made a motion toward the far wall area. Will went to investigate. Placed on a shelf in a zero status field was a small egg looking object. The Tigun reach in and took it out, he grabbed Will's hand and turned it palm up and placed the egg on it. There was an odd tingling in his hand.

"Why does it make my hand tingle? Moreover how does it speed up the pregnancies, and is it safe, those are my grand-babies after-all" Will asked?

"I assure you Lord Garrett that it is completely safe and we all know well that this is your progenies offspring, and as such we have taken the greatest possible caution with their safety. Beside this tech is not dangerous in anyway, the most that could happen is that is would not work. But it did work perfectly; you should be able to hold the infants in a day or two.

Will and Navar went to tell Tana the news, she loved babies and her own son's children would be an immense joy to her.

VAMPIRE WARS

SHANE

CHAPTER FIVE THE LAW BROKEN

Two day later the first baby was born to the Aussie girl. The baby a boy; was a red head like his mother and had piercing green eyes, also like his beautiful mother. Will learned that the girls name was Gwen and the baby was to be called Raz. Will thought it was an apt name for the alert infant.

Four hours later the lovely Kadi gave birth to a perfect baby girl, Aria. Like her mother Aria had dark skin and green eyes, but her eyes were rimmed with red around the green. Will picked her up abruptly and went to where Raz lay mumbling. Will put the babies in the bassinette together and looked at Raz's eyes, they had the same ring of crimson around his green coloring. Will opened the little fellow's mouth and found a pair of sharp wee fangs, Aria also he tiny choppers. Will showed Navar but said nothing to anyone but the mothers, whom he told to be careful when you nurse your babies they bite.

Will took Navar up to his own chamber and turned him. Navar screamed and fought the pain for two days, then gave over to the embrace and changed. His passing was nearly as bad as Will's was, likely because he would be a king himself one day. Tana cried and could not watch her baby suffer like he had, so she left on the first day. Victoria kept Mya away forcefully. Mya did not understand why she was not allowed to help.

Navar showered and donned his new armor that Will made him and was offered blades of his choice, made by Brian. The Prince chose a hand and a half sword with a double pointed guard and a pair of daggers. When the Garrett men emerged from the quarters Mya dove at Navar with desire, and the prince was extremely needy at this moment, however it had to wait. Ogre grabbed Mya mid-air and hauled her over his shoulder and turn to walk away.

Navar made to move to stop him when Jay and Will barred his way.

"She has broken the law son, she must be judged" Will said to Navar's confusion. "Go see your babies, look into their mouths".

Navar satisfied his desires with the mother's of his children fully. The Tigun Med-tech accelerated the ladies healing in a few hours as if they had never had babies. So Kadi and Gwen's bodies were hard and fit again.

When Navar who had to be careful with his new body not to kill his lovers was finally able to calm his hunger for his soon to be brides, he went and held his babies and when they yawned his heart sank. There in their tiny little mouths were perfect wee fangs. He knew what it was that Mya had done. He turned to Gwen but she answered his gaze.

"We know, we are both stronger and more agile than before the babies, we both gave birth to vampire babies, their blood mingled with our, so your mother told us we are likely immortal, but not vampires" Gwen said "You don't have to be so gentle with us".

Navar kissed her on the lips and handed Aria to her, he was running in a streak of light. He came to the meeting hall and his father was saying something. Ogre stepped in front of Navar to stop his entrance, but Navar back-handed him, sending him flying into the bulk head. Jay stepped forward, but stopped as Tana grabbed his wrist. Navar would have killed him by the look of it if he challenged him. Even mighty Steven Ogre was not a match for her furious son.

"What have we here" Navar said in an unmistakable deadly voice?

"The law was broken son, and you will hear it all before we decide what is to be done. You and I" Will said.

Navar was caught off guard, he was to decide Mya's fate? Freedom, what else could he decide, he loved her as much as Kadi and Gwen, he might be a greedy man, but he genuinely loved them all and they cared for each other as well. He would not let her come to harm no matter what even if he had to fight his father and everyone on board this bucket.

"Sit here by me son" Will said.

Navar sat down between his father and mother, the only two strong enough to contain him if he blew up. Victoria sat next to his father on the other side and Salen DeathKill Mya's sire stood by the vampire knight accused. Ogre and Jay closed the doors and stood there, the vampire knight brothers stood just behind them facing the door swords drawn against attack.

Will stood and spoke.

"We are here to speak the law. I will hear the words of all who wish to speak and when all has been said, judgment will be given. Mya bite my son before he had children, and the babies of other mothers were born vampires. This is a dangerous thing to do, as children have no restraint and can't fight their desires with other pleasures as we do, also Gwen and Kadi are in some way immortal now, without a proper clan. They are under my protection until that is ironed out" Will said sternly.

"I protest, they carry the blood of my clan as do the infants, they are mine by right of blood" Salen said.

Navar almost lunged at her, but Tana was as strong as her son and she held him down.

"Not yet son" She whispered.

"Your claim is noted...but don't get your hopes up, they are part of my family period" Will said letting the menace show in his eyes.

"Lady Victoria will be presenting the evidence. Please proceed" Will said.

Victoria got up in a single silky movement; she looked at Mya and then Salen.

"Where did you bite Navar" She asked?

"On the bottom of his left foot, not enough to turn him, but enough to make him strong enough not to be kill during our passion" Mya said miserably.

"Remove you boot Navar" Victoria ordered.

He gave a mean look at her but did as she bid him. Sure enough there was a tiny indent on his foot where Mya said she nibbled on him.

"Why did you break the law Mya, you knew that Navar loved you and he was already in your grasp, so why risk final death like this" Victoria asked?

"I just didn't want anyone to take him from me, I have never in my 157 years known a love like this, I could not loose it, it is the reason I breathe, it is everything to me. To be without him is agony for me, I am nearly as close with Kadi and Gwen, I love them too" Mya answered sadly.

"Is there anyone who wishes to speak" Victoria said.

"If I must loose my knight to this fiasco I claim her blood and death" Salen Said.

Salen was lunging forward to deliver the death strike to Mya. She never even got close Navar had her dangling by her throat at the end of his powerful left arm, Salen's knight began to move toward him. Victoria snarled and fifty of her elite knights came out of nowhere instantly.

"Hold your ground or be slain" Navar ordered.

Salen's knights were no match for the violet eyed avengers of Victoria's clan, who were only second in strength to Garrett itself.

Even Will was surprised by the insane speed of his son and the ferocity of his words. Victoria was not surprised and she was prepared for this it would seem. Will thanked God for the day she decided to love him and Tana.

"Son you can't kill her for claiming her rights, but I am not inclined to grant her request so do put her down gently" Will said.

Navar was on the verge of murder when he let Salen down to the floor; she chocked and coughed a couple of times. Salen gave him a murderous look and stood up to her full height which was still short of his by several inches.

"I will meet any challenge you wish bitch" Navar said as he leaned forward.

Salen wisely moved back and away, she was good but once again, she was facing a Garrett, and their power was paramount among the clans.

"Is there anyone else that wishes to make a statement" Victoria asked.

"We would" Gwen said.

Gwen and Kadi were standing next to Lee and Chad, they were holding their babies. Lee moved to sit by her mother, Chad at her side.

"You have no voice here I am afraid, only the clans may address the assembly" Victoria said sympathetically.

"I will allow it because they were involved without their consent, it is only fair to hear from the other victims" Will said.

An immediate outrage started.

"SILENCE"!!!

There was an immediate silence and many were shaking in fear, Will was standing and the glow from his eyes was blinding, it seemed like two red search lights were aimed around the room. He was positively pulsing with energy; that only Victoria had seen before.

"So Will can do it as well as Brian can, I wonder about the son" Victoria said softly to herself.

"Your will be still and listen to the girl speak or face my wrath" Will snarled.

The silence was crisp and still. It was finally broken when Gwen placed her baby in Will's arms. The baby caused a sudden change in the King's body attitude, he softened and smiled and nuzzled Raz. Will looked up and there was surprise and confusion and yes fear as well. The Lord high King Will Garrett was a mystery to them all, and that made him dangerous. Will looked at Gwen and winked.

"I am not a victim, I care not about your laws, we love Mya she is ours and she did not sin out of malice but love, we ask, I ask for mercy and common sense. I understand the gravity of making a baby vampire, we will all have to be vigil now and make sure that no harm comes to the human population" Gwen said an stepped back.

Kadi took her place holding little Aria.

"I agree with Gwen, It was Mya that brought me into the circle, she was what I desired, so I was willing to share with Gwen and Navar. I fell hopelessly in love with all of them, we are meant to be. Mya did what me and Gwen could not she claimed Navar in a most private way. Without Mya our hearts are not full" Kadi explain. Her face grew hard "I am not as strong as you or as fast but the hand that harms my Mya will be rent from the body which it is attached"!

There was no mistake that she meant it and would do whatever it took to kill anyone who harmed Mya. Will was worried this would lead to war. Great passion causes great pain and it is the perfect reason to fight and kill...for the ones you love. Will could not fault the girl her heart felt warning, moreover in Gwen he saw the same tough leather in her soul, she would wage war if Mya was killed, no doubt about it. Will could not allow harm to come to them; they were family now and his wards at the moment. If he did not stop this Navar would slaughter half the knights in a single day bare handed.

"Your words have been heard and noted ladies. Jay, Ogre take these girls to my quarters and stay with them" Will said.

Jay understood this was a dangerous time for the clans and more for the immortal girls and their vampire spuds. Jay was alert in the front of the girls as they headed for the door; Steven Ogre came up behind them his massive blade drawn. It said don't follow me or else. When they had gone, Will turned back to the assembly.

"Is there any more speakers" Will asked?

Strangely it was one of Victoria's elite knights that spoke; it was a handsome young vampire male with blond hair.

"I wish to speak lord" The vampire said.

"Granted, speak freely" Will said.

Victoria's face was showed surprise, and Mya's face showed dread. From Mya's face Navar guessed that this must be a lover. The knight turned to his Mistress Victoria and bowed very low, and then he spoke.

"I beg your pardon Lady Victoria, but I must speak. Mya is precious to me as well and I would ask the court to show leniency toward her, she is often misguided but she is true of heart and generous as a companion, never would she harm anyone who did not challenge her safety or those she is sworn to protect" He explained.

Navar was on the verge of murder as his jealousy boiled through. Will was again worried about war among the clans, but this was Victoria's knight who spoke for Mya?

"Why do you care knight" Salen said?

"I answer not to you witch" The elite knight answered!

Salen snarled but made no move toward Victoria's knight, wisely.

"Nonetheless son I need to know you reason, the why an elite knight would risk his own status for one of Salen's knights. Are you lovers" Will asked?

The entire room was startled when the handsome vampire laughed deeply and loudly at the question. He tried to catch his breath and answer but he was unable. Navar took to angry steps and went to grab him by his throat, but Mya stopped him.

"No".

"What is this shit Mya, is he your lover" Navar screamed in anger?

The knight was not laughing when Navar took a step toward Mya, he snapped his blade out in an instant and had the point on Navar's throat.

"She is my sister, prince or no prince, king or not, lady or lord, I will defend her to the last" Erik growled.

Victoria cautioned the room not to move with a gesture from her hand. Even Will could tell the vampire boy was special and deadly serious. Navar however was not about to back off, a Mexican standoff. Mya decided it.

"Stop both of you, do you think I could love a man who killed my brother, or a brother who killed my man. NO" Mya shouted "Back off".

She hit both of them in the chest knocking them back. She glared at Will as if saying silently help me please.

"Okay, that is enough debate. I will speak with Navar, Tana, and Victoria to decide Mya's fate" Will said solemnly.

For a long twenty minutes the heated debate took place. Finally, they decided, although Navar was pissed about it. Victoria had a few last words of wisdom.

"Erik is my sparring partner, he may be the 6th most powerful vampire alive, he is supernaturally fast, maybe faster than even you Navar and he is deadly and able to perhaps kill even you. Let me deal with him before we exposed the sentence to assembly" Vicky advised.

"Do it" Will said.

Victoria walked over to Erik and put her hand on his shoulder and then hugged him. She turned to leave and chopped down hard on the occipital plexus, Erik was out before he hit the floor.

"Disarm him and lock him up in the brig for now" Victoria commanded.

Four knights did as they were bid and Erik was taken away. Will cleared his throat and all was silent. He looked at Navar, the prince looked ill.

"It is our decision that Mya's life as she knew it is forfeit, she is to be taken from here by myself and drained dry of all life's blood until she is dead" Navar said with bile in his voice.

Not a single person moved or spoke, the look on Navar's face forbid it. Mya was not trussed up, rather she got up and went and held Navar's hand and waited to be executed. Navar took her to his families common area where there would be no intruders, the penalty for entering the Lords private area was instant death. Navar stripped Mya of all clothes, with tears in his red eyes "Goodbye my love", he sank his teeth into her neck and drained her of her precious life. At the point where she was slipping into the void Will stopped him. Navar was crying so profusely he almost could not hear him.

"Stop son, save her now, give her your own blood before she dies a final death" Will said.

Navar looked up with tears of blood running down his neck. The boy ripped open his forearm and force Mya's head back and let the blood down her tawny throat. She convulsed harshly and paid a terrible price as the Garrett blood crushed the last remnant of Salen's blood markers. The pain and agony was nothing like Will and Navar endured, however it was way beyond what any vampire knight had ever had to endure before. Navar was so glad he did not have to kill Mya; his love would have taken him to the grave with her after she died. Tana smiled at Will, she approved of his use of a loophole to save Mya from death and remove her from Salen's control in one move, brilliant.

SHANE

"Brilliant my lover" Vicky said with a twisted smile.

Later that night Will decided that is was time to teach Salen who was Lord of the clans, all of the clans. Victoria and Tana encouraged him to rape Salen mercilessly, until she learned her place. They did not like the thought of her touching their man, but there was no other way but this unless he killed Salen, and that would bring war.

"Don't think about it like a task, but a pleasure, Salen was after all an extremely desirable female" Tana told Will, but her eyes said more.

"I could just kill her you know" Will said in earnest.

"No just fuck the bitch until she swears loyalty and be done with her skinny ass" Victoria growled.

"You are about the same size and build darling" Will said amused at her jealousy since she told him he had to do this.

Will left after hugging Navar as he rocked Mya who was still burning up with a wild raging fever. Will made his way like a leopard on the hunt. He made it to the area assigned to Salen Deathkill and her clan. There were many guards, but no one could match Will's soft lightning fast steps when he moved. He slipped by them easily, and on into Salen's bed chambers. Luckily, she was alone and slept in the nude as most vampires did due to the sexual nature they could not resist. Will carried no weapons and wore only linen pants, which he took off. Will walked over to where Salen was lying on the bed and slipped the satin cover off her awesome body. Will could not help the powerful lust that come over him, he truly did not want to bed this woman, but he had not had sex at all that day because of matters of state. Vicky and Tana usually were pretty worn out by time he was satisfied. Now Salen was going to have to manage all of his incredible needs alone.

"OH, sure, do it" Salen said in her sleep as she rolled over on to her stomach and cat stretched.

Will was on her, he rammed his personal sword fully inside of her vagina, she tried to roll and toss him off, but he was a Garrett and as such many times her strength. He put a hand on the back of her neck and shoved her face into the mattress so she could not yell for help. His left hand was on her hip as he plunged in and out of her, but not mercilessly like Victoria advised but in a pleasurable way that was intoxicating to Salen's body. Salen did not even know when Will's hand on her neck was moved to her fit hips. She moaned and leaned back into his body, suddenly he jerked her up and fondled her firm heaving breasts; he rolled her nipples gently and nibbled on her ear. Salen began to build a deep internal energy, which was released when Will made her come violently on moment later.

"My God Lord, your visit is unexpected, I would have thought you would rather kill me than bed me" Salen said in a questioning yet grateful tone.

Will did not answer, he flipped her like a pancake on to her back spread her legs and began to taste her tender parts softly and he hummed as her licked and suckled her. Salen's whole body trembled with pleasure as she came and came and came uncontrollably. When she thought he was done he pinned her knees to her beasts and loved her more aggressively, she wondered why he was gentle and then suddenly rough with her body. It was a complete turn on for the nymphomaniac Salen; never had she had a lover than could master her like this. He was deeper inside of her than anyone had ever been, her body contorted with pleasure and she came yet again. He however, did not.

"You are a good lover Salen" Will finally said.

He turned her so his throbbing manhood was near her face; he tilted her head back and slid it down her throat as his warm mouth went back between her legs. Salen loved the way he ate her and was only happy to suck the color out of his tool. Salen inhaled his manhood hungrily as he pleasured her with his tongue and lips. She was so turned on she began to come non stop and sucked him as vigorously as she could; Salen wanted nothing more than to please her master. She totally submitted to him, she was his slave by this point. Will was enjoying her oral efforts but his mind was on Tana and Victoria, he wanted to eat one while penetrate the other, so he need to finish this up and go back to his own bed. He knew the moment that Salen was his slave, now he only needed punish her a little, cum and go home.

"Turn over on your belly and raise your sexy ass up Salen" Will said softly.

She eagerly did as she was told. When she was positioned Will grabbed her above elbows and stuck his manhood in her tight ass, and bent her back into his movements, she made a weak effort to resist but stopped and let him have her, she wanted him to do it strangely to her, so she rose up her hand and knees.

"Hold still Will, let me do it" Salen said,

She crawled backward into his lap and rode his throbbing tool until her legs got weak from the most amazing orgasm she ever had. Then she pushed him on his back, she mounted him like a cow girl riding a bucking bronco, she moan and put her breast in Will's mouth, he chewed on her nipple and then came hard inside of her body. Salen collapsed from exhaustion, Will took a brief shower, and he went to carried Salen into the shower and washed her body and put her back to bed when he was done.

Will went to his bed and found his lovers waiting for him holding each other. He crawled in between them and made their desires bloom as they coupled ferociously in their mad love. The new day started but Tana and Victoria were eager to stay in the embrace of their true love. Will wanted nothing more than to stay in their loving arms and let the world go away. However he was king and leader of a task force to save his planet, so he pushed himself up and dragged his mates up and into the shower with him. It is a good thing that each quarter has its own water recycling system, because they stayed in the shower long after they were clean, continuing what they had started on their bed.

Elsewhere on the ship Lee and Chad were preparing for a wedding. Chad was terrified when Will asked him if he wished to dine alone with him. Chad thought after looking into Will's eyes he was to be the meal. That was not even close to what happened. Will was a good host and he asked the regular fatherly questions. It was a little unnerving to look at a man; who looked no more than twenty five and think of him as soon to be wife's father. In the end Will gave his consent, despite Lee's age. Will explained that this may be a one way mission for many of the knights and soldiers on the ship, So his daughter who both Tana and Will believed truly loved Chad, deserved to be as happy as she could be before possible tragedy occurred. Chad liked Will he thought about things in a practical way, looked at options and better ways and he was not a tyrant, although he could be.

"Hey are you listening to me" Lee asked?

"What, oh yes" Chad said sheepishly and smiled.

Lee smiled back and slipped her arm around his waist and put her head on his chest, she listened to his heart quicken as he held her. Chad could not image how hopelessly he was in love with this girl; he even faced off with the deadly giant to be with her, foolish but so worth the effort. Since that day Steven Ogre and Chad had kind of fell into a close friendship, they played games, such as knife throwing. Ogre still watched over them, and Ruby the girl Ogre adored was at his side most of the time. Ruby was an odd mixture of sexual and deadly, you could not be sure which it was with her until you were dead or in bed Ogre told Chad.

"So do you want to invite the ship or just family and friends" Lee asked.

"Small please" Chad said.

Lee only kept smiling because she knew that he was aware Tana and Victoria had big plans for them. What she did not know was that Chad asked Tana to help him with a ring. You see Vampires are great craftsman, and Tana's delicate hands had created many fine arts and jewelry as well as her own person weapons. Chad's face darkened for a moment and Lee could feel the change before she saw it on his face.

"What is the matter" Lee inquired?

"Once we have a baby your going to be turned and I am going to get old" Chad said.

Lee did not tell him how completely wrong he was, like her mother was turned by her father, Lee would not let Chad grow old; she needed him so she would take him with or without his consent or her father's. Chad was her man and her heart could not survive in a world that he was dead in. No, Chad was to be turned and that was final.

"Hey we should be careful right now because of what happened to Mya, we should eat something and retire to my room for some...cuddling" Lee giggled.

(In Navar's quarters)

Mya woke up and she looked at Navar who was still crying, only they were tears of joy rolling down his chiseled face. Mya was confused, why was she alive, was she not sentenced to death. She kissed Navar softly on his lips, all questions were suddenly lost as an inferno of desire washed over her, she had never felt a desire so intense before. When she was turned she felt it then but not like this, she nearly exploded into Navar, she grabbed him and threw him on the bed, she ripped his clothes off like a wild beast. She slid her body over his and the love making began. They switch spots and angles many times, but what they did not do was speak, it was not necessary; their hearts spoke for them, as did their eyes.

(SCREAMS)

Gwen and Kadi jumped on the bed with tears running down their gorgeous faces, they like everyone else thought Mya dead. Mya kissed both of them and hugged them so tight if they did not have superhuman abilities thanks to Mya's misguided bite early on Navar's foot, they would have had their backs snapped like dry twigs. The Joy in being a quartet again was immense. Kadi who had been a Lesbian before Mya brought her to Navar's bed was more overjoyed than Gwen; although Gwen loved Mya very much. Vampires are usually bisexual, most of the female vampires are and a third of the males are as well. Mya was very happy with men or women, until she met her hearts desire. Mya told Gwen and Kadi that she would never want to be parted with them either; and she would never bed anyone else again because of the love she had for her new family.

"We are united once more my loves, but how is this possible" Mya asked?

"My Father is a wise king and kind Mya. He tricked Salen out of you and still upheld the law. You did die baby, but then you were reborn a Garrett. You are Mya Garrett my mate. You two have to choose, stay as you are stronger and faster than a normal human and your life will no doubt be extended, but your not a true vampire and still vulnerable to attacks. My father has left it to me to decide your fate, but I will not. You will choose; if you choose my way of life, then you will be part of my eternal family, my mates for life. You must understand once my blood courses through your body you will be bonded to me and me only until we are dead; you wont be able to control it and if you wanted to leave me, us, you are free to leave but you won't want to. I want you to be sure this is what you want; because once I turn you it can not be undone. I love you, all three of you with my entire being and I will protect and defend you as long as I live. That is my promise, my pledge to you" Navar said seriously.

"I want to say something Navar. I was so lusting after Mya in the beginning; I never wanted a man, not with me or inside of me. When you touched me my world changed and I fell deeply in love with you, I wanted to carry your baby. I fell in love with Mya and Gwen as well; lust plays no part for me anymore. I want to be with you always, all of you. You are my family now. Turn me" Kadi said with her pretty smile.

"I went to other way; I like a strong man to hold me close. I have never been one to give it up though until I met you three, my drawers were on the floor the instant you asked me to sleep with you. I know your want of me was more than lust Navar and I learned the joy of sharing with another woman, and how good if felt to be part of something special. I want to stay with you now and no amount of blood magic would change my true heart. Take me into your world and make me yours forever boyo. I could not stand loosing any of you. That is why as scared to death as I was, I spoke for Mya even though I knew I was not allowed" Gwen said.

Mya went to bite Gwen and Navar stopped her. She looked at him, but he shook his head and stood up.

"If Gwen and Kadi are turned it has to be by me, a true born Garrett, it will make them more powerful. I want my parents blessing first, understand I will turn you no matter what, but I want to get a blessing if I can" Navar explained.

A few moments later Navar saw Ruby walking toward the science docks where the marines kept there big guns. Ruby was popular among the human military because she was friendly and gentle spirited, they really had no idea. Navar ran up to her, he had to slap away her lightning fast dagger thrust.

"Watch it Ruby, I already shaved today" Navar said in a silly tone.

Ruby smile and jumped on him and hugged him tight. She kissed him but it was a nice innocent kiss, she knew his heart was stolen away by three beautiful sirens, she was happy for him, and Ruby was not a home wrecker, she had more than enough pleasure for her little self.

"How goes it man-ling" Ruby asked?

"I am good Ruby. Hey do you know where the old man is" Navar asked.

Ruby snickered.

"You two look like brothers. Yes, he is arguing with the military over lunch today" Ruby said.

"Thanks" Navar said and he leaned down and kissed her on her soft lips, turned into a blur and was gone.

Will was not arguing, he was listening to them argue like infants. The Army brass was bitching about training schedules and the marines were in their way too much, they needed to change that right away. Will saw Navar out of the corner of his eyes and smiled deeply, rescue had come to him just then.

"Gentlemen I must take a recess and speak with my son. Please continue without me, and fella's no blood ok" Will said

The son hugged his dad, and noticed they did look like brothers. He two Garrett males walked away to the main staircase and began to climb.

"Dad I...I want to turn Gwen and Kadi" Navar said tentatively?

"Why"?

"Because I can't bear to be without either of them, life would be empty without my family around me. I intend to have three mates, to your two and Lee's one" Navar said.

"I believe it is the right decision son, turn them now, today. I have been worried about their safety" Will said.

Navar went up and put the bite on his mates literally. Mya held Kadi during her passing and Navar cradled Gwen. They turned in no time and there was little pain, however the part of the old Mya that was in them caused a fever as it was crushed by the Garrett blood. Mya, Kadi and Gwen all had Golden-red eyes, the telling sign that they were Garrett's.

VAMPIRE WARS

SHANE

CHAPTER 6: CLAN GARRETT

In the three days that followed Mya's execution Erik has nearly broken the holding cell apart. Lady Victoria went to calm him everyday, he was calm when she was there because he was loyal and he truly loved her, but like a big sister. When Victoria left Erik would fly into a rage within the hour and begin to beat the wall to odd shapes. Erik never hit the door because his sire put him in the cell and here he would stay until she let him out or until Victoria herself was threatened, then he would go from this place and not before. He beat on the walls because his little sister was dead and he was not.

On the fourth day after the trial of his sister Mya; Erik was sprung from jail by his master; Lady Victoria. He put on his armor and sword and followed her up the assembly hall. Erik stood statue still as all the clans waited for Will and family to enter the hall. No one was ready for what they saw. Will entered holding Tana's hand, they both winked at Victoria. It was common knowledge that she was their mate now; she was part of the Garrett clan because of it, if not by blood then by choice of bonding. Salen also got a wink from Will, not the same quality however. Salen was very loyal these days and only a few people knew the real reason, but many thought bribes, they were clueless.

"WHAT" Screamed Erik!

Mya walked out holding hands with Navar and Kadi. Gwen was on the other side holding Navar's other hand. Mya's eyes were the red of the Garrett clan and so were the new mates of Navar. Even Victoria did not know Mya lived. Clan Garrett was growing and it's already insane power was gripping the clans tightly within their iron fist. Ogre, Jay and Ruby came in behind Lee and Chad who were to be married the next morning.

The vampire brother's guarded the door behind the king as usual. They were the silent security that Brian sent to watch over his kin. They were Brian's knights, not Will's but they were part of the bigger clan, so they were family and they were good at their job.

"Yes, I see questions on your faces. I will answer them by explaining why Mya stand where she is. Navar carried out her death sentence, it is the law. However, at the point where she died, I had him remake her as his own mate as a new Garrett, you have to only look at her eyes to see the truth of my words. I am not without a heart or mercy, yet the law was read and it had to be done to protect us all. Within her and the other two brides of N, flows the blood of Garrett, she is his and his alone, no claim on her will be tolerated, except...by her brother Erik" Will said.

Erik was floored, so was everyone else. Mya let go of Navar's hand and Kadi stepped over and put her arm around her boys waist and put her head on his shoulder. Mya touched her brother's face and he touched her's.

"Are you still my baby sister" Erik asked unsure?

"You silly boy, of-course it is me Erika" Mya said.

"Hey don't call me that" Erik said. Then his eyes open all the way up in revelation. "Mya it is you"!

Erik swooped up his sister and hugged her tightly. Mya hugged him back fiercely; it was then that Erik came to understand the difference in power between the Garrett clan and everyone else. Mya was fast and had great endurance for a vampire but was weak, now she was stronger by far than he was and likely faster as well. He made a mental note not to ever pull a weapon on the prince again, especial since he saved Mya from death.

Victoria walked up and sat next to Tana; they held hands and waited to see what else Will had to say.

"I want to thank you all for coming here. Tigre wants us to learn all we can in the next few months so that when we meet the Korv in battle, it is they who die and not us. I am not going to send any clan to their slaughter, if I am unwilling to go into an area to fight, then neither will any of you go there. You are all my family after a fashion and as such important to me. We should all be able to go home together, but alas some us will die in the valiant fight to protect our cousins the humans, and are brothers and sisters back home. I do not want any of us to fight each other; I wish you all to save the fight for the Korv. I am also going to encourage contests of skill, and betting on the contestants, there will be no killing, it is forbidden, if your opponent dies you will follow them into the veil" Will said.

"Well said Lord Will" Salen answered for the group. "I will arrange the first contest for later today; Garth will take on all challengers".

The assembly broke up and the five clans went their own ways. Salen grabbed Garth by his enormous arm and held him back off to the side. Salen was his master so he asked her no questions; Garth just followed Salen's lead. When the assembly area was clear Salen turned to Garth and spoke.

"I want to disrupt clan Garrett, by driving a wedge in the Garrett sleeping arrangements. Navar would kill you if you tried to taste any of his brides and they travel usually together as a group. If I had you touch Lee, Will would certain to kill our entire clan. Victoria is too powerful to rape. That leaves Tana, she is a vampire and subject to our customs, so if you force yourself on her, Will could not attack us without the wrath of the other clans" Salen said with grim satisfaction.

"It shall be done" Garth said.

Garth walked down the hallway trying to figure out what the hell was going on here. Will would most likely kill him for this insult, and that damn prince, as well as Lady Victoria would challenge him openly and kill him in a blood match. This was a bad idea, except for the fact that Garth wanted to get his huge hands on Tana's amazing body. She was so tiny and desirable; nearly every knight had fantasies about being her lover. Therefore Garth would risk death to get a chance to penetrate her body and force her to pleasure him.

Tana was in the shower washing up after her afternoon exercise. Garths slipped in and watched her gently, but vigorously wash her nude form. Garth was a big man and he was randy by the time Tana was rinsing the soap off her breasts. She turned her back to him and reached for the water shut off valve. Garth was on her, he pinned her to the wall while his other hand traced her bottom and as he began to move his hand to the inside of her thigh, when he got a huge surprise.

Ogre ran into Tana in the corridor, she was furious and towing what was left of Garth down the hallway by his ankle. Ogre snapped his fingers and Ruby came out of nowhere and they trailed Tana from behind weapons drawn. Tana continued on to the clan Deathkill's common area, she walked up and tossed Garth at Salen.

"If you ever send another person to rape me, I will cut your fucking heart out and eat it while you watch bitch" Tana said as her red eyes glowed with anger. "Worry not I have forbidden revenge against your clan".

Tana turned on a heel and walked lithely out of the area on whisper quiet bare feet and naked body. Ogre placed a hand on Tana's little shoulder and put his giant tunic around Tana, she did not seem to mind his touch or company. Ruby stood looking at Salen.

"Yes Ruby" Salen asked?

"Watch for me girl, I take no oath of friendship, I follow no man's orders, or woman's either" Rudy answered with a smile that was not friendly in any way.

When the time came for the tournament all the clans filed in and took up positions to either watch or compete. Salen was the host of the first contest so she was already there and set up in her area with knights ready to jump into the area and fight. The last to enter was clan Garrett; chairs were set up for them as the ruling family. They took their appointed seats. Ogre and Jay took up positions at each side of the family as usual. Ruby knelt just in front of Will.

"Welcome to the first of many contests, as host I will send the first knight to an open challenge" Salen said gesturing to a fit knight with a thin sword.

The knight stepped into the area in the middle of the assembly hall and was greeted by some hoots; he was known to be a fine fighter and a good technician. The crowd were startled when Tana got up walked to the edge of the area, dropped her dress. Tana had sleek red-black armor on her arms and legs, she wore only a black leather thong style micro bikini. Tana had two long curved daggers, sheathed in guards on her firm thighs;, she walked to the middle up the area and back handed the knight, who flew like a lawn dart at the wall. Tana pointed at Salen.

"Stop fucking around Salen and come to the ring yourself" Tana said in a satin smooth voice.

"I am host, and you would not stand a chance against me youngling, my sword is legendary" Salen scoffed.

"Chicken-shit coward" Tana whispered.

Which means everyone heard it.

"Fine"!

Salen looked at Will, his face was curious not angry, he did not know about Garth. Salen walked into the ring her mighty sword in one hand and her Dirk in the other. She began to circle Tana, but only Tana's eyes moved, her sexy body was statue still. Salen got around the back and lunged sword point straight at Tana's spine fast than a blink. Tana's movements were too fast for most of the knights to follow. She back-flipped over Salen's body, and blocked her sideway jab with the dirk. Tana knock the dirk to the ground by hitting Salen's wrist with the handle of her dagger and then snapped an elbow into Salen's nose, shattering it.

"I'll kill you" Salen screamed!

Tana was not finished and Salen broke one of the first rules of combat, don't talk when you should fight. Tana stepped in a sweep the front of Salen Bra off, taking her left nipple right off her body, she reversed her strike slitting Salen's throat on the left side. Salen gasped. Tana was a machine, calm look on her face, she drove a knee into Salen's ribs with lightning fast accuracy, launching her off her feet, Tana grabbed her wrist flipping Salen belly towards the roof; that was when Tana ended it. Tana drove her dagger through Salen's back and out her stomach. Tana held her there above her head height and whispered in her ear.

"The next time to cross me you will not survive to tell the story" Tana whispered.

In a fast movement Tana flung Salen off her right dagger and scalped her with her left and football kicked her into her clan, launching more than half off their feet. She just stood there red eyes glowing in triumph.

"Is there any one else" Tana asked?

Tana scanned the assembly.

"Is there nobody else to cross blades with me" Tana asked?

   Tana scanned the crowd, they were all shocked at how effortlessly Tana had taken down a master swordsman and clan chief. Will was even shocked and amazed at his tiny brides wild new abilities, not only sexy but deadly as well, it would be a fool who attacked her again after this display. Will loved Tana even more if that were even possible, his heart swelled with pride.

"I will cross blade with you darling...a friendly match please" Victoria said.

   Victoria was not wearing her armor because she did not intend to fight, so she striped naked and had Erik get her sword. Tana smiled as her lover walked naked into the ring with her, Victoria came up and kissed Tana on the lips.

"I will fight you for position, you win I will massage you, I win you pleasure me first, deal" Vicky asked with a smile?

"Sounds good" Tana said as she dropped her brief armor to match Victoria's nudity.

   The contest was so fast and deadly, that the clans thought they were trying to kill each other even though it was common knowledge they were lovers and mates. Will watched in awe of them. Everyone else was terrified at their insane speed and skill. These two goddess, bodies bare, blades blazing, they were a tornado of death, they cut each other some but mostly they looked like Chinese acrobats practicing at high speed.

   Victoria stepped back and tossed her sword to Erik who caught it effortlessly. Victoria stepped forward with her arms open wide and she wrapped them around Tana's little body.

"I am lucky you were only playing, or I might be dead now. It should bring me no surprise at your skills; you were the first knight that Will turned. Navar is already feared, I don't know why anyone thought you were less powerful than your son, you are the Garrett Clan queen" Victoria said loudly.

Tana sheath her deadly daggers and put her hands around Victoria's waist and let them slip down to her muscular ass, which she squeezed suggestively.

"Why don't we go wash our bodies and snuggle until Will is done here and can join us for a different kind of combat" Tana giggles.

Victoria turn her radiant smile on Tana and pulled her little body into her side and together they walked up to Will who kissed them passionately while fondling them shamelessly, he let them leave with a firm crack on there asses. It made them giggle. Will walked out into the middle of the ring and turned with a grand smile to look over all clans.

"I sincerely doubt I could top the display my lovers just put on, I am constantly amazed by Tana, who would have thought her so fierce and skilled. I should not want her as my enemy; your life span would be reduce. Nevertheless, we are here to match skills not kill one another, would anyone not of my own clan cross blades with me in a friendly contest of skill" Will asked light-heartedly.

"Aye, I will have a go Lord Garrett" Said a big sandy haired man.

The man was at least 6'5 and 250lbs; he had blond sandy hair and blue eyes and a big smile. He was finely muscled and moved like a cat. He was the leader of Clan Aussie (Branagan, actually). He walked up and pulled a mighty cleaver from his back, and then he stopped and held out a hand.

"I am Rip Branagan leader of the Aussie's and I will be happy to cross bladed with you Lord" Rip said.

"None of the Lord stuff Rip unless we are in a counsel or in the War room on official business. Hang on a moment Rip" Will said as he walked to his clan.

Will stripped to the waist; he tossed his armor on the chair except his wrist guard and ankle guards. He reached for his weapons and stopped. He turned and pulled Ogre's giant dagger out of his belt.

"May I borrow this Steven" Will asked?

Ogre just smile and looked over his head at Rip. Will punched Ogre in the chest.

"Thanks big guy" Will said.

Rip was waiting in the ring patiently for Will with an amused look on his handsome face. Will smiled back, neither men looked smug; they looked like old friend about to play a favorite game.

"May I use a second Blade Will" Rip inquired.

Will nodded his head. Rip did not even look he just held up a hand and there was a strange fang bladed knife in his right hand. Rip noticed Will's interest and handed it to him. Will was shocked at the weight, there was none; it was so lite that if you were not gripping it, you would not know it was even there. Rip smiled and handed his sword to Will. The sword was large, near the equal of Ogre's mighty blade and it weight nothing either. Will decide not to attack hard or he might shatter the bladed and kill Rip back accident. Rip would dispel that notion in a minute for Will.

"Ready Will" Rip asked as he took his sword back from Will.

"At your leisure Rip" Will said.

Rip was as fast as a cobra and ten times more deadly, Will was caught off guard by the speed and precision of Rip's attacks, they were so fast you would have thought the man had four talented arms instead of two. Will blocked them all however, that only made Rip smile and step up his game. Will began mixing in martial art, none blade attacks to the utter thrill of the crowd, who began to bet on whether Rip could cut Will before the king dropped him. Rip was just as talented with his feet as he was with his hands, so he deflected most of Will's attacks but not all. Will caught him with a front kick that launch the Aussie into a black-flip, Rip twisted landed on his feet and was on Will again in a half of a heart beat. They went around with Rip's knife raking Will's chest and Will's borrowed blade cutting the inside of Rips arms and legs. The contest ended when Will stepped in so fast that nobody could follow his movement but Navar who gasped at his father's acceleration. Rip was disarmed as Will raked down on his arms, literally ripping the weapons form his hands and simultaneously hitting Rip in the center of his chest with a palm strike that big Aussie flying into Ogre who braced and caught him with a smile.

"MY GOD" Jay hollered "Damn boy, that was PHAT baby".

Rip was put back on his feet, he turned and grabbed hands with Steven Ogre and smiled.

"My thanks Steven, good catch Mate" Rip said.

Will stood waiting for Rip to return to the ring. Rip walked with his head up, he never thought the contest would end any differently; the fact that the king had beaten him completely and Rip was not seriously injured made the leader of Branagan feel he could place his clan in this man's hands and they would be safe as safe as in his own.

SHANE

"I am defeated Will" Rip said with a deep laugh. "My I retrieved my weapons, I will not attack again, the day is yours"?

"Go ahead; I can see you're an honorable man Rip. You are a perfect choice to be one of my advisors, interested" Will asked?

Rip stood up and all humor left his face. He looked around the assembly area, where more than three thousand Vampire knights and their human guests. Will could see worry in his eyes.

"You have my complete support and loyalty, the same as I gave Brian, sire. My clan is with you no matter what" Rip said very loudly.

Rip turned his back on Will and tossed his sword over his shoulder and walked to his clan, but he called over his shoulder.

"Complete support...NO MATTER WHAT" Rip said with force to drive home his meaning to everyone.

Rip was an odd duck, very funny and never seemed to serious. He was however nearly omniscient when it came to knowing what was going on. Point in fact he warned Will that some of the military were pissed about their ranks joining vampire clans, like Chad for instance. Nevertheless, Lee was getting married in the morning and Will was expected back in his bed before long. The contests went on very friendly for a while longer with no more mishaps.

The night went very pleasantly. Will was surprised that a blade could cut Tana's skin, but Victoria's sword was enchanted, it was made by Brian Garrett as a gift to her so that when they sparred she had a more far chance. Honestly, there was no chance; it was just more of a challenge. Anyway, Tana and Vicky were talking softly when Will got out of the shower and came to sit on the end on the bed. Tana crawled up behind him and wrapped herself around him; she put her head on his shoulder. Victoria slid around the side and put her head on Will's lap. Will absently ran his fingers through her hair.

"What do you know about Rip Branagan" Will asked?

"He is solid man, damn fine fighter, elite, one of the best in the world. He was one of Valor's best pupils, even Val had to try when he spars with Rip. Rip has a silly charm and good humor about him. However, he is a most intractable enemy, ruthless once he decides to opposed you" Vicky said. "Why do you asked"?

"He sparred with me just a few moments ago, he was magnificent, if I was not a Garrett with all the entails, I might not be able to have beaten him. He was over matched but his tactics and strategy were so well thought out and applied" Will said. "I asked him to be my advisor; do you think he is a good choice"?

"I think I want to make love and talk shop in the morning" Vicky said in a mewing voice.

(Laughter).

(Snuggling and intense loving)

Lee was up a 5Am and Chad was running like he did every morning with his platoon or cell since he was a Ranger. He was scared of not being ready to be a father and a husband, but he had such a deep love for Lee, he would walk a hundred miles through broken glass and fire for her. Her family were the strongest on the ship and planet Earth for that matter. It was a little daunting to think of the power and focus of just Lee's father. Tana was another complete issue, she was small and breathe taking. Chad did not know anyone who did not want to bed her, even he thought about it before he met Lee, now all thoughts of anyone else were gone. Lee stole his soul and he was more than happy to let her keep it. Lady Victoria, the deadly beauty was Will and Tana's lover and mate, she was just as gorgeous as Tana and she was playful and teased both Lee and Chad mercilessly. Victoria made their combine passion go nuts whenever she was near them; Lee said Vicky did it on purpose.

"Hey Chad" A loud Voice called out.

Chad looked in the general direction on the voice and saw Ogre waving. When Chad got close enough the giant began to talk in a more normal tone.

"Hey Chad-o, your general told me you were off duty from today until next Saturday. So, I thought you should be getting ready to married the princess by now, cold foot problem lil' buddy" Ogre asked?

"Yes, I am off, no I do not have cold feet. I am simply working out as usual" Chad said in a huff.

"Hey, calm down. I have a gift for you, I want you to wear it today at your wedding and there is one for Lee as well, it is a matched set" Ogre said.

The giant held out a small box for Chad to take. Chad opened the box and there was two tiny jeweled pedants inside. They wear miniature curved daggers. They were fabulous but Chad could not see wearing them for his wedding and was about to say that when Ogre spoke.

"Hold them point to dagger point" Ogre said.

Chad did and smiled. When they were put together they made a very delicate looking heart. Chad suddenly got it there was a message in this gift. Together he and Lee were one heart complete, apart however, was like having a dagger in your chest. Ogre was a big softy and thoughtful as well.

"These are great, where did you get them" Chad asked the giant vampire?

"I made them for you myself, Tana taught me how" Ogre said.

"Wow, thanks Steven".

"Hey you're like the little brother I always wanted and Lee is my baby sis, so it was a small token of my esteem. You should seriously move your ass though, time is running out Chad and your wedding is just about upon you" Ogre replied.

Victoria had some fine silk and lace under garments made for Lee. They should off and flattered Lee's nice breasts and firm young body. The wedding dress was a tad too transparent for Lee's taste being a non vampire she was still a little shy, so she used a long floor length satin slip under her very sexy wedding dress. Lee's legs were bare up to her high thigh, and the neck was cut down to her belly button. The train of the dress was 10 feet behind her. Lee was mouth watering according to Vicky. Tana teased Vicky and told her to stop hitting on her daughter. Tana looked more like a sister to Lee than a mother. Victoria told Lee that if she was not madly in love with her parents, that Lee and Chad would have been her second choice. Lee knew this was not a joke, she really loved Lee and Chad, although it was only in the heart, Victoria was extremely picky about bed mates, so much so she went without a lover for a thousand years, now that is some will power.

A quick note about the Tigun ship, it was big, really big, the size of a city big. It was built with human needs in mind, it had apartment like quarters, shops, gyms, assembly areas, offices and conference rooms. There were shuttles from one part of the ship to the other and lifts. No transporters, sorry. The Tiguns as a race were geniuses with machines and technology. Tigre was the best of the best and he seemed to be more than just an engineer for the ship, Will suspected that Tigre was royalty or something in that way. Tigre seemed to work around the clock and never rest. He however stopped his duties whenever Tana and Will were around; he seemed to have a hero worship going on. Tigre watched both Will and Tana fight in the ring and now he was awe struck around them, because they were so nice and gentle, yet they fought like the devil himself when evoked.

"Hail Tigre" Will said "You ready for the wedding my friend, you have to stand next to Ogre so you wont miss anything because your size. Please invite all the Tiguns for us, they are most welcome".

"I would not miss your lovely child's bonding ceremony today Lord Garrett" Tigre said.

"Hey now, none of that lord poop, you're my friend Tigre" Will said as he placed a hand on the tiny grey man's shoulder.

"Sorry it is hard for we Tiguns not to be formal, it is our way. I am pleased that you count me among your mighty friends, Will" Tigre said.

"You are as mighty as they are Tigre, without you brains and technology we would have been slaughtered by the Korv before we even knew they were coming for us. You personally designed the ship and built it in record time to suit the needs of humans and vampires alike. Your synthetic blood manufacturing alone is a marvel, it tastes like real human blood, but without the drama of biting anyone, genius" Will explained.

"Actually Will I used Real human typed AB Negative as the foundation and just cloned it and replicated it until I mastered the process" Tigre commented.

"How long did it take you" Will asked?

"Nearly two hours, it was a challenge, it took longer that I would have guest" Tigre said as a matter of fact.

Will just stood there mouth gaping open in awe of this tiny grey fellow's genius. Tigre thought that two hours was too long to design and produce synthetic blood. On Earth his method would be worth billions to the health industry and vampires alone. However, this fine person did not think much about it, we had a need and he met it; that was his genius, he made things that were impossible, possible and usable in a short period of time. Tigre was not vain; he saw what he did as a utility service not an invention or break-though. Will would have asked him if he wanted to be a vampire but was not sure his race could survive it or would even want to be something like that.

Will and Tigre went to get dressed for the wedding, they met Jay and Ogre who was helping Chad get his snow white tux and tie all straightened up. The Tiguns made huge Steven and Jay custom red and black tuxedos to match Will's. They all dressed in a traditional style for marriages down on the Planet Earth, to please Lee. Navar came later and dressed in his tux as well to please his little sister.

In the dressing room for the ladies, Tana was supervising the dresses and hair styling for the bride's maids. Tana had the help of a few gay vampire males, they were fast and knew how to make any hair do better and more fetching. They started with Lee's long red-brown hair, they made it curly and springy looking and it framed her lovely fame perfectly, draping down to her cleavage. It turned out that the dress style did not allow for a bra, so Lee was happy she was firm breasted from hard exercise. She did however, wear the sexy panties that Victoria made her; they were more comfortable against her tender skin than she would have thought. They were a fine gift.

VAMPIRE WARS

One hour later the large main chapel was filled with the human and vampire peoples, with a few dozen Tiguns. When Tana walked in wearing a shorter version of Lee's sexy wedding dress only it was red and announced it was time and could everyone be seated.

First the bride's maids come down the isle with a grooms man, ladies in mini red dresses that showed off their legs and cleavage, men in tuxedos. When Tana and Will took their spots and Victoria who was the maid of honor, and Steven acting as the man of honor were in place, Chad walked in. Last to enter to a strange mix of music was Lee. Chad smiled so big that his mouth nearly touched his eyes. Lee had little golden shoes that were open except across the bridge of her feet. She wore no nylons, her tan leg were bare and she walked slowly and with every step as her stomach muscles flexed, you could see them through the ultra tight gown. Even with a room full of vampire females, Lee's splendor stole the show. Lee had the little dagger necklace hanging between her full breasts. Ogre smiled at his little adopted sissy and a tear crawled down his cheek.

Chad reached out for Lee, He took her hand and placed his other hand around her waist and guided her up the three steps. The pastor was all smiles. Chad and Lee were as beautiful of young couple as he had ever seen. Likely they were the most beautiful. The pastor was asked to keep it simple. So he greeted the crowd and they addressed Chad.

"Chad Sorren do you take the woman to be your wife, will you protect her and provide for her and cherish her for all the days of your life" The pastor asked?

"Yes I will, and I most certainly do" Chad said excited.

The pastor turned to Lee.

"Lee Garrett do you take this man to be your husband, will you guide him and help him through the hard times, with

you grant him children and love him the rest of your life"
The pastor asked?

"Yes with all of my heart I will and I do" Lee said with
enthusiasm.

"Then with the power invested in me by God and the US
Army, I now pronounce you man and wife you may kiss the
bride.

   Chad picked Lee up off her feet and kissed her. The fact
that her legs were bare made in possible to wrap her right
leg around the back of his left leg and press her body
against his, there long kiss was gentle but sultry and
passionate.

   Tana and Will had tears in their red eyes. Most of the
crowd did. Tana regained her wits and started organizing a
receptions line. Will and Navar kept people away from Lee
while she enjoyed the embrace of her husband.

   The reception was an event unto itself, there was food
of every kind, and dancing to music from many countries,
none of which was part of the planned party. It did not
matter, there was laughter and joy and love and friendship.
It was a common sight to see couples or even groups of
people off to the side making out or even more. To be
honest the reception turned into a love in.

   After Chad and Lee cut the giant cake, Rudy took a
thousand photos of them doing everything from eating to
fondling each other. Then Ruby, Gwen, Kadi and Mya
passed out cake and drinks to the guests. It was not known
when Chad carried Lee away, but he did. Their new
combine quarters were down the hall from Will's, as befit
the princess and her new prince. Chad and Lee did not
leave their room for the entire five days. You could hear
giggles and laughter coming from their apartment but they
never came out. They were completely happy.

VAMPIRE WARS

The wee babies of Navar were growing nicely, they were plump and happy. They had one advantage over human babies, their minds developed faster and so did their coordination. The crawled all over and then escaped from their play room and made their way into the human population. Of-course super cute babies always get picked up and played with. It is a bad habit to put your finger in a baby's mouth, especially when they are vampire babies. Raz and Aria innocently nibbled on what ever was put in their wee mouths. Each time they drew a little blood, but the healing properties in their saliva closed the wounds and since there was no blood to see, it went unnoticed. One of Gwen's fellow soldiers saw Raz and went and got him and Aria, she took them back to the nursery, and Gwen came in at the same time and saw her with the babies.

"Why do you have my babies" Gwen asked?

"They were wondering around out in the gallery, people were playing with them. I saw the kids and worried that they might get hurt so I brought them back" The Jana said.

"Oh shoit, they must be able to escape the little Crocs, well let's see who is minding the nursery and chew their ass and warn them about the babes being able to slip out aye" Gwen said sweetly to Jana.

The woman running the nursery was a very military type, ex nun by the look. Gwen came up looking down at baby Raz and began to speak.

"We need to watch my little ones more carefully, they are able to escape due..."Gwen was saying when she was cut off.

"Well if you were a better parent and gave them more discipline maybe they would stay where they put" The woman growled "Perhaps if you gave them a good beating"?

Gwen was about to grab her by the throat when Jana bitch slapped her across the face. The woman was aghast, completely speechless.

"Idiot, first they are babies not kids, second, they are vampires so you must watch them closely for they own protection, third, I just saved your worthless life" Said Jana as she pointed at the sour face and red burning eyes of Gwen.

"If you so much as yell at my baby I will toss you out an air lock, and since the king is my father in-law don't think you going to get any help consider that is Will's grandson" Gwen said in a flat venomous tone. "I am a doctor just like Jana, the idea of hurting a wee babe, is against my morale code" Gwen snarled.

Jana picked up Arai and the little baby bit her on the finger not hard, but hard enough for Jana to notice, she unlike other people realized the implications of that nibble. Jana pulled Gwen away gently and spoke to her in a low whisper.

"Aria just bit my finger girl" Jana said.

"Oh she wont hurt you, she is just playing" Gwen said.

"Think like a doctor not a mother Gwen, I was just nibbled by a vampire" Jana said sternly.

"Oh, that might be a problem; they are to small to turn you Jana, but who knows if any ill effects, we should put our heads together with Tigre in the med-lab and see to it that if there is anything that needs to be done, it is done immediately" Gwen said. "We should take the babies to Lee".

CHAPTER 7: TROUBLE

Several days after Jana had seen the babies out of the nursery they escaped again, they truddled off the gallery where there were a lot of sounds and colors to entertain and enthrall the babies. Just like the last time the babies were out they were picked up and cuddled and played with. It did not seem to dawn on anyone; that these kids had the lightest green eyes you ever saw and they could practically walk at only a month of age. The babies without knowing it were mesmerizing the people who held them; it is something full grown vampires can shut off, however the wee little babies did not even know they could do it yet.

It started that afternoon, the human population began to get high fevers for no reason, and at first the Doctors thought it was a virus. However, Jana knew better and she told the USAF general what she knew and that imbecile leaked it to the other services.

Jay had been seeing Jana often; it started because she met him when she was working with Gwen on the baby issue, which they were keeping hushed. Jana while waiting for Gwen to pull herself away from Navar's bed early one morning took up a conversation with Jay, who gave her the best cup of java she ever had.

"So are all vampire nympho's; I mean how much is enough" Jana said?

"I could say yes, but you would still not really understand Jana. We have desires a thousand times stronger than you do, I have only been a vampire for this voyage, before that I was just a boy in the hood. When you get turned, you get so hungry for physical pleasure that if a none vampire was to come near you, they would literally be loved to death; it would be an extremely pleasant death, but death nonetheless. Therefore, Will is very careful about how it is done, to protect the innocent from harm. Will also has forbidden anyone to be turned without their consent, or if they have not had time to have a baby, because being immortal without a family is a lonely road. Lovers are not the same as family" Jay explained.

"Well, what about deceases, what if you get VD" Jana asked.

"Not possible" Jay said.

"Can you be a carrier" Jana asked?

"No, our blood kills and defeats every virus or bacteria" Jay said.

"Okay but why so many lovers; why not choose one and do it with just them" Jana asked?

Jay walked over and picked Jana up and kissed her neck. Jana gasped and was instantly aroused. Jay sat her on his lap and kissed her gently. Jana had an orgasm from just kissing Jay. She was embarrassed because he knew and she knew he knew. He was pleased that she liked being with him. Jay wanted Jana to understand fully and this small demonstration was not sufficient to do that.

"Would you come back to my crib and make love with me Jana, I wont hurt you in any way baby" Jay said?

"Yes" Jana said in a fog.

Jay placed her on her feet took her and led her to his quarters. Jana was surprised because the first thing Jay did was put her in a cold shower. Then he asked her again if she still wanted to be lovers. She was naked and nervous but her scientific curiosity and plain old fashion lust made her mind up for her.

"Yes" Jana said.

In a blur of movement Jay was naked and in the shower with her, the water turn warm and soothing as he ran he hands expertly over her body. Jana was not a vampire, so she was not near her own personal perfection, however her body was fit. Jana had beautiful full C cup breast and they were firm with small button nipples, her butt round and narrow, her pubic area was clean shaved. Jana was not a flirt or easy to bed, but Jay was charming and risk free, she would not get pregnant or a decease so she want to let go for once.

Jay took Jana out of the shower and dried her off, and tickled her playfully. He kissed her gently on the lips with his hands on her hips.

"You're going to like this" Jay said.

Jay flipped Jana up side down, her knees went over his shoulders and his warm lips and tongue were now kissing and tasting her other lips expertly, she was not much for oral sex but Jay had her hot and bother in ten seconds. Jana could not help herself, since his manhood was in front of her face she reach out and grabbed it and without a second thought her mouth and lips were covering his shaft, she sucked on it with a vigor that surprised her, since this was not her thing. She wanted to keep nibbling but he laid her on his big bed. Jay was a big man, and he was also well equipped, so when she took a more careful look at his manhood as he was about to enter her body she was not so sure that this was as good of idea as she thought aroused or not. Once Jay was working steadily like a motor, long gentle penetrations her body began to vibrate with desire and there was no pain or fatigue only ecstasy. Jana never wanted to stop, but Jay did stop every so soften so she could catch her breath.

"Your heart is beating to fast doc, I don't want your heart to burst, so let's slow down and calm you down" Jay said softly as he kissed her neck and suck on her earlobes.

Jana decided to get on top and she made an error, she put Jay inside of her body again and dropped her hips down to begin, it was right then as her was completely inside of her, that Jay was not giving her all of his tool before, he was too big to fit inside of her. Now she was on top and could control it her passion began to over ride her judgment, thank God Jay was clear headed, because he stopped her.

"You're going to bust your insides baby, and since I am digging you girl and I want to take you to my bed again, I don't want to ruin you this morning" Jay said.

It was that moment, not the best most power sexual experience she ever had, but the concern for her person, in spite of the fact that she was pleasuring him, he was more worried about her than his own desires, that made her fall in love with him. Jana was aware instantly that she lost her heart; it was Jay's for the taking and he had not tried to push up on her, but that is all she wanted right now.

"I will work on stretching so I can get all of you in me comfortable without killing me, because Jay, giant Black vampire knight, I want to be in your bed as often as will be allowable and I want you to get the most out of it you can" Jana said.

Jay carefully made Jana find the woman in her eleven times and then he rolled her up in a quilt and let her sleep while his powerful arms held her. She smiled the whole time in her sleep.

In the nursery Gwen was waiting for Jana who was late, and Jana was never late. Jana was very organized and punctual. Gwen waited and played with her son and her goddaughter Aria. Jana came bustling into the nursery, she was about to speak but the look on Gwen's face said that the explanation would be unnecessary, Gwen's button nose sniffed the air and she smiled.

"How is my mate Jay this morning love" Gwen asked.

Before Jana could stop herself she told Gwen the entire story play by steamy play.

"He was amazing, why didn't you tell me it was like that" Jana said?

"Jana, I fell in love with my mate before either of us were turned, after it was so incredible, there is no way to explain it, you have to have a taste to understand. If you think it is good now, you should make love just after you have been turned, it is a thousand times more intense. I have three lovers, my man and two girlfriends, we are the wives of N, or so we are called. It makes my heart pound to be near any of them and twice that when we are all together as lovers" Gwen said with a dreamy look on her perfect face.

Other parents were bringing their babies in to the room now so Gwen stopped talking and just smiled. They left and went to the med lab, where they were accosted as soon as they entered. All of the military brass were there and they were yelling about bites and a fever. One of the Navy commanders grabbed Gwen and jerked her around.

"Don't you ever touch me again" Gwen said as she lifted him off the floor by his throat and held him there with one hand.

"Look, there is no danger we can see or the Tigun medical core can find it is just a fever, we are still doing tests, but so far as we can tell it is nothing more than that. Gwen please put that fool down" Jana said.

"Now GET OUT, this is a medical facility not a war room"!

Gwen tossed the marine on the floor and looked at him with disdain. Jana did the same thing; they turned and went to the research lab they set up to study the fever issue.

(Elsewhere on the ship)

Jay was still pretty happy with his morning; he made love to a beautiful woman, and then went and practiced his blade work with Ogre and Ruby. He face the brothers three on one and did excellent, they scored on him but he did even more scoring on them, Will would be proud of him, strangely that was really important to him. Tana greeted him as they meet in the hall with a jump kiss on the cheek as usual; Will was a lucky man to own her heart. A loud set of shouts caught Jay's attention; he went to see out of pure curiosity. Navar's babies were in the middle and a buzz cut headed jar head was screaming, Raz was snarling and blocking the path to Aria. The marine drop kicked Raz into the wall.

(SNARL!!!!)

Jay bulled through the crowd like a runaway bulldozer, he grabbed the marine by the back of his neck and threw him at the far wall fifteen feet off the ground. Jay swung his arm backwards and flattened twenty some soldiers.

"Back off" Jay snarled.

Jay took one step toward Aria and a bullet bounced on the ground just in front of the baby; this was a bad thing. Jay took two bullets in the back, they did not even penetrate his skin, and he was completely without his armor, he always had his sword though, as a knight he was bound to protect as needed. Jay lost his temper and was going to kill the one who shot at Arai, but Ruby came flying like a whirl wind into the shooter, she disarmed him and kneed him in the face then snapped his feet out from under him in what looked like one move. Jay was suddenly in Ogre's iron grasp; his mighty oak tree arms went around secure the irate Jay.

(SNARL!)

Ogre let the loudest growl out Jay had ever heard it sound like a lion. The humans backed off, one made the ultimate mistake.

"Hey freaks, stop where you or I will slit this little bitch's throat" The marine said with a cocky grin.

You could hear a pin drop when the marine died. Chad saw from a distance what had happened and Arai was his niece, first the baby was nearly shot; and now her life was being threatened. Chad was a ranger and not just any ranger he was the best. He stalked up and snapped the marine neck and snatched Aria into his waiting hands as the marine hit the floor dead.

"If any of you no good sons a bitches ever touch one of my family again, especial these tiny babies, I will make you pray for death. Steven guard my back" Chad growled between his teeth.

Chad walked over to where Raz was laying against the wall stunned from being kicked. Raz knew Chad and went happily into his uncle's warm arms. Chad was grim faced when he went to find Navar. Chad thought it best to tell his brother in law first hand what happened. There was going to be terrible retribution for this, the peace was broken. Bullets were fired and there were dead.

Navar was not the problem Chad had thought; Lee, Mya, Kadi and Tana were even a greater problem than expected.

It was going to be bad when Gwen and Victoria were told; they had extremely testy behavior when the kids were involved.

"Who shot at my baby" Kadi screamed!

"I think Ruby busted his face over it" Chad said. "I killed the man who put his knife on Aria".

Aria was still nuzzling Chad's neck, half asleep. Raz was asleep on the bed that Chad was sitting on. Lee sat by Chad with tears in her eyes, what if Aria would have been killed, what if they hurt the little ones, what would her family do? They would kill everyone in anger.

Will came up the hallway with Victoria and Rip talking about training sessions and minor clan disputes, when he stopped and looked at Tana's taut face.

"What has happened to make you look like that baby" Will inquired?

The entire tale was told with a few minor additions. Will's face was grim, but calm. Only his glowing red eyes gave away his wrath. It is common knowledge that Will loved kids and these were his son's babies, so there was no hell deep enough to save the guilty, yet Will seemed less mad and more worried.

"Rip, take your clan down and secure the armory, no killing but take it and hold it. Victoria find out who was involved, all who were involved and arrest them, no killing but don't take any guff either, disarm and stop anyone trying to interfere. I will be holding court in one hour. Please be ready by the, if you need help call and I will get that help to you. Chad stay here, Steven, Jay and Ruby protect them no matter what" Will softly ordered.

Chad was about to protest but Steven Ogre cut him off and stopped him from approaching Will, with fear in his eyes. Even Jay who was Will's best friend was nervous about getting to near Will at Present.

"Chad" Will said?

Everyone looked at Will.

"You are a welcome member of my family, I am proud to call you son, you protected your family, I could never ask more than that. You will not be on trial or allowed to be harmed in any way" Will said.

"I had no choice, family is everything to me" Chad said.

Will only nodded and then turned on a heel and burst to speed.

(ESLEWHERE ON THE SHIP).

"Oh MY GOD, are you nuts, your men shot at and hit one of Will's clan, worse they kicked and shot at his grandchildren. We are luck to not be hanging in a meat locker right now. There are five clans on this ship; each clan has about five hundred knights and a clan leader. Each one of those knights is stronger than twenty normal men, they can't be killed and poisoned, or suffocated, and until today they were all very friendly and accommodating to us. Now we will be lucky not to be slaves or worse, dinner" The Army general Brad Franklin yelled at the brass.

Gen. Franklin was the ranking officer so he was in command of all human personnel. He was troubled, because he was under Will's authority per the UN and President Obama. Therefore, he was in a super hot spot at the moment. What the heck was he going to do if war was declared on the humans? The marine commandant should be whipped unconscious, but he couldn't do that either. The overall brass was very upset about this, come on shooting at a baby, so what it is a vampire, the whole damn ship is full of them.

"Gentlemen, this may be a huge craft with plenty of room for stupidity, but shooting at the most powerful family of vampires and the ships ruling king and commander of the entire ship is ignorant beyond explanation. What do you propose we do to make this right before we have a rash of killings" the Gen. asked?

There was no answer to that question.

"Gentlemen"?

The room was instantly startled by the sound of the one voice they feared to hear just then. Will Garrett's.

"I think we need to talk boys about why there are marines shooting at my grandkids, and why when forced to stop; they felt ok with shooting my best friend in the back" Will asked in a deathly calm tone?

"I was trying to ascertain that as well just now Will. I cannot apologize enough for this breach of good judgment. Are the wee ones ok, they are hopefully not injured or traumatized" Gen. Franklin asked?

"They are well enough...physically. It is their view of normal humans, not homo superior vamparis; that bothers me. If they grow up seeing you as the enemy it could lead to disaster Brad. I want to know what caused all of this before my clans are compelled to wipe out the marines to the man" Will said in a matter of fact voice?

All faces turn to the marine commandant waiting for a viable explanation.

"It has come to my attention that your brats have been biting my people and others as well, now they all have a roaring fever; that no medication can reduce. It is your fault that this happened Garrett, if you could keep the little bastards under control none of this would have happened" The marine said in a haughty voice!

(Insane laughter).

The room was surprised by Will's sudden burst of laughter; they expected that the Commandant's life was toast but laughter? Will composed himself with effort; then he smiled and spoke.

"Aaron, Ian, Evan". Three knights appeared behind Will with blades drawn. "Go fetch Raz for me, bring him here please" Will said with a smile.

The three brothers were gone and back in what seemed like a breath and no more. Ian was holding baby Raz in his arms. He stepped forward and handed the sleepy elf to Will, then bowed and backed away. Will smiled at the cherub in his powerful hands.

"Brad do you trust me" Will asked not looking away from the baby?

"Yes of-course, you know I do" Gen. Franklin answered in haste.

"Then let Raz bite your finger" Will said handing over the baby to Brad.

The General took baby Raz and put his finger in the little baby's mouth Raz began to gently nibble the finger and suck on it. Around the table the brass gasped. Brad looked around but did not understand what the deal was.

"Your hair was blond-red as a boy, wasn't it Brad" Will asked; with a knowing smile?

"Yes, how did you know" Brad asked?

"Do any of you ladies have a mirror on you that I could borrow for a minute" Will asked?

An USAF major handed over her compact over to Will with a smile. Will smiled at her and squeezed her shoulder. When Will held the mirror out to Brad to look at himself, it was silent in the room.

"Wow, what happened to me" Brad exclaimed?

"You will be running a fever soon Brad. The little guy is introducing a weak version of our venom into your body, not enough to turn you, but it is enough to caused regeneration and increased strength, endurance and vitality. If you were a smoker it would cause your lung damage to be undone or reversed if you like. If you have any decease or diabetes or whatever, you will like have just been cured...for life. The endurance and enhanced strength might wane but the cures will remain" Will explained.

"I feel great. How long will the fever last" Brad asked?

"It will last until your body is running perfectly, then you will just feel great, better than you ever have" Will said.

"Now, on to a serious matter. My family was attacked by marines and the person in charge is an asshole who thinks shooting at babies is justified. It is my decision and order that he be striped of all rank and tossed into the brig until time that I see fit to release him" Will growled and everyone flinched.

"You can't, you don't have the right" The marine argued.

"Fine I'll just kill you now if you would rather, it is our law, to attack the king is a death sentence and you attack my grand child, do you really think I will let that go" Will snarled?

SHANE

So fierce was Will's face and eyes that the entire room was pasty faced and perspiring, Will looked every bit the substance of nightmares just then, Deep crimson back lit eyes, and snow white fangs.

"Will do you think, we could explore a different punishment" Brad asked shyly?

Will looked at him and Brad's knees almost buckled from fright. Will seemed to realize how angry he was and settled himself, with a sour grimace.

"What do you have in mind" Will asked?

"Well, he is a seasoned soldier and has good battle skills and judgment based on war craft. I would suggest a reduction in rank to captain and ten lashes, 30 days in the brig, then a return to duty under my personal supervision" Brad suggested?

Will seemed to ponder this for a minute and then he smiled and looked directly at the marine.

"Fifteen lashes, five from Navar, five from Kadi, and five from Gwen. And no brig, infirmary for as long as it takes for him to heal up, and no vampire venom to speed his healing and pain control" Will said.

"Ha, I can endure the first five then I have nothing to fear of some little girls" The commandant spewed!

Will just smiled at the fool.

"I want you to know something up front, education I suppose. A normal vampire knight is 20 times stronger than you are, normal humans. A vampire with Garrett blood in their veins is fifty times stronger than you are, Navar is likely seventy five times as stronger as you are, and his brides somewhere close as princesses of my clan. You will be luck to live thru the whipping at all, the first five lashes will likely take your life" Will explain calmly.

The face of fear and dread settled on all of the military brass faces, they were trembling visibly. Brad was the only one that did not seem effected; he did however want to say something.

"In that case, how about one lash per parent, so he does not die, that would be a release from responsibility, not a punishment" Brad asked?

"Granted, one lash per parent and one from Lady Victoria, because these are her adopted Grandchildren and she is pissed off greatly. That is the final decision, no more negotiating" Will finished.

Later after Will left the marine commandant began to spew his poison on the military leaders.

"Why are we listening to this guy, he is a no good blood sucker. Let's arm up and go kill him and his kind, we don't need them anyway" the marine yelled.

Brad gave him a Wuthering look, and pointed at the MP's then to the marine.

"Arrest that idiot and toss him in the brig until Will is ready for his punishment. Here is why we don't do what the fool suggested. First, the armory is guarded by Rip and his crew, second you can't kill vampires with bullets alone, third, Will just explain the power difference to you. Will himself was not included in the explanation because he is powerful beyond explanation; he alone could destroy all of us with all of the best armaments we could muster. Lastly, it was his grand kids that were hurt, so we are lucky he was so generous with us. He won't be next time, this is a warning, if you missed it, let me make my own. If any harm comes to his family or clan, I will have the culprit spaced" Brad said.

VAMPIRE WARS

The following morning the former marine commandant was strapped to a metal frame and stripped bare ass naked. Navar walked up and looked at him with deep pools of crimson lava; he stood looking into his eyes for a moment. The punishment and charges were read off; Navar just stood and looked at the marine.

"You got off lite, say your prayers buddy, you are going to need God after this" Navar whispered.

Navar was handed a leather bull whip, he turned it over in his hand and then he turned to his father.

"One strike with this and he will die father, we need a lighter whip if you want him to live" Navar said as he tossed the heavy braided whip to Will.

"Tigre do you have a smaller lighter whip we can use" Will asked?

"Not at the moment" Tigre said embarrassed.

"Here we will use this" Victoria said.

The lady of the Clan Elite stepped forward and produced a canvas belt about four feet long, soft and sturdy. Will took it and inspected it. He then tossed it to Navar who shook his head.

"He will live I think with this, but the belt will be a mess after" Navar said.

"Are you going talk me to death or beat me you cowards" The marine screamed.

Navar smiled.

The crowd held their collective breaths as Navar lined up behind the prisoner. He brought his hand back and was about to step in and lay in on, but he stopped, looked at

Tana, then Gwen. His arm came back painfully slow, he just flicked his wrist and the belt hit the marine. Blood sprayed the crowd in front of the prisoner. The place where the belt the man, was a wide open wound and the pale white bones underneath were broken.

"MY GOD" Brad said

Kadi took the belt and it cracked the right thigh of the prisoner. Blood sprayed and the leg was broken and the meat was hanging off. Gwen was not as gently, she whipped the belt at angle and she hit both arms and his face expertly in one strike, the marine's arms and jaw were broken. When Victoria stepped up to give the last blow; she tossed the blood soaked belt at Brad's feet.

"Victoria, alive please" Will said. It was not a question but an order.

Victoria stepped up and slapped softly, for her anyway, down the marine's face and chest dragging her fingernails. There were four bloody trails that would leave good scars for the rest of his life.

"You were shown mercy dog, don't forget it or I will visit you in the quiet of the night" Victoria whispered in his ear, though he was out cold, he shuddered.

That was all of it, Brad got up and made a speech about unity and cooperation and good will, and the law.

A week later all the soldiers who had fevers were so healthy and strong that they could not sleep, they worked and trained like never before and they always smiled. Many of them took vampire lovers, because they were not afraid to be killed during sex anymore. In spite of their new strength there was some sex related injuries because they over estimated their abilities and so did the vampire lovers. However, they healed up at an amazing rate and went right back to bed with the lover who hurt them happily. The good cheer and friendships bloomed like spring all over the city-sized ship. In the days ahead when the met the Korv in battle, they would need that closeness and brotherhood to over come the trials that would thrust upon them all.

VAMPIRE WARS

CHAPTER 8: BLACK PLANET.

It was the beginning of October, four plus months since they started out for the war effort. The Tiguns had the ship moving at a rate of speed that was unfathomable by man. They had given the best up to date intelligence to Will and the command crew. It was the sudden appearance of a planetary body of the port side of the massive ship; that clued Brad Franklin that all the training, meeting and planning were about to come to a head. He called to Will, Navar and Tigre to join him and the bridge.

"Tigre, are the Korv on this planet? If so where is the ship or ship that brought them here? Do they have surface to air guns, or missiles that can hit the ship" Brad asked?

"There is no weapon I know of that can damage my ship, the one you are currently on. I built this ship special for Will's grandfather Brian, I am not one to brag, but I am a quick thinker and this ship, unlike others my race has built comes with guns" Tigre smiled mischievously. "Yes, there are Korv down there, their ship is either on the ground down there or on the far side of the planet, they have guns as well, but they are puny and useless against this ship. On the planet they can be used against troops though; so be watchful of the skies. If we can, we will pump some shot in their ass, as Ogre says, or is it bust a cap in their ass, like Jay says" Tigre told Brad.

(Laughter).

"Those are both apt terms Tigre, and we appreciate your genius and your peoples help. Earth would have been caught without your warning" Brad said.

"Will, Navar how are we going to play this, scout first or attack" Brad asked?

The Garrett men just smiled and looked at each other; it made Brad both nervous and happy at the same time. These men were made of a strong metal; they were likely a force of nature as regular humans, but now...

(In the food court)

Tana sat with all the ladies of Clan Garret, her daughter, all three daughters in-laws, Ruby, Aria and Victoria her lover. There were all the female knights as well; who were under Tana's direct command per Will's order. Her immediate family was only loosely under her, Ruby was too independent, and Victoria was a clan chief, but they would follow Tana in to hell if she asked it.

"You're among the strongest fighters in the universe, some of you are stronger than the men who share your beds, or the women for the matter. (Snicker) Only Victoria's ladies rival our own. However, it falls to us to lead by example, we will fight until no Korv is left breathing, or we are not. I will not ask you to be canon fodder, and you better not spend your lives foolishly trying to shield me, I am stronger than all of you and nearly as invulnerable as our king, my husband. I will not be a hindrance to my man or my son when they go to the battle field, you must be stronger willed, and fight like a demon, that way it will give the Korv pause if they turn on a female because they think our smaller size is a sign of weakness" Tana said in a stern voice.

"Well said Tana. I am the oldest vampire on this ship, older than Rip who is also ancient, and I have seen many wars, fought many, I have never known defeat and only Valor, Tana and Will have ever equaled my ability with a blade, I will lead my clan as is my responsibility, but if you should need aid or direction I am at your service, if you fall in on the battle field with my clan, follow my orders until it is safe or feasible to return to your clan or squad" Victoria explained.

Plans were laid and squads were formed and it surprised the human military that Will decided to mix the clans into the human soldiers. Will explained that the human were no match for the Korv hand to hand so they should stay to long arrange attacks and support the clans as they engaged the Korv at close quarters. The Humans felt a little insulted but Gen. Franklin gave the order and called it plain common sense, Will was concerned and providing for the safety of all the ships company not just his own Knights. The general called this the mark of a great leader and man. After his short speech that was broadcast over the entire ship, Will was greeted warmly by everyone no matter who they were as their leader and commander of the ship.

The planned move to scout the surface and attack based on the knowledge obtained was set for the next morning at 0500.

Lee found her mother and Brother discussing muster arrangement and deployments for the following day. Lee walked up; Navar leaned over and kissed her head then looked down at her and sniffed the air. He smiled and looked at his mother. Tana looked at him strangely.

"I will see you later mother; I think baby sis has something she wants to speak of" Navar kissed his tiny mom's head and left.

Tana looked at Lee.

"I am pregnant momma" Lee said!

"Small wonder, you and that pretty boy of yours have more sex than I do, and that is really saying something. How far along are you" Tana asked?

"Two months" Lee answered.

"Why don't you speed up the birth like your brothers wives did" Tana asked?

"I want to do it the regular way" Lee said.

"Honey, I love you but we are at war, and we... no Chad could get killed at any moment and he will never get to see his baby, so could you. You are helpless as you currently are baby, just think about it" Tana said.

Almost on cue, the entire ship bucked.

"The Korv horde have finally noticed we are here, the ships shield has been adjusted, there will be no more vibrations, we are sorry for any problems the shock might have caused" The Tigun officer's voice said over the Com.

"Lee" Tana said?

"That works for me mom, I am off to the med –lab now, find Chad for me and send him" Lee said as she booked off toward the med-labs.

The last clan of vampires on the ship stayed to themselves; they were not pretty like the other four clans. They had blue eyes and super sharp monster teeth, pointy ears like a bat; they hated light areas, but were not affected by light or anything the other clans weren't. They were the monsters of legend. It was said they were ugly because they ate people and Brian Garrett had placed a curse on them. They were not bitter about their appearance; in fact they loved it. They were by far more dangerous in unarmed combat, because of their longer claw-like fingernails and shark like teeth. It is not that the dark ones were unskilled with a blade; that would be a fatal error. They wore long flowing hooded black robes. When they moved it looked like they were floating. The governed themselves mostly, as a clan they were pissed off about Brian making they follow Will on a suicide mission.

Will and Rip went to talk with the dark clan, which is the name they gave themselves. When Will entered their common area, fifty knights came out of the dark weapon drawn, they did not bow to his authority, not yet anyway.

"Why have you come" Asked a five foot Dark one?

"Your services are needed boys, and we have come to fetch ya" Rip replied.

"We refused to..."The dark one started to say.

A left backhand sent him careening off the bulkhead. Before any of the dark ones could move, Navar who Will had not known was there until he moved, was knocking the stuffing out of all of the gathered dark ones too fast for them to defend themselves. Navar continued until a blade snaked out and nearly cut his throat. That was a mistake pulling a weapon on the prince. Navar simple slapped the blade away and in one fluid movement drew his katana and tanto. He would have cut down his attacker but Rip had already flattened them and made a bright light appear above the room suddenly.

"I just saved your life mate" Rip said to the ugly Vampire on the floor. "That is Navar Garrett and Will Garrett the king. You are not strong enough to stand against either one, now heal toe or die boys".

"Are you indeed the Garrett's, and if so by what right do you order us to do anything, king" A old nasty looking vampire asked?

Will realized this was a test of some sort and he needed to pass it in order to gain loyalty without blood shed, the dark ones were notorious about revenge. Will looked at Navar and motioned to put up his deadly blades. The prince was carrying a new set of blades, not the usual big blade he liked, strange.

"I think you know why you should follow my rule and orders" Will said.

"Because you are Brian Garrett's whelps I suppose" The old one said?

"No. You will follow me for the best reason ever, self-preservation. I believe that is one of the few things you truly believe in. Am I wrong" Will asked with a smile.

(Laughter of the many).

"You are wise Will Garrett, we will follow your rule for this reason and I swear the loyalty of my clan freely from this day forward, even above Brian, for I believe you are his equal" The old one said.

"Your efforts will be welcome, my dark friend" Will answered.

"I am Grom, I lead the dark ones. You have come to us for what purpose" Grom asked?

"I need your clan to do what you are best suited for, spy. I do not want you to fight the Korv unless you have no choice, do not risk yourselves if you can help it, I do not want your blood on my hands. I except your loyalty, but would have you continue to enjoy your own lives" Will said.

"I take it back King Will, we will follow you because you see value in us and would not throw us aside because of our looks and waste our lives foolishly because we are considered worthless" Grom said.

Will and Navar's faces clouded over in anger, Grom was suddenly confused until Navar spoke.

"Grom, your worth has nothing to do with your looks; your life is no less precious to us than any other person on this tub, save our own mates and kids. I can't make up for the BS you probably had to endure over the years, but that dog wont hunt with us, you're an important member of our team, we need you and your clan to get us intelligence, you may fight some but that is not what we want from you, information and sticking to the shadows, you are all experts in being unseen, this is your task and it is vital" Navar said.

Not only was Grom floored but so were all of his clan, they came out into the light and there were a lot more than the five hundred the other clans brought. The exact number could be figured out later. As if one mind they all tossed back the black hoods to show their faces, a sign of respect among their clan, then they all took a knee and bowed to Navar and Will.

"Come now, none of that shit. You are all part of my bigger family, go on get up and let's talk over our plans for the Korv" Will said.

Once again Grom was surprised, what kind of a king was this. He cared more for the dark ones than even Brian does, he called them family and from his eyes both he and the prince believe this to the bone. The king for all his power and authority, did not seem interested in taking his royal due, he wanted your loyalty freely, even though he could just force it. A strange and wonderful man; Grom felt his clan would be in good hands with this man.

"I need to sneak you on to the planet without the Korv knowing your there, once you are planet side, I need to know troop strength, gun placements and size, weight and images if you can. I would like your opinion on what their weaknesses are as well" Will said.

"You want my opinion" Grom asked?

"Yes, you are an expert assassin are you not, then yours is the opinion that I need the most, because it is your nature to see openings and opportunities for the kill" Will answered.

Rip stood and watched how easily Will and Navar won the respect and loyalty from the elusive dark ones who hated everyone. It seemed to Rip that this set of Garrett's were the best history had ever grown, Brian should be proud that his blood line produced these men and their women. Rip was proud to call them friends. Will seemed to grasp the very thing that people were good at and then ask them for that, he did not seem to want his knights to go against their natures for the sake of his orders, soon he likely would have no choice but to ask for that very thing, but for now he did not have too.

The next morning Grom and his son Sect went to the planet after Tigre shelled the shit out of the Korv guns that were shooting at the city ship; it was child's play the Tiguns said. When the Korv's attention was away from the ship because of the pounding they were taking, a small scout ship with two hundred dark ones on it landed on the planet and spread out with Tigun coms to report everything they saw.

Salen finally was brave enough to show her face again. Garth was a proud man and he came to Tana, got on his knees and kissed her feet and then her hands. He told her that he was ordered to attack her and confessed that her beauty made him want to do it. He asked for her pardon and swore loyalty to Tana over everyone including Salen and Will.

Tana accepted him as her friend and told him that when the time came to act with out thinking, he would know what that meant when it was time.

VAMPIRE WARS

"You have my word my lady" Garth pledged.

(Down in the Human Military staging area)

   Victoria and Kadi had been organizing the human Special Forces; since Kadi was one of them, her former Captain was a friend and when he was told he would be under her command he only laughed and told them, that her hands were a good place to be. Kadi always thought that he loved her but he never tried to address that issue, but Navar did as did Mya so it no longer mattered.

"You will fall in with us during battle, the Korv like to fight at close quarters so shoot them in the joints while we try to cut them to bits, and try not to shoot me" Kadi laughed.

"You're not going to carry a gun Kadi" The captain asked?

"No Gamy I don't need one" Kadi said.

"Why is that" Gamy asked?

"Shoot me" Kadi said.

"What"!

"Just shoot me please" Kadi said.

   Everyone except Victoria backed up. Gamy shot Kadi in the leg and it made a bruise but did not penetrate her leg, and then the bruise began to fade as if nothing had ever happened.

"What the hell was that?" Brad yelled into the com.

   Kadi smiled and answered the general.

"Sorry sir, we were working on tactics down here in the loading bay. All is secure." Kadi said.

"Very good." Brad answered.

Kadi turned in a complete circle and looked at every soldier.

"That is why I don't need a gun, and I am not a very strong member of my clan, well compared to Tana, Navar and Will. I believe I am stronger than Ruby or Gwen, but I would hate to live on the difference. Mya I don't really know about, she seems reluctant to open up right now, since she was returned to us" Kadi said with her full lips pursed.

"You always were one scary girl Kadi; now you are so pretty and perfect; like her" Gamy said pointing at Victoria. "I never thought you could be any more lovely and then you were, however you are... marvelous really" Gamy said.

"Buttering me up wont help you Gamy" Kadi said teasingly.

Victoria scowled, it seemed to her that Kadi wanted to bed this weakling, it was a clear insult to Navar who was the second most charming beautiful man on the ship, not to mention the second most powerful, and Navar was a seriously jealous fellow. Yet, Vicky kept her own counsel in this matter. Kadi noticed her look as they were leaving the staging area and decide to set her friend straight.

"I was a lesbian before Navar, Victoria, I would never have bedded Gamy or any man, Mya linked me to my man and I will never have any desire for another man no matter how cute or charming. You would have a better chance of bedding me" Kadi said as she slapped Victoria on her butt.

"Fresh" Victoria said as she giggled at her own foolishness.

"I flirt a lot, but it comes to nothing, because I desire nothing but what I have already. My heart and soul are full" Kadi said with a smile and conviction.

The two vampires walked in an easy gate the grand staircase that served no real purpose but was pretty anyway. It was twenty feet wide and as tall as the ship itself. It was positively Gone with the Wind in style, very grand.

"You know that most of the human military will not survive this war Kadi. Your friend Gamy is too gung ho to survive. We have faced other vampires in open war, but humans never have, they are unprepared for the speed and strength of an enemy like this. We can neither protect them nor leave them out of the fight, therefore, we must accept they will die in battle' Victoria said solemnly.

"Perhaps not, but then again with the baby venom fiasco, we might be able to give the humans a chance to live longer, Gwen and Jana are perfecting the trials even now" Kadi answered with a twisted smile.

Victoria led Kadi to the med-lab where Lee was about to have her baby. Tana and Mya were out front, and they looked like they were guarding the door, Mya had her sword cradled in the crux of her arm unsheathed. Tana looked distressed, but when she saw Kadi and Victoria her face was serene suddenly.

"What has happened, your face says much little lover of mine" Victoria asked as she pulled Tana into her warm embrace.

"Not long ago a few human soldier, at-least we thought they were came up here with guns drawn and tried to take Lee from us, because they said we were vampires and the child was not safe in our hands. I told them Lee is my daughter and the baby my grandchild and they would not take her. They tried to shoot me, but Mya attacked them from the side disarming and break the arms of all the attackers. Mya would have thrown over the rail to their deaths if I did not stop her. Will would not approve of the murders, although he would not have said so because of me. Mya has not moved from this spot since that time. Gwen is with Lee and Chad now, so even if they had gotten passed her and me; Gwen will finish the job. Chad is furious but Lee forbid him from doing anything until after they baby comes" Tana said quickly.

"Will must be told about this. Where are the men who tried to accost you" Victoria said in a quiet voice.

   Tana looked at her mate and knew she intended in killing them for what they had done. There was blood lust in Victoria's violet eyes; they were nearly fluorescent. Mya said that Brad had come and slapped the taste out of their mouths and threw them in the brig, without medical care. Victoria was about to leave and Tana held her firmly to her body.

"No, stay with me Vicky. Lee is having a hard birth and I feel so helpless" Tana said.

(WHAAAAAAAA)

"Not anymore Tana, I believe the baby has arrived" Vicky said.

   Sure enough when Tana went into the med lab there was Lee covered in sweat like she just ran the Boston Marathon, and in her arms was a perfect pink baby, nuzzling her for warmth. Chad was standing leaning over the bed kissing the baby on her tiny head.

"What name did you decide on" Tana asked?

"Pepper" Chad said.

"So welcome Pepper Sorren Garrett" Victoria said as she bite her own finger and made a sign in her blood on the baby's forehead.

"That is not her name" Chad said in a huff!

"Why do you say that Chad Sorren Garrett" Vicky asked?

Chad looked at Victoria, tall and regal with a very confused face. He was not a Garrett, he was a Sorren, so what was with the name change? He was about to ask when Will walked in and answered the unasked question for him.

"All of our family carry the Garrett name at the end of their given names as a identifier, even those who marry or mate with us since we are the ruling family" Will said. "May I hold baby Pepper"?

Baby Pepper opened her little blue eyes and looked into Will's and she smiled, not like an involuntary one but a toothless smile that lasted as long as Will looked into her eyes. Chad was suddenly nervous the way Will was looking at his baby, he stepped forward but Lee grabbed his arm and clamped down harder than he thought possible.

"There is no safer place than in my daddies hands Chad, can't you see how much he is in love with Pepper" Lee asked?

Chad looked up to see tears in Will's eyes; Chad could not believe this was the same mega power that he envied, crying.

"You old softy" Jay said from the edge of the room.

"Yup, he cried like a baby with Navar's little ones as well, Will loves kids and these are his grand babies, so they are special" Ogre said.

Will handed the baby to Chad.

"She is beautiful Chad, well done. You and Lee made a lovely elf. Now it is about time you were knighted Lee, as soon as the Tigun doc sets you free" Will said as he turned and walked out.

"Wait, where are you going" Lee yelled?

Ruby and Jay looked at Tana and then silently left on Will's heals.

"Guard my family Ogre" Will called from a distance.

"You got it chief" Steven yelled back.

Mya walked out beside Ogre and stood next to him sword drawn, silent. Ogre looked at Mya; she looked troubled to him and distant.

"You want to talk about it Mya" Ogre asked?

"No".

"Bull shit, you're chomping at the bit to say it, look at you. If you don't want to tell me then say your piece to someone before you explode baby" Ogre said as he looked away.

Tiny perfect tears ran down Mya's breath taking face. She did not look at Steven but; he was right she knew that; so Mya took a leap of faith and explained her heart to the giant. If he laughed she vowed to cut his throat.

"I can't have a baby for Navar" Mya said.

"What" Steven asked?

"I am sad because I can't make a baby with Navar. Kadi and Gwen gave him kids but I can't, and moreover, they were nearly killed. Now Lee's baby was almost taken. If I can't make a baby, then I will protect the ones there are" Mya said.

The trim Asian vampire was shocked when Ogre's giant arm scooped her up and held her close to him and rubbed her back. Mya let the damn break and balled her eyes out. Ogre did not say anything he just comforted her. Gwen came out and looked at Ogre and Mya confused. Ogre put Mya down and turned her to Gwen; Mya stepped forward and held out her arms. Gwen came forward and embraced her tenderly.

"Tell her Mya" Ogre said as he walked ten paces away.

"Tell me what" Gwen asked?

Mya explained herself to Gwen and by the time she finished Gwen had tears as well on her glowing face. She held her mate close and kissed her tears away.

"You know Raz calls you mamya, to him the mean mama Mya. He loves you, I know that is not the same thing" Gwen said.

"Raz said that" Mya smiled.

"Aria addresses you as my Mya, or didn't you ever notice. Kadi and I love you and so do the babies" Gwen told her.

Mya cried her heart out, but there was joy in her heart now; where there was only a void before.

(AT THE BRIG).

Will punched his fist thru the hatch and ripped the door off the hinges, because the guards would not let him in. Since he was absolute commander of the ship, this surprised him. Jay was sure his best friend was about to kill someone. Will was livid.

"On whose authority did you decide to lock me out" Will asked?

Jay put his hand on Will's shoulder to calm him and stepped forward. The guards went pale at the big black man with bright red-orange eyes. He glared at them meaningfully, and then spoke in a deep voice.

"Get stepping fool and bring the idiot who locked the door on my king" Jay said in a low growl.

The guard stood frozen to the spot, perhaps it was fear, maybe stupidity, but Jay feared for their lives if they did not start leaving.

"NOW" Jay screamed!

The soldiers ran so fast they tripped over each other and fell several times on the way. They returned with armed marines. This was clearly a mistake, Ruby pulled her sword and move in a blur, Will snatched her by her elbow and stopped her dead in mid air leap.

"No".

Brad Franklin Gen. of the human forces nearly fell down the stairs trying to catch the marines.

"Jay" Will said pointing at Brad.

Jay moved so fast it looked to the marines that he just disappeared, he was back standing next to Will hold Brad in his arms. Jay put the General down and stepped back. Brad collected himself as he stared down the marines.

"What in the name of God is going on here men" Brad said in ire.

A marine 1st Lt stepped forward.

"We are acting on the orders of the Captain sir, we were told that any aggression on the part of the vampires was an act of war. We tried to save the human girl and her baby from these freaks" The man said boldly.

Ruby snarled and lunged; once again Will snagged her and held her in place. Ruby looked at him, he shook his head, but he did not let her go. Brad was red faced and totally beside himself.

"Which Captain gave the order son" Brad asked?

"The former commandant, sir" The Lt answered.

Will was gone in an instant and so was, Ruby, Jay and Brad. In what seemed like one breath they were at the Med-lab where the injured, beaten former marine commandant was supposed to be resting. Brad was told that they let him go, after the Tiguns healed him of all his injuries. Brad was beyond angry.

"Will what are we going to do" Jay asked?

Will only smiled as he leaned over and lift the com off the wall.

"Blood hunt" Will said softly into the receiver.

(AHHHHHHH)

The instant the words left Will's lips several thousand vampires roared in delight at the same time. Will walked down the grand staircase and waited as soldiers and vampires mustered in front of him.

VAMPIRE WARS

"The former marine commandant has attacked and order new attacks on my clan and all of our extended family. He has cause disharmony and mutiny on my ship. Therefore, per my last ruling, where we were forgiving in our punishment, if he caused anymore trouble his life is forfeit. I declare him traitor to all humanity, and say blood hunt. Bring him to me alive and able to speak" Will ordered.

"What does blood hunt mean" Brad asked?

"It means he lifted the restriction on killing and drinking that guys blood. He is to be caught and drained of all blood to strengthen our family. It is not a lite thing that Will does, it is his highest law that forbids biting humans, to declare this man's blood open game means that there is no chance of reprieve" Ruby explained.

"Is it only him or all humans that are open game" Brad asked in fear?

"No baby, only that idiot" Rudy said as she kissed Brad on the lips softly, making him blush although he did not pull away.

(On the Planet)

Grom was keeping to the shadows and the planet was hot, too hot for most life. The Korv either killed or ate everything or this was a dead world. Sect was on the far side of the planet and Grom was conversing about his findings when Sect went silent. There were sounds of battle over the com. Even with their amazing speed Grom could not get there in time to help much, so he suffered not knowing if his own son lived or died just then.

A Korv sentry walked by Grom; who was hidden in the shadows observing the Korv troop placements and strengths. The Korv were seven to eight feet tall and weighed between 400 and 600lbs. They had four brawny arms with four fingered hands. Their heads had two black eyes and an abbreviated nose. What stood out was their mouths, they had a long jaw that opened up to two rows of sharp points teeth instead of one set. Grom did not see any ears, but the Korv could locate the tiniest noise and attack the area it. It led Grom and his assassins to believe that they were movement or pressure sensitive not sound sensitive.

"Father, (Cough) you would not believe what we found (cough) down here (cough), we must let Navar know now" Sect managed to say.

The sound waves, as small as they were alerted the Korv who barrel into the dark and it's own death. The Korv were not easy to kill, but they were not as hard to kill as a vampire. Strength wise the Korv were stronger than an average vampire, but not as fast, so it evened out.

Grom canvassed the area before he called Will.

(On the bridge of the city ship)

"This is Grom, I need to talk to Will and Navar now" Said the voice in the com.

"Confirmed, this is Tigre, wait one while I summon Will" Tigre answered.

The Tigun coms were excellent and they were easy to use and had a zero failure rate. When you spoke on one, it was as if the person was with you because it was so clear. Will and Navar were alerted. They raced to the bridge. Grom told them Sect found something that the King must come planet side to see with his own eyes. Will acknowledge he was coming, Tigre set the coordinates and made the arrangement for the king to drop on to the Planet.

Rip and Erik were walking from the practice area, when they caught the scent of a human hiding near by. Now humans are everywhere around the ship and it was not uncommon for them to be in the training area for blade training and martial arts practice because the older vampires were all masters of both disciplines. However, this was different, this human reeked of fear. Rip motioned for Erik to circle around the other side of the corridor and stop the human from running that way. Rip just reached into the dark where the human was hiding and lifted his shaking form out and held him up for all to see. From Rip's mighty left arm hung the marine they had all been looking for.

"Come little traitor the king awaits your pleasure" Rip laughed.

Will was indeed surprised by Rip walking in carrying the traitor like a dirty shoe, out away from his body as if the captain stunk.

"Well hello there former commandant" Will said in a friendly voice that fooled none.

"What now Will" Rip asked?

"A moment of indulgence only Rip then you can kill him anyway you like, feed him to your clan if you like since you found him" Will answered.

"Nay my king, I will not taint my blood with his, nor will any Aussie of my clan" Rip said in honest disgust.

"Erik then" Will asked?

"I refuse on Lady Victoria's behalf our king, this filthy traitor's blood will not be spilled by us either. I will kill him for you if that is your wish though" Erik said with a bow.

VAMPIRE WARS

"Are you going to let these blood sucking bastards eat me and do nothing" The Marine screamed in fear?

(BANG)

The marine just stared as the ground rushed up to meet him. All eyes turn to the end of the table where the War planning was being held. Brad stood there with his 45 Colt pointed at the marine. Brad shot the marine right between his eyes.

"I beg your pardon Will. Rip and Erik your's as well, but I could not let this traitor live, he had undermined both your authority and mine. I can't allow that, we are at war gentlemen so that piece of shit had to go" Brad explained. "Toss his ass out an airlock, with Will's permission of-course"?

"Yes, please do" Will said.

The invasion plans were well made when Will and Rip left to have diner with Tana and his family. When Will came in baby Pepper was between the other babies sleeping. Raz and Aria had their tiny arms around baby Pepper in a protective way. Pepper for her part was sleeping with a smile on her face. Lee was watching them closely with a sad smile on her lovely face.

"Our babies will not bite Pepper Lee, I promise" Kadi said.

"No, I am not worried about that. I am going to be turned today and I am afraid. My brother who is as strong a man as any whoever live suffered terribly, I don't know if I can handle it" Lee explained to Kadi.

"Gwen will give you Morphine like I did to Tana when I turned her, so you will sleep thru the pain" Will said.

"Oh, I guess I am being silly" Lee said.

"No, it hurts like a mo-fo baby, but you will be stronger and healthier than you can imagine after the change. One more thing, your going to be starving to death sexually when you wake, don't kill Chad by accident, restrain yourself or you will" Will advised his daughter.

"I will get the drugs and Chad" Gwen said and jetted off to do that.

Lee picked up Pepper and breastfed her baby for the last time. Her body would not be the same; her breasts would have no milk in them for her baby.

"Dad, how am I going to feed Pepper after I change, there will be no milk" Lee asked?

"Tigre took a sample of your milk already didn't he" Will asked?

"Yes".

"Pepper will be drink milk that was made from you then, until she out grows the need for it and starts solid foods" Will said.

Lee looked at her dad, young, powerful and very beautiful if you could apply the term to a man. Lee thought that except for Chad, her brother and father were the most handsome men on the ship, perhaps all of humanity. In them she had the fiercest protectors imaginable, and the closest friends. She was very close to her brother and dad. She loved her mom, but they had a very different view of life, Tana was hard on Lee because she was a girl and expected more from her and was afraid for her all the time up to becoming the queen of all vampires. Lee knew that Tana was held to be the most desirable female on the ship and Victoria was a close second, it made her blush to think that her father had them both every day. It was the way of the vampire though. Lee wanted only Chad and he only wanted her as far as she knew. Will brought Lee back to reality.

"We should start once Chad gets here" Will said, "You know this is to make you powerful enough to protect your own family, it is not a punishment. Lee you don't have to accept the kiss of the vampire baby, you can say no and we will take turns protecting you".

"No, I want to stay young and strong and I want my daughter to have the chance to be young and strong as well some day. The vampires I know are the most interesting people I have ever met. Some of them are thousands of years old, and the ones that have permanent mates, have never been parted in all the time, their love has never weakened at all, I want that" Lee said.

Chad and Gwen came back and Will took Lee to Tana. Tana was going to embrace Lee, but Lee said no. She wanted Will to do it, so she would be as powerful as Navar her brother. Will smiled and told her that if Tana did the honors Lee would just as powerful.

"OH MY GOD, Thank you Lee. I did not want to do it myself, I will however not leave you until you wake, then you and Chad will need to be alone" Tana giggled.

Lee began to strip and Chad looked aghast. Will stopped her.

"After I embrace you baby, your mother and sisters will remove you clothes for your protection, so you don't strangle and you are going to have to be chained up, because your going to be so strong you could kill yourself or some else when your in your coma. Chad you will not be allowed near her until Tana says it is safe for you" Will explained.

"You have no (Gag, choke)" Chad started to yell when Will grabbed him by the throat and lifted him off his feet.

"Chad understand this, Lee will be this strong and out of her mind, she will not know you, you can not reason with her, if she grabs you then you will die. Simple but so true" Will said, and then he put Chad down. "Look Chad you're my second son, I don't want you to get killed even by accident, so please listen to us, or I will have Gwen knock you senseless, and Kadi sit on you. I would sick Navar on you but, he might kill you for touching his baby sister" Will said jokingly, but still firmly.

Will decide to take Chad with him when he went to the surface. Navar and Jay came as well. Ogre and Ruby were left to back up Tana. Rip took command of the ship until Lee was passed her coma and Tana could come out to take command of the ship.

(On the surface on the planet).

Will met Sect instead of Grom, because he had something dire that Will and son needed to see. Will met the small dark one on the edge of a rocky mountain slope, Sect looked at Chad with humor, and then he saw Jay's burning eyes and got that Chad had a bodyguard that he was unaware of.

"Show us little brother what we need to see" Navar said with kind authority.

Sect smiled and so did his twenty knights. Sect led them down a crevice in the rocks that was hidden to all except the assassins. It was the dark ones stock and trade to find such places and use them to their advantage. The end of the rocks came abruptly to a final against metal. One of Sect's knight slipped by like a ferret, and into the whole in the metal that was impossibly small for his body yet he went thru it anyway silently, it was obvious it caused him great pain to Will and Jay.

Jay was about to speak when Sect's hand was silently over his mouth and he shook his head no. Sect took out a small soundless pad and wrote (Korv hunt by vibrations as far as we know; your voice will bring them down on us in seconds, **NO TALKING** and be careful not to touch anything or step to heavy). Sect looked at Chad. Chad glared back and pointed behind Sect. All heads turn to see the little Dark one had opened a hatch.

The inside of a Korv ship was very similar to the Tiguns, too similar in fact for Will. Navar noticed the same thing and looked at his father. Sect led Will and the rest to a room that looked down on what looked like a factory. It took a second to get what they were being shown.

"Oh shit, this is a nursery" Jay said out-loud softly.

Sect and Will's faces jerked around, just as Jay realized his error. The sound of huge heavy feet running toward them from two directions confirmed they were found out. Will turned to look at Sect.

"Get us out of here Sect, now" Will commanded.

Sect grabbed five of his knights made a sign and they ran down toward the corridor on the left, Sect did the same to the right and made us wait until we could hear fighting.

"Okay we can run for it now" Sect said.

Sect turned to run and was off his feet hanging from Navar's powerful right arm.

"Did you just send our cousins and brothers off to die so we can escape" Navar snarled in Sects face!

"Yes of-course, you the royal family, it is my duty to protect you with my life and that of all of my clan, I would be put to death by my own father should you fall in my care" Sect said unashamed.

Navar dropped Sect on his feet, slapped Jay across his chest and ran down to the left sword drawn; Jay ripped his sword and dagger out as they melted into the darkness.

"Navar is right, no sacrifices Sect, you are NOT expendable, your family, now let's go save our kin son" Will said as he pulled both of his deadly blades. "Chad stay behind me at all times.

Will picked up Chad like a doll and tossed him over his shoulder and ran so fast Chad could not make out anything at all. Suddenly Chad was on his feet and in the middle of a blood bath. Chad slammed his P-90 into the back of a Korv and pulled the trigger, the Korv jerk around and Chad had a knife in his left hand, he danced to the side and slit the Korv's throat nearly temple to temple. Still, the Korv went hit Chad as it died, but the wily ranger back flipped away in just a fraction of enough time to save himself from being beheaded. Suddenly Chad was yanked flat.

"GET DOWN" Sect screamed as Will launched himself like a tornado into the Korv.

Footsteps behind them brought Chad up off the ground gun first. Navar ran passed him and Jay ran up carrying four dark ones who were dying, his face was grim, but he did not look behind him at all like there was no need to. Nevertheless, Chad had no intention of letting his guard down; if you did the Korv would kill you. Sect never left Chad's side, the wiry vampire was smiling, Chad thought he looked terrified.

"Son, take the back guard, Sect & clan; protect Chad, Jay your behind me" Will said!

Will went down the corridor slaughtering the Korv. The last one popped up just in front of the hatch they had come in through, Will kicked the Korv sentry in the stomach so forcefully that when it hit the hatch it blew the hatch right off the hinges. Will jump out after it and pulled Jay through since the big vampire was carrying four men in one arm. Navar was stationed on the inside of the ripped hatchway and he was so still that he did not look alive, until the Korv showed up.

"Come on son let's get the hell out of here" Will hollered at Navar.

Chad would never forget the first time he looked into his brother in-laws glowing red eyes, which looked more like neutron stars than eyeballs. Navar looked at his father and shook his head no.

"Run for it dad, get them out of here safely. I will keep this trash off your back until you're safely away. I will cut and run when your gone, and go find Grom" Navar said as he turned and went back into the dark after the Korv.

Sect started to go back in and Jay stopped him.

"No man, you will get yourself killed and just be in his way" Jay told the small dark one.

Ok let's move, run as fast as you can, we have injured that need medical care" Will said as he grimly looked at the Korv ship.

The last thing we heard was inhuman screams of terror coming from deep in the Bowls of the ship. None slowed down, none spoke, on they ran until the cloaked ship was airborne and they were on the way back to the city ship.

"Tigre" Will snarled!

"Confirmed Will, go ahead" Tigre answered.

"Track Navar's com and hit that area with every fucking thing you got" Will growled.

Will looked dangerously close to loosing his cool. Only Jay was not afraid. Will's eyes were burning like Navar's, if anything even more brightly than the son's had. These Garrett's were a scary lot when angry. Jay patted his friend and leader's shoulder.

"Hey man, none of those toads can even scratch that boy, he is amazing. I will contact Grom when we get to the ship and confirm that prince charming made contact" Jay said punching Will in the arm.

Sect was dying to say something, but was afraid Will was going to explode if he spoke.

"I know Sect, I think so too. The technology on the Korv ship was not just similar, it was the same" Will said as if reading the Dark princes mind.

"Yes, master. I have a detailed report with visuals and technical data for your review later" Sect said in a rush.

"I would expect nothing less from a master assassin Sect, well done" Will said; in a final tone that spoke of his desire not to speak further.

Tigre was at the landing bay when Will's shuttle landed. When the Tigun saw the look on Will's hard face has was terrified, he went as far as turning to leave and then stopped, took a deep breath and went to face the king of the vampires. Jay hauled the injured dark ones out and rushed them off for medical care and blood transfusions. Sect, Will and Tigre faced each other for what seemed to Sect to be forever. Therefore, it was Sect who decided to move things along.

"Can you explain why the Korv technology is the same as the Tigun's" Sect asked. "I have technical specs if you need proof".

"We were once the same species, more than two thousand years ago. There was a point were a few of our people mutated and the Korv were born. They were big and strong and useful, so we were actually in the beginning thrilled. The Korv are not mindless, they are as smart as we are and ruthless. So when we saw the evil starting to seep through so we segregated ourselves from them and developed new stronger defense technologies to keep them from wiping us out. Now they destroy any race that might ally with us and eat them. Disgusting" Tigre explained.

"You don't think that little bit of information was important Tigre, my own son sacrificed himself to allow us to get the injured to safety Tigre, if he dies I will raze the planet to dust" Will said softly, which made it far more menacing.

Tigre and Sect shuddered in fear.

"Will, what is below us is the famed Black planet, the breeding grounds of the Korv. We Tiguns have searched for it for nearly eight hundred years, we must wipe the surface clean of the Korv horde if we can. I will do anything to stop them here and now" Tigre slobbered out. His tiny face was manic.

VAMPIRE WARS

CHAPTER 9: KORV

On the Black planet the Korv were not happy. They had just gotten the first taste of the powerful new allies that the tiny Tiguns brought to fight their war. What astounded the Korv was that the small creatures were as strong or even stronger that they were; not to mention the insane speed which these creatures fought at. The Korv were mighty and loved to fight handed to hand, but they might have rethink that with these well trained fighters. Kurl the leader of the Black Planet Korv breeding complex; was worried. He knew that the Tiguns were going to destroy the small lab they had infiltrated, but the main underground facility was in no danger.

"I want to know about these new menaces, yesterday. They are to well groomed to be mindless drones, so that mean they are intelligent. We can not therefore take for granted that we can best them in warfare, we need to out think them" Kurl said.

The science of super procreation was invented by a Tiguns; but it was tailored for the Korv by Kurl himself. He was every bit a genius, and he was a first rate fighter as well. Kurl had overseen the process for centuries, every since he was taught it by a Tigun genius, the only person Kurl acknowledge as his better intellectually. Kurl like the tiny fellow and they were he guessed friends, so when he was ordered to kill the Tigun he was conflicted. During the big Korv's indecision; the Tigun made his escape and was never seen again.

The Korv breed the same way humans do, there are females and males, yet, the stronger the male and female pairing the greater the off-spring, so they do not couple for love, but for powerful children. The Korv are not devoid of emotions, and they experience love for their children and often they come to enjoy their mating partner as a companion as well as a mother or father. Female Korv are only slightly smaller than the males and they are faster moving. If they were both armor-less you could tell them apart easily, because of the female's breasts. However, the Korv wear armor almost always.

The education the Tiguns gave the humans and vampires; was incomplete and biased. Later, Will and company would realize this.

(On the City ship).

"Grom" Jay called?

"Grom are you receiving, if you can't answer because of Korv danger, flip you com on and off" Jay ordered.

The com assigned to Grom blinked off suddenly and then popped back on. Jay smiled to know Grom was still alive down there on the planet. Rudy was with him scanning the surface, except for a few dozen patrols the surface was clear. Rudy thought everything must be under ground for protection form the elements. Point in case, there was a huge storm coming Grom's direction. Rudy pulled Jay over and showed him.

"Hey Grom, you better find a deep hiding place, there is a big ass storm coming your way soon. Also did Navar make contact yet" Jay asked?

The bridge was silent as they waited for Grom to answer Jay in some manner.

"No Navar, digging in for storm Grom out".

The grim look on Jay's face said it all. When Will told Tigre to shell the Korv ship, the tiny genius did that. The only thing left where the ship used to be was a smoking crater, Tigre never does anything half assed, so the area was nuked so to speak. Jay looked ill, Rudy looked sorry for him.

"Better you tell them than me baby" Ruby said.

"Thanks" Jay said as he stalked out of the bridge toward Will and Tana's quarters.

Lee woke up from her coma two days after Will embraced her into the vampire clan. Chad had just gotten released from the med-lab. During the on planet fight Chad had killed three Korv, one he shot, two he fought in close near the ship, Sect tried to help but Chad screamed at him to get on the ship. Chad cut the throat of both of them, but he his own ribs and shoulder were broken. The entire ship knew of Chad's valor before he was out of bed. So deep was the respect for him by the vampires, they began calling him the human prince; and they bowed when he passed.

Lee woke up to see Chad sitting by her; she attacked him with a vigor that scared Chad.

"Hey baby, be careful, I am only human" Chad laughed.

"Do you want me to change that Chady" Lee said as she ripped his clothes off.

Lee was always very playful and intense as a lover but she was so far beyond what Chad believed was possible, and strangely she was being careful with him. She pleasured him orally to begin, she sucked so strong and vigorously that he came always instantly.

"Hey spin around here so I can lick you while you're making me cum" Chad said breathlessly.

Lee did just that, she placed her silky thighs around his face and lowered herself expertly so he could taste her easily. She moaned as his mouth and tongue went to work on her soft moist parts. The oral sex did not last too long because vampires need deep powerful penetrations to help satisfy their insatiable hunger for physical pleasure. Chad tried to get on top, because Lee liked it that was usually, not that she was unskilled on top. Not this time however.

"Sorry baby, I want to drive. Don't move, just close your eyes and enjoy it" Lee said as her eyes got more deeply red.

Lee pushed Chad on his back. Chad's tool was so hard and engorged he thought it would split, Lee did not help. Lee reached down and ran her tongue up and down it twice and them swallowed it whole, now mind you Lee is a small girl, with a small mouth, and a tiny Huhu. Her breasts are on the medium to large size scale for her frame though. For Lee to get his entire manhood in her mouth meant most of it was don't her throat, he was appalled at first, but it felt so damn good he was not capable of speaking. Suddenly, Chad's tiny wife stood up on the bed above him, she reached down and held his tool in her delicate hand, she bent her knees until his tool was touching her juicy little hole then she kicked her feet out and dropped. Chad was instantly deeper inside of his wife than he ever dared be before, and Lee was raise and lowering herself on him faster and faster, Chad wanted to scream it felt so good. Chad could not image anything this erotic or passionate. Lovemaking for Lee and Chad was very good before, but nothing compared to this. Chad final passed out form hyperventilation.

Three day after the wild love making with Lee Chad woke up with a new set of red eyes. He turned to see Lee naked sitting on their bed. She patted the bed next to her suggestively. Faster than Chad had even moved before, he had his tiny wife dangling from her hips upside down as he ate her vigorously, she return the oral favor and again they made love, but this time neither had to hold back for fear of killing their lover. It was the most incredible thing they had ever felt, the passion was a thousand times more intense.

Chad would later wonder how Lee held herself back, his desire was like a cocaine addiction, he had to have her, again and again, and it was uncontrollable.

Later when Lee and Chad went to see Pepper who was laying on her back while the other two babies tickled her softly. Lee went to pick Pepper up and the baby shied away with a confused look. Raz and Aria even as babies knew what the change in Lee and Chad was; they could feel it in their blood even if they could not put it into words with their tiny list of words.

"Mama, Pepa, dat da mama" Raz said pointing at Lee

Pepper looked skeptical, which on a near two week old baby looks pretty cute.

"Papa, Pepa, da-da. You da-da. Mama and dada" Raz muttered as he pointed and held Pepper's tiny little fist.

Even at the baby stage Raz and Aria knew to protect little helpless Pepper and they never bit her even by accident, and no one could pick her up but a Garrett or baby Raz would go berserk and alert a Garrett instantly. He was holding his wee soft baby companion, when Aria rubbed her face on Pepper's cheek. Pepper turned her chubby face to look at Arai.

"Ma ma Ee, da-doo Ad" Aria whispered in baby talk.

Pepper raised her baby eye brow on her right eye, and then she held out her wee hands to be picked up.

Chad lifted his daughter up and smelled her. Her scent was so rich and wonderful, she smelled like the lite soda of his tiny wife. Lee smelled like the most wonderful scent in creation, it drove his senses wild, his daughter smell very close to that. Chad could track this scent across the universe and never loose them. He took a deep breath enjoying the aroma of his girls, when he was startle.

Baby Pepper leaned her little face in and was sniffing him the same way. Chad busted out laughing; his love for this tiny baby was so complete in that moment. If Chad lost his life anytime soon, he would go to his reward satisfied with his lot in this life, his heart was full and his soul was singing to him of pure joy.

"Come to mommy Pepper" Lee said.

Pepper let Lee lift her gently out of Chad's vise grip hands. The baby leaned in and sniffed Lee like she had done to Chad. They all laughed again, because her little nose was flared in the effort to inhale big like her papa did. Raz and Aria were laughing to; Chad picked them up and cuddled them as well.

"What are you little monsters up to? Thanks for baby sitting my Pepper, Razy and Airy" Chad said.

The cousins kissed Chad on his cheeks. Pepper saw and was making a jealous face now that she knew that was her daddy. Lee laughed sweetly at her baby.

"I love you Pepper and I always will" Lee said. "Let's get something to eat Chad.

"What do we eat, and what do these babies eat" Chad asked.

"They drink milk, we eat whatever we want" Lee said with a smile the melted Chad's heart.

(In the food court Galley area).

Tana was sitting with Will their faces were grim and Ogre was standing by Ruby when Chad and Lee came up.

"Hey family" Lee said brightly!

"Oh hey the kids are up" Steven Ogre said walking toward Chad.

Raz literally leaped at Ogre, one gigantic hand snatched the falling baby right out of the air, and Ogre reached over and took Aria as well and began to juggle them around. The babies laughed so hard they had tiny tears coming from their wee eyes. Ogre seemed to truly adore the elves. Pepper was fussy because she was not getting juggled.

"No baby, you are not indestructible like they are you could be hurt" Lee said.

"Bull shit Lee" Ogre said as he deftly took Pepper out of her hands and juggled her with the other babies and she giggled with pleasure as well.

Lee was about to hit Steven when Pepper squealed with delight. Chad just put his arm around Lee and smiled at the spectacle. Lee sat down by Tana with Chad taking the spot next to her. Will looked at Chad appraisingly, so did Tana and Vicky. Ruby was less restrained; she gazed at Chad with open bare lust.

"Sorry but my eyes only see Lee ladies" Chad pointed out in a casual tone.

"I understand Chad, I see only Tana and Will, the way you see Lee" Victoria said with a lovely smile.

"You did well for our family on the Black planet son, you risked your human life for us, it was foolish, but damn brave. You have earned the respect of myself and everyone else on this tub. Now for the bad news; we are going down that God forsaken rock and putting the Boot to the Korv and I need you Chad, you are one of the strongest Members of the family, number five if I am not mistaken, right behind Lee, just ahead of Ogre and Jay. I want you to go with Sect, he likes you and is loyal to you on a friendship level and find the main facility, the one we were in is small potatoes according to Tigre. You're going to be in co-command, you're the muscle and Sect is the experience, so work out a game plan with him and be careful, these Korv are not dumb beasts" Will advised.

Tana looked at Will with longing she knew he was up to something she was not going to like. Yet, the queen said nothing; such was her love for her man, that she would follow him and do what was necessary to make the mission and their lives a success.

"Jay you will take Gwen and Kadi and go find my son, alive or dead I want you to bring him back little brother. Kadi you will take your friend Gamon and his band of merry men with you as back up, try not to get them slaughtered" Will said.

"I will find him, no matter what man" Jay said. He smiled at everyone and turned and left.

"I will get the merry men up to speed and be ready when you call for us" Kadi said as she went to inform Gamy of their orders.

Will turned to Victoria and addressed her.

"Vicky, my second mate, I need you and Erik to be ready at a moments notice to attack the Korv when Chad roots them out, and don't get killed, our love for you is immense and your loss would damage us" Will said.

"I will not let my guard down for an instant, my clan and guard are among the very best there is or was. We will be ready" Victoria said.

"The brothers, Ogre and Rip's entire clan are with me, we will face the Korv in open war in two days, to buy time for Salen and Victoria and everyone else get into position and entrench on the planet. I will have Tigre communicate a challenge to the Korv. One important note, make damn sure

Salen leaves this ship before we do or she will make a play for the control over the forces we brought with us. I am leaving Lee, Mya, Ruby to support Tana, with the three of you nobody would be able to stand against you. Besides, Lee is Chad's, Ruby is Ogre's, Mya is Navar's and Tana is my lover so this makes the forces balanced in that way" Will said.

There was general agreement that was a good plan, the group broke up and went to their own personal tasks before deployment.

(In the Med-lab)

Jana, who was the head of the human medical practitioners, was gearing up for the coming war effort, and the wounded or maimed that would bring into her ER. Jay walked in and lifted his girlfriend off the floor and carried her to the counter and kissed her until she was dizzy from oxygen debt. Jay reached out and took a syringe and slid it into his arm and drew some blood out, which is not any easy task for a invincible vampire, their skin is extremely tough. Jay practically willed the 16 gauge needle to enter his arm. Jana was about to ask what he was doing when he explained it to her.

"Baby have you studied the properties of vampire blood" Jay asked?

"Yes, why"?

"It will make a person faster, heal from any wound, kill any decease, and keep you from aging" Jay said.

"Yes, but what does that have to do with anything Jay" Jana asked?

VAMPIRE WARS

Before Jana could do anything, Jay pushed her flat on her back on a bed that was beside her only a moment before. He was kissing her neck and then her breasts, suddenly Jana felt a needle go into her arm and the blood in the vile entered her. Jana tried to pull away but Jay made sure she could not move. He held her down and kissed her tenderly, and then he tossed the empty syringe in the Sharps container across the room expertly without looking.

"I am sorry Jana, but I love you baby and I need you to be as strong as can be while I am at war" Jay apologized.

"I told you I don't want to be a vampire, at least not yet Jay, and now you took away my free will damn you" Jana said looking at her arm.

Jay only laughed at her, which made her mad. She hit him in the chest and he could actually feel the impact. He smiled even bigger; he pulled Jana to a mirror and showed her. Jana's back and chest muscled flexed by themselves and her breasts lifted about an inch higher as she watched. Her whole body was tighter, much more fit and way stronger.

"You're not a vampire Jana" Jay said.

"What, but you embraced me" Jana said?

"No, I gave some of my blood. Your eyes are pale blue now, and for about a year or so, you are going to be super human, need to sleep very little, hunger will not be a problem, neither will endurance. I gave you this gift, so you can do your job better, faster as the need arises" Jay explained.

"It that all" Jana asked?

"No, if any vampire comes near you, they will smell me on you and back away, any human that decide he wants you; had better ask you for sex, if they try to take it you will beat them to death; your five times as strong than a normal man now" Jay told her.

"You're protecting me even though you are not going to be here to do it in person. I think I truly love you Jay, vampire or not" Jana said.

"I would like to hold you close before I have to go, and with your new strength, love making will be extra special little girl" Jay smiled.

Jay carried Jana to his quarters because hers were among the military and there was no real sense of privacy there. Jay and Jana made a deep impact on their already serious love affair, she was scared in the beginning when Jay attacked her with a fever, her body should have broken. Jana could feel Jay actually using some of his river of strength to pleasure her, yet she felt great and wanted more not less. Jana lost herself in passion and spurred Jay to greater heights, and she herself tossed caution to the wind and gave herself fully to Jay without holding back for the first time, she felt no fear, no reservations, not pause. Jana wanted to be in Jay's powerful arms and in love for all eternity. Jana was ready to truly be embraced. She was not yet a full vampire and her heightened everything from Jay's blood showed her what that life could be, and she with no reservations wanted it and she believed in her heart that was what Jay wanted as well.

(In the armory of the Special forces).

Gamon was pleased that he was going with Kadi to the black planet, she was his best friend and they knew each other's mind in combat, it was safer for his men and women to go to war as a unit with a known leader and Kadi was not just tough, she was clever in the field, she would not risk her friends recklessly and they all knew it, so if she asked for more of them they would jump into action without a second thought, and Kadi would lead them herself right up front. Jay and Gwen however; Gamon did not know and was not sure he wanted to follow their orders, since they were not seasoned soldiers. Well, Gwen was, but she was a doctor not a fighter. Jay was big and fast, Gamon saw him toss a marine like a Frisbee once, it was awe inspiring and terrifying at the same time. Hopefully, Kadi would be in charge.

"Sorry, Jay leads this merry band Gamy" Kadi said as she popped him on the butt.

"Why him and not you" Gamon asked?

(Laughter).

"He is number seven among our clan, in strength and ability. He could whip my butt without breaking a sweat. He is faster than I am and a brutal fighter, Will is an expert in Kajukenbo, Chinese martial arts, and he taught Jay long ago to defend himself, so he could protect Will's back. That was when they were human. My father in law has never lost a fight and Jay has lost very few and those were due to them ganging up on him. Jay has my trust and my friendship, we follow him no matter what the order is" Kadi said sternly smiling.

"Oh".

"We are going to search for my man, the prince of the Garrett's, he is no doubt up to his eyes in danger knowing his temper and sense of justice. If we find him dead" Kadi did not finish, the fire in her eyes flared.

Gamon backed away from her trembling. Gwen was standing behind him and she put her small steel arms around Gamon and hugged him to her.

"Best give our mate a little space at the moment. She resisted our original union because she was not into guys, but Mya encouraged her to open her heart to Navar and I. We found her heart to be as beautiful as her body. Now that Kadi has bonded to us, the fear and ache of loosing Navar is more than she can bear. She did not want a man in her life, only a special girl, so the guilt she feels makes her dangerous to you and everyone. She loves Navar deeper than a pure human could understand, our passions are a thousand times stronger, and so is our wrath" Gwen explained.

Gamon tried squirmed a little to see if he could move the pixie sized girl who held him. He could not move her at all. It was not unpleasant in her arms, she smelled like strawberries and flowers and she was strikingly beautiful. So, this is one of the brides, the doctor. Gwen smiled and kissed his cheek.

"Are you as dangerous as Kadi" Gamon asked?

"I am faster and more agile; she is stronger and a more fierce fighter. We make perfect hunting partners because we balance out as a couple; we compliment each other's style and skills to perfection. Only Tana, Will and our own husband could survive a fight with us" Gwen said as she let Gamon go.

Kadi as if supporting that view came up to Gwen and held her in her arms, putting her head on top of her tiny mate's head.

"Don't worry Kadi, we will find him, and I doubt deep in my heart if anyone or thing could kill my baby, he would not let anything stand in his way to coming back to his family" Gwen whispered as she leaned back into Kadi's longer body.

"I know sweaty, but our bed is cold without him, I am incomplete without him" Kadi whispered back.

VAMPIRE WARS

CHAPTER 10: NAVAR

The black planet was not as nearly lifeless as the Tiguns had alluded to. The prince of all vampires was hit by an unknown type of weapon and he had to fight his way out of the valley where the small ship lab had been after his father had it blown up. Navar had his blood running down his face out of his mouth. He had to slaughter an entire small army so he could disappear into the rocky hills. He also did something he found personally disgusting, he took a smaller Korv and skinned in carefully and crawled into it and traveled the surface as a Korv sentinel. It was an odd sight, because the lower arms were the Korv's natural ones and the upper arms had Navar's inside of them. Strange, the body did not seem to be decaying at all. The smell was not bad either; kind of a well wore leather scent. Navar had to find a place and hide while his body repaired the damage from the weapon that ripped into him. Navar never thought he was invincible or that anyone was, but he was surprised when his insides were blasted out of his body with no warning. The worst thing about it was Navar did not know what hit him, so if he lived through this he could report very little to his father. Will would be hard jawed and angry at the loss of his only son and he would make the Korv bleed hard for it, but Navar's thought were for his family as he laid down in a rock cave in the dark to rest.

Navar dreamed of holding his little babies and making them laugh and having them fall asleep in his mighty arms. He dreamed of hold his mates and tasting their sweat lips and the feel of their hard silky bodies pressed against him. He tossed in his sleep; it made his serious wounds gush blood again. Immortal or not Navar needed blood badly if he was going to live.

There was creeping sound in the entrance of the cave mouth. Navar was instantly awake, his dagger in his fake hand. The sound of claws scratching the stone and the space between those sounds gave Navar the impression that the attacker was big and not a Korv. Horrible breath was on Navar's Korv skinned covered face, the thing was sniffing him.

"SNARLLL"!

The beast backed away confused, but ready to attack at any moment. Navar sat up slowly and pulled his vampire face out of the Korv skin and looked at the beast with his own eyes. The cold air kissed his tired face; he sighed and focused on the massive predator.

The thing was either a large wolf like creature or something very close to a saber tooth tiger. The hide was nearly the same as the rocks, so it was hard to know which impression was correct.

"Well, jumbo are you going to attack or leave, please attack I need the blood amigo" Navar said in a quiet huff.

(Growl)

The beast crawled forward slowly, but was not poised to spring, when it got close enough it stopped and laid flat and smelled Navar thoroughly. It raised it's head and peered intently into the vampires red eyes. It seemed confused, Navar notice the red tint of the beast's eyes and guessed that this monster was trying to understand what he was. Navar decide to take a chance, he reached slowly over and scratch the monster under it's chin. They sat there for a few minutes until Navar's blood loss was making him woozy, so he lay back down and decided to let the beast make his own choice about attacking. Navar was out cold in a few moments. The beast laid down next to Navar, providing a fur coat to keep him warm as the night turn extremely cold, cold enough a human would have died.

When Navar finally woke in the dark hours of the early day there was a rustling sound in the front of the cave. Navar who was delirious with pain and bloodlust from blood loss crawled out to see what the hell the din was. The giant beast had a smaller less powerful beast backing up toward the cave mouth. Before Navar thought about it he was on the back of the creature with his mighty teeth sank into it's brawny neck. Rich thick blood ran down Navar's dry throat, he did not spill or waste a drop. When he heard the heart begin to flutter and the beast was about to die; he let it go and looked at the giant who just saved his life in all likelihood. Navar stepped back and the giant predator grabbed the other animal and snapped the neck easily. Navar had been correct, the giant was saving him, why he didn't know, but there was no doubt. The giant ate the other beast in a short amount of time and only the big bones were left behind. When the Tiger-wolf was finished, it walked forward nudged Navar in the chest with it's massive head. They looked at each other for a moment and then the monster sprang into the rocks and was gone.

"Good hunting my wild friend" Navar said after it.

The planet was big and as Navar traveled to the east, at least he thought is was east, there were patches of green, trees and grass after a fashion. It was not until Navar found the oasis with water that he was sure that life on this planet was actually thriving. Around the water hole were several types of beasts, they were not fighting or hunting as if this place was sacred or off limits as a hunting spot. Navar was thirsty and this time not for blood, water would be nice to wash the dust out of his mouth.

There were a few low growls when Navar came near the water; that turned into full attack snarls. Navar realized he was still in the Korv skin, and these animals must hate the

Korv. Navar shed the Korv hide and walked unmolested right up to the water. The animal's seemed shocked. Most of them took test sniffs to ascertain what he was. Navar looked at them and smiled.

"The Korv are not the big dog on the dirt ball anymore, I have come to town boys" Navar said as he leaned down and tasted the clear cool liquid in the small woodland lake.

There was a distant sound and all the creatures at the waters edge froze, even Navar held his position and listened with his vampire ears to see if he could hear what was coming this way.

(Off to the East)

"What do you mean we can't find the prince? We must find him, Will demands his only son is found, he is challenging the Korv to open war to give us time and confusion to speed our search" Grom growled at the Dark ones assembled!

The dark ones did not like being pushed in their task, they resented it. Grom was not about to loose favor with the new king, Will was a man like no other, and he and the son had called them brothers, his family. Grom would not let this feeling of worth be lost, they would find prince and protect him no matter if it cost him all the dark ones lives. Will would surely be pissed off if he knew that, because he did not want anyone to waste their life for him. It was what the Dark ones wanted to be heroes, not monsters.

"Grom, we are so few and this is a large planet, we will not rest until we are successful, but we must be careful not to be reckless and draw the enemy down on us, or we will not be helpful to anyone" A dark ones said sagely.

"You are right, haste without caution is a waste and a danger, do your best my knights" Grom answered in a wiry voice.

The dark ones did not know how close they were to finding what they prized the most, a chance to maintain and bolster their own personal honor. They set out to search moving systematically west alone the mountain range and foot hills. A drifting sound caught the dark clan's ears. They knew that it meant trouble. There were only two choices, go back the way they had come, where the prince was definitely not. Or they could go forth and face the Korv hoping to find and rescue the prince before the Korv found him.

The great predator watched the Korv coming toward the water giving place and it's giant fierce eyes narrowed. It roared and they valley was filled with a rich rumble, heard for miles.

A riotous roar made all the animals around Navar jerk their heads up in the direction of the mighty bellow. They looked at Navar and then took flight. Navar wondered if he was to blame, but he decided that since he offered them no harm; he didn't dwell on it much.

The skin of the dead Korv lay out beyond the border of the oasis; Navar walked out to where it was and cut in a way they made it look as if a huge predator got the hapless Korv sentinel. Navar took inventory of his weapons and went toward the noise drifting in the wind; no doubt it was the Korv hunting for him or Grom's clan. Little did Navar know that just around the valley to his northeast, Grom was heading straight into jaws of death at the Korv's hands?

The Korv were being noisy; it was a ruse to bring the Vampires into a trap with laser eye beams to set of the motion detectors. Kurl had thought that if they could catch a few of the invaders to study and dissect, he may be able to put his people back on the offensive, with an at-least equal playing field. It would be a success if he got just one of the invaders alive.

The great predator watched Navar begin to gain the high ground, the beast was not dumb animal, he saw the alien with the red eyes was clever and wanted to flank his foe before attack or retreat; this was a wise course of action, study your prey and then stalk them until they make you kill them. The giant tiger-wolf moved down just before Grom's group came into view or he would have seen them and ran to his small friend and alerted him, that another foe was coming his way.

The laser sensors were tripped because they looked like rocks and plants, and the Dark ones were not looking for Tech in the wilds of this type, they would never make that mistake again.

The Korv waited until Grom and his group was in their web and then they sprang the trap. Korv popped out of hidden bunker and blinds and they didn't attack they wanted to gas and spray the vampires. Grom's clan began to gag and some felt flat one ground, Grom held his breath and pulled his blades and began the dance of death, the Korv tried stop his killing onslaught, but Grom was old and he was strong.

Navar got to the top of the rock where he wanted to be to observe the coming Korv. He almost had a heart-attack, if his heart was capable of that now. Grom's clan was being murdered. Navar was still weak from his injury, but something inside of him grew beyond the limits of his body, he pulled his shoto and katana and became a blur.

The Korv should have been trying harder to watch everything and everywhere, because Death was screaming threw the rocks above them silent as the grim reaper. A shadow flew passed the Korv captain's head and he did not react at all.

VAMPIRE WARS

Navar landed with his blades crossed over his chest; he snapped his arms open and all the gas disappeared in a mini hurricane. Navar began to move like a snake, the Korv who had tried to capture the dark ones had no illusion about who Navar was or whether they could catch him. They simply tried to kill him. Where Navar's deadly blades did not strike his knees and elbows did, the Korv were taking heavy damage, they scored a hit or two with their spear-lances, but they were not equal to Navar's skin or speed so they bounced off. Navar never stopped moving he was unhinged, he thought that he had lost an entire clan to the Korv and he was determined to take them all with him.

A Korv not in direct combat took aim with a rifle like weapon right at Navar's unprotected back. He heard a sound behind him, so he stopped and turn just in time to see a huge beast's teeth clamp shut on his head. The Tiger-wolf was in motion and airborne instantly picking off the next attacker at his new friends shoulder. Navar saw the monster out of the corner of his left eye, so he turned away making sure not to let his flying blades cross the beast's path. Side by side the vampire and monster beast fought in perfect harmony, the Korv were petrified at the sight. The red eyes of juggernaut and the king of all the black planets beast were fighting together, Kurl must be told. If the Guardian was with the invaders then Kurl would have to reassess his plans.

Grom finally succumbed to the gasses effects and fell.

The guardian as the Korv called it turned on the last few Korv that tried to make a run for it and took them down. Navar was so unhinged that he did not even check to see if there were any survivors, after he killed all the Korv. The guardian came back and looked over the field, out of the two hundred Korv sentinels none were left alive. The alien fights like a beast the guardian thought. His enemy is my enemy, therefore he is my friend. The Tiger-wolf could tell the Grom and some of his clan was not dead, but since they were not a threat and they too fought the four armed blight, they were not to be killed this time.

Navar cleaned his blades on the uniforms of the Korv, and then he selected a small dead Korv, probably a female and began to skin it like he did before. Navar took the leather smelling hide and turned to the guardian and spoke for the first time.

"Let's hunt" Navar said as his eyes continued to flare dangerously.

The guardian understood the alien somehow and they burst to speed and were in the mountains minutes later. God help any one who tried to stop him from his new life mission, to wipe the Korv out...completely.

CHAPTER 11: WAR BEGAN

In the counsel chamber Will and Victoria sat with Tigre who was explaining the mechanics of the challenge as far as the Korv were concerned. The Korv understood honor and warfare as well as Will did. But they have a few different ways of showing it. In open war it is an all out free for all. In a person challenge, the challenged gets to choice the form of combat and all the rules; so don't choose this option ever; it is a trick to get to kill you, and then eat you, while your troops watch. It is very disheartening.

"I want a blade for blade only war, no beam or projectile weapons, bombs or grenades. I don't think we will get to destroy them all at once. What we need is time to wipe out the breeding grounds, labs, all of their science technology" Will said. I will see what I can do to set up the contest between you and them" Tigre answered. "We will send Salen and clan Deathkill to stage the battle area prior to going there ourselves Victoria. It will give Salen a sense of her pride and self-respect back after Tana nearly sent her to final death" Will said holding her hand gently. "Will, I worry about Tana. Should we leave her here" Vicky asked? Tana will have Lee, Ruby, and Mya backing her up. With Jana and Brad pulling from the human military side and Tigre running the ship, it would be nuts for anyone to cross her" Will said with a chuckle.

Tigre relayed the message to Kurl and the Korv entrenchment. Kurl was if anything impressed and overjoyed at a straight fight, this covert attack on his sentinels was cowardly. The area for the battle was agreed to and the sides of the plains where each army would stage were decided. The battle would start at mid sun the following day.

"Navar lives and he is pressing our host's buttons" Will laughed deeply.

"Salen report to the landing bay for deployment" Victoria said in the com.

Will and Victoria ran all the way to the Garrett common area where the family and knights were breaking down their roles of responsibilities. Tana had Aaron, Ian, and Evan in the corner yelling at them.

"If so much as a hair is harmed on my husband, you three will be spending an eternity without your balls gentlemen, do you feel me" Tana said sternly.

The famous vampire brothers looked at their tiny petite slip of a queen and each took a knee to look at her eye to eye since they were all tall men. It was the youngest who answered her.

"We have never failed in our duty to the Garrett clan in three hundred years, we will either return as Will's shield, or on his shield Tana. You have our word, our lives for his, our choice our duty, it is our purpose" Evan said pleasantly.

"Well met Evan" Tana answered.

Tana liked Evan very much, he was a gentle spirit, but had a ton of Loki in him if you know what I mean. The other two brothers were too serious for Tana's taste.

Will ran up to Tana and told her what he found out, it made her practically sing. In less than two minutes the entire ship knew Navar was putting the boot to our enemy and they were smarting for it. The most happy were Navar's lovely mates who all cried at the news that there prince lived and was still as valiant as ever. They insisted on continuing on to find him as before. Will fully agreed with that view.

VAMPIRE WARS

(In the common area of Clan Deathkill)

"What do you mean you refuse to go" Rip snarled!

Most of Salen's clan was backing away, the usual happy go lucky Rip Branagan was a powerhouse and even Salen was no match for him in combat. At present Rip was furious.

"Go tell the King; that I refuse to waste my clan on his worthless war. Be gone boot licker" Salen screamed at him.

"If it were my choice Salen your head would already be on the floor" Rip growled. He turned as if to walk away and then bitch slapped Salen off her feet. "Watch who you call boot licker you little whore, or I might get offended". Rip smiled as he walked away.

Rip met Erik on the way and the grim set of Rip's jaw meant that Will would not like what was coming. Erik had become very close to Will, they played chess and drank together and sometimes they practiced with blades. Erik was sure if it were not for Victoria that his allegiance would be to Will directly instead of through her. Clan Elite and Garrett were at presented practically one Clan. Never in Erik's years had he ever know such close relationships between clans as now.

Rip stopped in front of Will and waited to be addressed; even though Rip was Will's close friend. Rip respected Will deeply and never traded his friendship in for liberties.

"What is the matter Rip" Victoria asked with her eye brows raised.

It took a lot to anger Rip, he was a joker. He laughed and sang even when he fought you. It was very disturbing to see the fire burning in his eyes now. Rip looked at Will, and Will nodded to go ahead and speak his mind.

"Salen has refused to deploy or even participate in the war effort" Rip said softly, the barely control ocean of ire was evident to all who listened.

"Well, I guess I will have to go change her mind" Will said.

"NO"!

All eyes turned to the pint sized Tana; her beautiful face was as grim as Rip's. She looked at Will and stepped forward to take his hand in her own.

"You charge me with the running of the ship and all aboard her. Salen is not questioning your authority my love, she would not dare. This is my test, mine alone. Clan Deathkill will go to war or out the airlock" Tana said.

Tana turned and walked down the hall, Lee and Mya were right on her heels. Ruby smiled, she kiss Ogre on the chest, popped his butt and skipped after Tana.

"Should we go with her" Rip asked?

"Only if you want to beaten, I would not interfere with my little wife right now, she is seething. Besides with Lee and Ruby backing her up, she is hardly in danger, not to mention Tana is only second to me in power and ability" Will answered.

"What about Mya, Salen was her former master, is she to be trusted" Rip asked honestly?

Oddly it was Victoria who answered and not Gwen and Kadi who were Mya's mates. She put her hand on Gwen's shoulder but looked at Rip.

"Mya, was never Salen's creature, she hated her with her entire being, but her blood ties kept her from leaving or rebelling because she was weak. Mya is no longer weak, she is stronger and more fierce that you can imagine and she has been training privately with Ruby, Erik and I. Mya is simply amazing in combat, she has supernatural focus and awareness. She will not let anyone or anything near Tana unless she is dead, and I guarantee that she will not go down alone if it comes to that, she will make sure Salen hits the floor dead before she does" Victoria explained.

"My sister is beyond loyal, her blood is your blood, her mate is the prince of the clan, she would never falter or fail to protect her family, for that is what Clan Garrett is, a family, your bonds are that of love, no servitude, it makes you far stronger that you could possibly know" Erik said suddenly.

Everyone looked at Erik, he smiled so rarely, that the rye lop sided grin on his face was novel indeed. He summed up the atmosphere in the clan to perfection, it was love that ruled the clan, they never fought each other and Will never imposed his authority on them. They talked about everything and then decided what was best. Erik saw all this and was glad to be part of Clan Elite and by extension part of Garrett.

"Are your Aussie's ready Ripper" Will asked?

"To right they are mate, you point and shoot and we will be the arrows" Rip said with his usual good cheer.

"Mama mad" Raz said.

"No I am not mad my prince" Gwen said as she lifted Raz out of Ogre's hand.

"No, Mama Lee, and Maama" Raz answered in a tiny baby voice.

"How do you know that little one" Victoria asked softly?

"I feel'd et" Aria whispered from Steven's massive arm. Aria was making grabbing motions at Raz.

Gwen placed Raz back in Ogre's hands next to Aria. The moment the babies were near enough the held hands and their tiny faces changed, they were seeing something else then what the group did. They both said one word in unison.

"POISON"!

Victoria was already gone before anyone else could react; Will and Rip were closing in seconds. They arrive five second later to find Mya choking; leaning on Ruby, her skin was grey. Erik came out of nowhere blade draw. Tana grabbed the blade with her bare hand and stopped him. Erik was shocked and froze in place so as not to harm Tana. He need not have bothered; his blades cut not cut her lovely skin.

"You will not intervene, any of you" Tana ordered. "See to Mya our daughter".

Mya's pretty ashen face smiled at Tana's comment and then her knees buckled. Will grabbed her up before she could hit the floor. He smelled her wound.

"Aaron I need you" Will screamed.

Three tall vampires snapped to a stop next to Will, all three of them weapons drawn, Evan walk over behind Tana.

"Just say the word, any word" Evan said between his grinding teeth.

Tana smiled at her friend and shook her head no.

"Sadly Evan this is mine alone to deal with" Tana answered him.

VAMPIRE WARS

Behind her, Evan's brothers were stand over Mya.

"Aaron can you smell the type of poison" Will asked?

Aaron took a knee and smelled the slash across Mya's ribs, and then tasted the wounds. He looked at Will and then at Salen.

"It is a modified form of Iocane extract poison; it has an anticoagulant to allow the poison to infiltrate the host body even a vampire. If Mya did not have your blood in her Master she would already be dead. She will be ill for awhile but the power of the Garrett blood will save her in the end. Now, I want permission to destroy Salen" Aaron said, his usual calm was fractured.

"Not my call Aaron" Will said looking at Tana's rigid back.

"Fine, I will beg for it then" Aaron said.

When Aaron left to ask Tana, Ian leaned closer to Will and spoke.

"Our mother was poisoned by a jealous woman and Aaron tried everything to save her. In the end we went to Brain Garrett and pledge to his service if he would allow us a single boon, the life of the woman and her family the killed our beloved mother. After some consideration and investigation, Brian granted our request. They were the only people we have ever killed for person reasons...until now" Ian said in anger.

Will was shocked by the extreme volcano of anger that erupted from the brothers. They were like Navar's brides, no one person could hope to beat them save Himself , wife and son, maybe Lee, but no other. All three brothers were itching to be let off the leash, they were not faking this, they were completely insane with anger.

"Sorry but no, Aaron" Tana said.

"Tana please, she intended that for you" Aaron screamed in Tana's face and pointed at Mya. "She can not be allowed to live" and he turned and lunged at Salen.

Only Tana's vise like grip on his arm and Evan's on his opposite arm save Salen from him.

"Rip, Evan, Ian, Aaron, Ruby, Lee and Erik block all the exits, if anyone tried to resist kill them" Will said. "This is your show baby, but I will see it contained".

Tana smiled and winked at her lover.

"I challenge you Salen for the leadership of your clan, to a death match, the winner gets to choose the course of the clan, the loser's dead body gets spaced" Tana said flatly.

(GASPS).

"You can't do that, it is against the ancient laws set down by Brian himself to keep anyone from being too powerful and ruling the world" Salen said in a huff.

"True Salen, but Mya was part of your clan and she could challenge you but you slashed her with deadly poison that was meant for me. If you would have succeeded Will would likely have turn your entire clan to dust, so I challenge you for Mya and by proxy take her place. You can not refuse unless you step aside and except my rule" Tana said sagely.

"You can not do this, we will fight to the last before we except slavery at your hands" Salen yelled.

These were the last words of her life. Garth took her head right off her shoulders and then reverse his sword and cut heart in twain. When Salen hit the floor in three piece; Garth looked at her on the floor and then knelt at Tana's feet.

"I gave my word and as Salen's second I surrender control of the clan to you Tana" Garth said.

Even on his knees Garth was taller than Tana. She smiled at him in surprise.

"I know you swore loyalty to me Garth but this is not what I expected when you made the pledge. I accept you and your clan" Tana said. "However Garth I want you to lead the clan, what say you" Tana said.

"If they will have me, I will lead them" Garth answered.

Garth got up and looked at his clan. They all pulled their blades and took a knee and put their sword over their heads in a show of support. One vampire woman of exotic dark beauty got up and approached Garth.

"We hated Salen, Garth and we love you and followed you all these years, never her. I love you Garth but never had the courage to say it out loud, now that the witch is no more, I would have you if you will have me" The girl said.

"Telsa, I have wanted you since I watched you turn, I will lead this clan, but I will not bear the name of that woman any longer. We are Clan Golden from here on out. What say you clan" Garth asked?

"AYE" the clan shouted.

"We will be ready to deploy and defend on your order master" Garth said to Tana.

"Be my friend Garth not my servant" Tana answered.

"I am both, as is my clan" Garth answered as he scooped up Telsa.

The brothers threw the remains of Salen into an air lock and spaced her.

Mya shook hard, so hard that Will carried her with increased speed back to his bed. Most of the immediate clan family followed him in and surrounded the bed. Will pulled his own dagger from his thigh guard; he cut his forearm and held it up to Mya's quivering lips.

"Drink daughter, I am not willing to take any chances with your life, so drink my pure blood and let it restore you" Will crooned to his lithe daughter in-law.

"I..." Mya could say no more, her eyes clouded oddly.

Tana lifted Mya's head and slipped under it, letting Mya's head rest on her lap. Will held his arm to Mya's mouth and let the blood run into it. Mya trembled and then weakly put one hand on Will's arm and the other held Tana's hand. Mya drank carefully, and tried not to waste any of the life giving fluid. Finally the wound closed by itself; Mya licked the blood off and then was embarrassed. The change in Mya was complete, her eye were not fogged, but a rich crimson like Tana's and her skin took on a golden tint just like Tana's lovely exotic hide. They looked like natural sisters. And Mya's vitality was increased greatly.

Jay walked in with Jana.

"Hey buddy we just dropped on the family power level list I think" Steven told him.

"Really, why" Jay asked?

"Long story, short version is Mya almost died, she drank Will's undiluted blood and it super charge her wee ass"

Ogre explained " She is likely even with Chad or even with Lee, I am not sure which".

"Well I am good with what I have, don't want anymore. As long as I can look after my family then I am fine with my strength, if I can't, then I will get stronger so I can hold up my responsibilities" Jay answered.

He pulled Jana to him and gently squeezed her. Ruby jumped up on Steven's shoulder and put her head on top of his. Ruby looked at Jana and then at Jay.

"I looks like things worked out right for all of us, I ended up with my giant and you ended up with the Nubian goddess you have there, still you were an enjoyable lover my friend, but she does not look like she wants to share you over much" Ruby said.

"Would you share Ogre with other women" Jana asked?

"Yes, Steven and I take lovers to our bed all the time, some human, but mostly vampire girls. It is an enjoyable experience. I love the big guy and he loves me, yet I am a nympho and he is close so we sample often the pleasures of others, but we are a mated pair now" Ruby explained.

"Mated" Jana asked?

"She means that they are bonded for life, no matter who they play with, they belong to one another and will never be parted until death" Jay explained. "Vampire marriage is like this".

"Oh, do you have other lovers I don't know about" Jana asked?

"Not since the first time I took you to my bed to show you what it is to have a vampire lover. From that day until this one, you only have shared my bed and my body, I want you to be my mate for life Jana, but you should enjoy the full sexual range of being a vampire before you decide if I am the right one for you, and there is something about vampire women that is so sultry" Jay said.

"I don't see that" Jana replied "I am not into girls".

"That Jana is because you have never had one seduce you" Will said as Mya sat up and hugged him.

"When Jay and Steven are gone Jana, you will share my bed with me at night, I will educate your mind and heart" Ruby said. "I am an excellent lover and your view of sex is very limited because you never allowed yourself to experience it until Jay took you. I still prefer men, I love men, but it is a good thing not to limit your capacity to love or feel".

"Well, I am not..." Jana started to say.

"Accept, you will enjoy it and I will be happier knowing you're in her arms at night, protected and cared for" Jay said.

"What if I decide I want her more than you" Jana asked playfully?

"Then you will have chosen wisely" Jay said as he kissed her.

That night all of the vampires and most of the human soldiers paired off or in groups made love for hours before the war effort the following day.

Will, Tana and Victoria turned in early after a good meal and began the long sweat farewell. Both Tana and Victoria cried, since they were in private they did not have to guard their feelings. They were only slightly afraid Will mighty be killed. It was more they had not spent a night without his powerful body pressed against them and his soft words in their ears as they fell to sleep each night. They wept for the longing for their man; that was coming after this night. They did not sleep this night at all. Victoria was determined to make this the best sexual experience Will had ever had, and Tana as well. Victoria had waited ten life times to find someone worthy of her heart and she found two people, she loved them so deeply that the thought of loosing either of them took her breath away and made panic swell in her breasts.

Chad and Lee made crazy love for hours and then held baby Pepper between them as she cooed. The fell asleep as a family holding tightly to what was important to them, each other.

Navar's mates did not let his absence stop them from having amazing group sex. Kadi who was a lizzie as a human had taught her mates to pleasure a woman as well or better than any man except Navar who had a way of topping anything she could do, Damn she loved him. Gwen and Mya both fell asleep in the early morning hours wrapped around Kadi's longer female frame, But not before Mya displayed her new lust for life.

Ogre and Ruby never slept when together, they were not capable of being nude together calmly, they wore out fifteen girls that night and were still shagging when Will came to fetch Steven in the morning.

It was much the same with Jay and Jana, but Jana wanted to talk about Ruby and the time Jay was going to be gone, during love play. Jana got pretty wet when Jay told her what Ruby was going to do to her, everyday. Jana even with Jay's blood came so violently she passed out twice. Jay never thought he could fall in love with anyone but Jana was just right for him.

The two strange vampire babies Raz and Aria always slept together in a big soft satin oval bed. Raz held his sister's smaller body in his chubby arms protectively. Aria could not sleep if Raz was not touching her, they were like twins, only they had different mothers, who were different nationalities, yet even as babies, they had as deep a bond as anyone on the ship. When they were grown it was going to be a Mo for anyone to part them.

Gamon was in the landing bay when Jay walked in and looked at him and said "No".

Kadi walked in behind him and her head jerked up when she looked at Gamon and company. Gwen smiled and shook her head.

"What" Gamy asked?

"You are so cute you guys, but all the shit your carrying get ride of it now" Gwen said sweetly.

"We need this stuff" a soldier said.

Gwen turned her crimson eyes on them and her smile disappeared and her teeth appeared.

"You question my orders again and I'll kill you. We are going to find and support my husband; we are going to be moving extremely fast for humans, slow for us. If you bring the stuff you will died of exhaustion in the first day. Repack for lite fast flight, ok" Gwen said flatly.

"Damn baby-girl, you are all jacked up aren't you" Jay asked?

"We are both already missing our babies and Mya. We are excited to go find our man Jay, but we are leaving behind much as well" Kadi explained.

Gamon came over and began bitching to Kadi about Gwen's threats. Kadi listened for a moment then grabbed him by the throat and hoisted him straight up.

"Gwen is my mate, my lover, my best friend, and she is co-leader of the band, I am tactical, Jay is command, you need to learn your role and do as you are told, the Korv are people eater Gamy, your food to them, we are your only protection from being killed, so stop bitching and do as you are told, or stay here. That goes for all of you, if you have no stomach for it, then stay here on the ship, I don't need coward or fools with me" Kadi snarled.

Gamon got up from where his body was tossed like as much trash by his friend and walked back to her and held out his hand. She looked at it and then stepped forward and hugged him.

"We care about your lives Gamy, and don't want you to be killed if we can help it, Will asked me to look after you and protect you. I know your tough, all of you are tough, I am one of you, but the Korv are not a regular enemy, they will kill and eat you so, we can't take any chance with slowing down and letting them catch us" Kadi said.

Jay coordinated with the Tigun tech and the group got into the drop ship and dropped away from the battle area. When the ship dropped them off it went back to the city ship for another mission.

The fifteen members of the band walked quietly through the country side, three vampires, and twelve rangers. Jay took the point because he was the toughest and if the stuff hit the fan; he would face it first saving the rangers. The two female members of his clan were in the rear as a tail guard.

A Korv sentinel popped out of the woods and shot at the band. Faster that they could blink Gwen and Kadi were all over it. The Korv soldier was rent apart completely. This was the first time any human had witnessed a vampire knight let go and fight, in almost four hundred and fifty years, it was terrifying to them and fascinating at the same time. Gwen looked at Kadi and she looked off to the valley just beyond Gwen. Gwen was like a wisp of smoke with sparks in it. Her bright red hair looked like a match being struck when she accelerate. Kadi went off the other direction and they swept the entire area in less than a minute.

"Jesus, Mary and Joseph" Gamon said to Jay "They are incredible".

"Humph, you think so' you should see Tana fight, or even Ruby. You would never be able to look at them again, without raw fear climbing down your spine. Victoria and Lee are just as awe inspiring, or terrifying if you would rather. Remember what you all just saw, the next time you feel like mouthing off to Gwen or Kadi, they could kill you by accident just as easy as if they were mad" Jay said as he kept going his eyes peeled for Korv.

Gwen and Kadi fell into line at the back of the line looking off to opposite sides. The soldier in front of them kept looking back at them. Gwen looked at Kadi. Both girls were dressed in sexy lite weight vampire armor, that would be at home in a lingerie shop. It protected their arms and legs, the center of their back along the spine and their breasts, the rest of their hard bodies were bare for freedom of moment.

"What soldier, is it how we are dressed" Gwen asked with a smile.

"Yes, ah No. I can't hear your foot steps behind me ladies, it scares me. If you were attacked or grabbed from behind, I would not know to yell for help" The ranger answered.

"I would know boy" Jay said "Even if we were in a fire fight I would know. I can hear everyone of your hearts beating, I know all your scents, so do the ladies, you can't be taken or loose us out here, we will know you and each other no matter what. Our senses are extremely acute and we are using them now to keep you alive. There is a company of Korv just over that rise. It is time to do some damage. You will watch only. I will face the Korv alone".

The band snuck up to the top of the rise and there were a hundred Korv at the quick count. Jay looked hard at all of them and then he looked at Kadi. She waved them all back to forest.

"Attack them from the west side, that will put their backs against the rocks, also it gives them almost no way to get away from you except through you. If they get passed you we will clean up, Gwen you agree, Gamy your thoughts" Kadi said?

"Your assessment of the terrain is exact as usual, but there is a way to the northwest that they could slip passed, let me mine it so they get a big surprise if the try to go that way" Gamon said.

"How long" Jay asked?

"Fifteen minutes no more" Gamon answered.

"Okay, Take two rangers and Gwen with you just incase. One way or the other Gamon in fifteen minute I am going in" Jay said.

It was fifteen minutes to the click when Gamon slipped back to Jay's side. The big black Vampire smiled at the ranger in appreciation of his skills and knowledge. Jay stood up and shook out his arms and pulled his big double bladed sword and dirk, he smiled at the band and said one word.

"ALONE".

Every face nodded that they accepted the order. Jay walked slowly into the camp. It took the Korv a moment to understand what was happening, Jay was huge, and the vampires they fought were only the smaller dark ones. They would learn moral fear a moment later.

"Come rangers you need to see this" Kadi said.

No words were spoken as Jay rent apart one hundred Korv in twenty three minute alone. Jay was not as fast as the girls but his speed was far two much for the Korv and his one arm was stronger than all four of the huge Korv arms put together. The Korv jumped on Jay. The rangers wanted to help, but Gwen waved them off. Next thing they saw looked like the Korv were in an outdoor blender, because Jay began to twisted and turn so fast that what every he hit, was chewed apart. Jay showed off some strength then, He grabbed a 700 pound Korv and tossed him into the sky until the rangers could not see where he fell. Then it was over. Only one Korv tried to get away, he ran into Gamon's trap and blew up. All the rangers cheered.

Jay returned to the band and began to clean his blades with a silk cloth and some oil; the rangers who were elite warriors were in awe of Jay's display of skill and brutal efficient killing methods. They would never think of a Garrett clan member the same way again. Kadi walked over to where Gamon sat looking at Jay and sat by him.

"Still think Jay is not right person to lead the band that searches for my boy" Kadi asked.

"Did you say that he is number five on the overall power list for you family" Gamon asked?

"Actually, I am number seven on that list, and Kadi is number eight, Gwen in number nine. We are a tough group; it is a privilege to be part of Will's family. He is my best friend, even if he were not I would still follow him, because before anyone could get to me they would have to crawl over him first. Good luck with that, even when he was just a man, a normal human, he was a hard man and not someone to cross lightly. He is one of the last of his breed" Jay said.

"What, there six more powerful members of your clan that you" Gamon asked in shock?

"Yes; and the gap in power jumps drastically in the top four. Me and the Ogre think we are about even, though he is physically stronger, I am a better fighter, so it is apples ands oranges there" Jay explained.

The look on Gamon's face was priceless, he was crossed between shock and disbelief but he regained his footing when Gwen asked him a question out of the blue.

"Why did you agree to come with us, you know that your at a hung disadvantage down here" Gwen asked?

Gamon looked at Kadi and was having a hard time focusing on how to explain his reasons when Kadi spoke.

"Gamy and I have been joined at the hip for ten years, it would be weird to have to go into battle without each other, at-least for me" Kadi said.

"Honestly I love Kadi, which is complicated because she never liked men at all and now she is a homo superior vamparis, married and bonded with two other girls, has a super-human baby...so it is complicated. I came because if I didn't and Kadi got hurt or killed I would blame myself for not having her back when she needed me" Gamon explained shyly.

One of the rangers came in and began to report in a low voice to Gamon about what the scouts witnessed near by. Gamon was miffed because the ranger ignored Kadi and Jay who were sitting right there and they were in command. Jay saw this and waved it off as nothing, he wanted to hear the rest of the report. The scouts found an entire field full of dead Korv and a few small ugly vampires laid out all over the place. The signs of battle were fresh but the pattern of kills made no sense to the expert soldiers. Some of the Korv seem to have been bitten in half or ripped apart, where others were slices cleaning into pieces expertly.

"The dark ones; are any of them alive" Kadi demanded?

"The what"?

"The small ugly vampires as you call them are clan dark ones; are any of them alive" Kadi snarled impatiently?

"No ma'am, at-least I don't think so" The ranger answered.

"Show us" Gwen said.

The area of the battle that the ranger lead them to was indeed strange. The kill pattern did not make since to the vampires either. Gwen looked at the ripped apart Korv and the obvious teeth makes and made a statement of theory about them.

"The must be a super predator here, the teeth maker are consistent with a tiger or another animal of that size and strength. But why are there no dark ones attacked, only Korv" Gwen pondered.

"Spread out and look for a trail away from here for us to follow, we have to know what did this. Will and the rest of your people are coming down here to fight, we can't let them get caught unaware no matter the cost to us" Gamon said.

"Right, make it so rangers" Jay ordered.

The rangers looked at Gamon for orders, and this time Gamon lost his temper.

"When Jay, Kadi or Gwen give you a fucking order, you better move your ass to do it or your going to taste my shoe, you feel me rangers" Gamon shouted!

"Yes sir" they answered.

The rangers fanned out expertly and combed the area. They found the trail easily as if the predator feared nothing and no one, it was almost like a dare to follow scenario. They did follow the trail and an impossible pace, not one ranger complained or slowed down, they did not want to be the weak link. They called in a scout ship to come and collect their fallen brother, the dark first.

(Elsewhere at the staging area for the Earth forces).

Rip Branagan and his Aussie forces were going where Garth directed them to set up. They did as they were bid, Garth was not Salen, and he was a natural leader and asked no more of you than he would be willing to do himself. Rip was pleased that Garth had heeded the call to leadership, he was well suited to the task, and his newly named Clan Golden were just that golden. They worked harder than anyone to make sure Will was not unprepared when the time came.

Will was the last to touch the soil of the black planet, not because he was afraid, but because he had so much to do that he could not go first and fulfill his responsibilities. Will made sure that there was no full human's in the battle force, this did not set well with Brad Franklin the Army General and overall commander of the human forces. Brad and Will decide together that the human forces could set up and be the rear guard, sniping any Korv that tried to sneak into their staging area. The military set up and placed their guns and snipers where they thought would be the most advantageous to Will's plans. Steven Ogre over saw the placements and he helped move the heavier guns into place, which the soldiers were happy about. The three bothers disappeared in to the wilds with Rip and Telsa right behind them. They returned and reported that the Korv meant business and they were going to cheat and use some sort of beam or pulse rifles. They would likely wait until Will was fully engage in combat before they began to shoot. Will considered this and called Brad to him.

"If they want to shoot at us after we agreed on bladed weapons than I think I could use some of your sharp shooting types to bust a cap in any of them who shoot at us. Aim for the eyes, they will be armored, so I want them to be dead not wounded" Will explained to the general.

"It would be our pleasure to support you Will. I will have the troops follow you in and take up position in the high ground and drill any of them who shoot. What about the ones who don't shoot, you want us to shoot them" Brad asked?

"No, if they want to fight us head to head, by the rules we agreed on, then we will oblige them" Rip said over Will's shoulder.

Will only smiled at his irrepressible friend and nodded that he agreed.

Thirty minutes before the battle for the black planet was about to begin, Will began moving forward. The Korv had been sneaking up on them all night; Garth knew and had everyone on alert. The Army Special ops from Australia and England moved into position to blast the Korv ambush forces unknown to the Korv. Garth as it turned out was a very fine tactical field commander; he left nothing to chance, and never guessed. If he didn't know, he quickly found out.

The three brothers slipped into the edge of the massive battle field area, where the thick groves of trees grew and ferreted out suicide squads that planned to jump on and harass the main earth body as they passed. Every single squad they encountered they killed quietly, and they kept moving. The brothers did all of this without being ordered to; they were experts in this kind of warfare and were not about to let anything get to their king without a serious fight.

The field itself was not flat, it had dips and gullies where the Korv could hide and attack. Currently the depressions were filled to the maximum with Korv sentinels waiting to attack Will and his knights. Garth and Rip had drawn the entire region on paper the night before and they studied the encampments and how to neutralize them. Therefore Will knew just what was waiting for them when the marched out onto the field at 1130Am. They stopped just short of the midway line of the giant battlefield area and waited for the Korv leader a giant named Kurl to take the field per the agreement, which the Korv were already breaking. Steven was less than impressed when the Korv finally made a showing. There were thousands more of the Korv than the there were of the Earth forces and still the Korv were acting cowardly, that made a mean street fighter like Ogre mad. If your strong act strong, if you weak, then you don't pitch shit to the strong.

"When they cross the rise over there we attack" Rip said.

"No, I attack alone first, then Steven, then Rip and Garth may lay to any way they feel is necessary" Will said.

Garth and Rip started to argue but Ogre growled low and dangerous. Will's eyes had changed and there was a power and majesty there that they had never seen before, both big men stopped and became silent, and Will never looked at either one. There was something going on internally with Will, you could feel the pressure in the air, see the waves running through the abbreviated king. Will was only 5'7 and one hundred fifty pounds and still he seemed bigger than Steven Ogre who was well over 7'5 feet tall and four hundred fifty pounds, when he brought his focus to bear. This very moment was one of those times. Only Steven had ever seen the light in Will's eyes before like this, the last time was when they got into it as humans with some bikers over a girl they were harassing. Will tore into them like a wild animal, Steven remembered the terror those bikers felt, they tried to fight back but it was useless, if Steven had not been there Will would have killed them all in his righteous anger.

Will took a deep breath exhaled and began to walk forward, Rip and Garth made to follow but Ogre blocked their path.

"If you value your lives, let Will begin as he said it would go" Ogre said in his deep voice.

"Are you threatening us Steven" Rip asked?

(Laughter)

"Boys if I were threatening you, you would not need to ask. I am warning you to do as you were asked to do, let Will begin alone, if it goes all wrong then you get to jump in and kill them all" Ogre answered.

The clans watched Will walk alone out to the Korv battle group and when he stopped and spit at their feet all hell broke loose. The Korv thought to draw first blood, they swarmed Will. The leader of the Garrett family just stood there and waited until they were within three feet from him. Will smooth as Butterscotch Schnapps pulled both his custom swords and made an X slash movement so fast that only Rip, Steven and Garth could follow it. In the direct path of the X the Korv were laid to waste. More, Will moved hard to the left in one fluid motion and the Korv flew up into the air as if hit by a Diesel truck, as they rose they flew to pieces. More than three hundred Korv were killed in less than a single breath. Will stopped and faced the Korv with blood dripping off his twin wicked blades. The Korv were incensed.

"Dear God" Rip gasped, and not in his usual jovial way.

VAMPIRE WARS

The three powerful Vampire warriors stood there is awe of what Will had done. Even Rip who was among the oldest most powerful of all the Vampire lords, had never seen a display of raw might as what he just saw. Rip thought he was at-least in Will's realm as far as combat ability went, he just realized that Will never used even half of his ability when they spared. Rip vowed to get stronger to make the Workout more enjoyable and challenging for Will.

"Come my knights and Lords, attack this vermin". Will demanded

One single shot rang and a hole was blown thru Will's chest. The three brothers burst out of nowhere and the onslaught they visited on the Korv holding distance weapons was a horrible sight. The first Korv had his leg cut off by Evan, his torso cut in two by Ian and his head take off by Aaron as if they moved as one body the brothers did not even hesitate to wait for the body to hit the ground. The Korv tried to get them in a cross fire, but it was like trying to shoot flies out of the air, the brothers moved so fast and every touch of their flashing blades meant death.

"Master" Garth lunged forward and took a laser bolt in the chest, he grabbed Will and spun to protect the King with his own body, Will understood the gesture and made an mental note to reward this man's unswerving loyalty to his family. However, Garth was not as durable as Will and He did not want the new lord of Golden to loose his life trying to shield him.

"I will be fine, you need to look to your self, you hurt Garth" Will exclaimed.

"Will you good" Ogre yelled as he stormed by.

"I am good, go get these four arms cowards"" Will yelled back!

VAMPIRE WARS

Steven Ogre was never what anyone would call a finesse fighter, so seeing him bulldozer through the Korv ranks, knocking them flying in every direction. Ogre did not even pull his big four and a half hand sword or even his sword length dirk, no he used his monster arms to beat the Korv to death and shattered their bones. Most of the Vampire stayed away from Ogre, they thought he lost his senses; because his blades were going unused. Will knew better, Steven Ogre was a giant, rude crude and mean. However, you would have to go far to find a man with a deeper sense of honor and duty. The Korv broke the deal, so he could take out his great cleaver and put them to death fast and clean or he could inflict a heinous amount of damage and subject them to unbelievable misery; that was what Steven decided to do, no quick easy death. Hell no, he was going to bring the pain as he frequently said.

The Korv were big and once they got over the shock of how powerful an opponent they faced they gave a pretty good account of themselves among the regular vampire knights, but against the lords, Ogre and the brothers they fell like wheat to the scythe. There was a pitched battle between the military and the Korv, a real shooting match. The Korv weapons packed a bigger punch but the humans were much more skilled with firearms so it was a Mexican stand-off. Brad had a 60 cal and was cutting the Korv up that got to close to his snipers. Brad ran out of ammo at the wrong time, He blocked a Korv lance with his rifle, pulled his custom knife the Will made him and stabbed the Korv in the eye, the Giant four armed menace punched Brad in the left side just before it's brain registered it had died. Brad felt his ribs give way under the sledge hammer blow. They hit the ground together, but only Brad got up.

"Reload" Brad coughed!

Telsa came out of no where and picked up Brad just as an explosion went off where he was standing. She half turned and snapped her right arm out, Brad almost missed the dart that she hurled into the trees, but he heard the result of a Korv's death gurgle.

"Thanks ma'am" Brad said.

Telsa looked at the blood coming from Brad's mouth and shook all over, so powerful was her bloodlust that she almost forgot that Brad was her ally; She turned away from him suddenly and jerk herself out of her stupor.

"You are welcome, we are all in the together after-all" Telsa answered. "Get your weapon reloaded General and watch your back, by the way you did well with your blade".

"Thank you" Brad cough up more blood.

"You better get looked at Brad, you are not one of us, you could die from an injury of this sort, your insides are busted up. MEDIC...MEDIC" Telsa hollered.

Two medical soldiers ran up and took the general from Telsa. She held his hand for a moment and then she disappeared into the trees again and Brad was sure he could hear the Korv screaming in terror as the slip of a girl sent them on to their final judgment.

It seemed to the human military that the Korv had an endless supply of sentinels to send against the out numbered vampires. The fight was pretty equal at present, the Korv were not as skilled or as fast as the clans, but they outnumbered them fifty or more to one. Despite the prowess of Will and his clan, who as far as they could tell had lost not a single knight, they fight was semi-hopeless. Will and Ogre did not fight like they thought of loosing, only vengeance.

"Hey stop them" Garth yelled at his clan.

The Korv had a few human snipers that they captured and they were eating them alive. Suddenly a swarm of dark ones came through the tress and took down the Korv, they snatch the humans and some ran the soldier to safety; while the others slaughtered the Korv. The Dark ones were berserk, mad with bloodlust. They fell on the Korv like a plague, clan Branagan were surprised, they never seen the tiny vampire fighting so fiercely before, they had reckless abandon. The Korv were instantly terrified, no matter what they did the tiny avengers slaughtered them with deadly efficiency. The other vampires got out of there way or herded the Korv into the meat grinder that was the tiny vampires.

"Shoit, what set them off, I have never seen them like this, ever" Rip said startled to Ogre.

"Grab one and let's see what is up with them" Ogre said.

Rip reached out and snagged a dark knight and herd him up, the tiny menace whipped his blade around and tried to stab Ogre. Steven just grabbed the blade with his bare hand and stopped it.

"Peace little brother, what has happened to your family to make them so fierce this day" Ogre inquired?

The dark one screwed his face up as if speaking were difficult and he spoke in a rasp of berserk words that were very close to the snarls of a wild animal.

"Those things took Grom and they are dissecting him" The dark one said.

"WILL...WILL" Ogre screamed!

In an instant the leader of the Garrett's was at his giant friends side, looking anxious, when he saw the tiny dark one hanging from Ogre's oak tree arm.

"Tell him little brother everything you know, we are family; if they have live members of that family then we have to get them back" Ogre told the miniature vampire knight.

"We were jumped out in the dry part of the wilderness by the enemy, they used chemical warfare on us, knock out gas and poisonous spray, we fought hard but the gases over took us. Grom held his breath and gave a fine account of us, but they ganged up on him. It took sometime for us to shake the effects of the gases, when we did the two princesses were there and they followed the giant Korv killing beast off into the forest, and pointed us this way toward you and the trail of the enemy that took our Lord Grom" The dark one explained quickly.

Will's handsome face turned dark and his thoughts were deep suddenly and deadly silent. Will took his com out and spoke into it slowly as if he was taking great care to choose his words carefully.

"The is Will, I need to be patched to Sect asap" Will said.

"Wait one" said the sing-song voice of the Tigun Bing named for an old earth actor.

"This is Sect".

"Sect, Will. I need you to triple your efforts, the Korv have caught some of your clan and I am told they are going to dissect them to find a better way to kill us. We can not let them keep our brothers. From this moment on we are all on one mission; rescue" Will explained.

"We are on it Will" Chad's voice sounded suddenly. "I will work with Bing to ferret out the unique foot print that the dark ones have and track them that way".

VAMPIRE WARS

CHAPTER 12: RESCUE

Tana was having no trouble running the ship, the military were all in love with her, and the vampires knew how powerful she was and indestructible, so they did not back sass her at all. Bing the smart mouthed Tigun singing technician had been making the babies a play structure to keep the wee babes busy while there parents were off to war. Bing also sang them to sleep more often than not. However, when Chad called for Bing to use the tracking system he just invented Tana saw very little of the wily little alien.

Jana had spent the last two nights with Ruby and Tana was told by Lee that she could hear giggling nearly all night. It Pleased Tana that her family and extended family were finding some happiness and joy in these trying times.

"Excuse me Queen Tana" Said a tiny crisp voice.

Tana looked down to see the smallest Tigun she ever saw. At first she thought that this must be a child, but the super alert face and eyes spoke of genius and experience that no child could have. She knelt down even though she was the smallest woman on the entire ship.

"Yes, sir Tigun" Tana said with a heart melting smile?

"I am here to fix or replace the com in your quarters ma'am but I am never to enter your area without your express permission" The tiny fellow said.

"What is your name my tiny friend" Tana asked?

"Your Daughter's mate Chad named me Tad, because of my diminished stature, also I can mend or fix anything so Tad is short for Ta Da" Tad explained.

"It is very nice to meet you Tad. And please feel free to fix anything in my area that needs it. I am not that private, only when the man is around then I do not want to be bothered by anything except Vicky and him" Tana said as she shook Tad's hand.

"On would you mind if I made an aqua slide for the little ones, it will be able to support even the giant Ogre, so all can enjoy it but it want to make it for the use of the children. It is a hard thing to have no world to play on, I would make life here more enjoyable for them, I want your permission to do these things, and this is after all your ship" Tad said.

"I thought the ship was a loan from your people Tad" Tana said?

"No Tana, this ship belongs to clan Garrett, Will and you; we only built it. Everything on this ship was built and tooled for your and your human cousins. We only work for you, in whatever manner you need. We need your continued alliance to be able to travel freely in the galaxy. The Korv technology is not as good as ours but, if they even find a way to beat it, we are helpless; where you are not helpless in anyway. We envy even your human cousins, who are seemingly nearly as fearless as you vampires are" Tad explained.

"I would never think to say a Tigun was helpless, it seems to us that every single member of your people is a genius in someway or form. I am surprised that the Korv are not terrified of you" Tana answered.

(Chuckle)

The tiny Tigun shook with mirth at the thought of anyone or any creature being afraid of a Tigun.

"Your minds and technology make you a formidable adversary; you only have to believe in yourself. We will look after you and fight with you and for your people as long as you still want our help, in return we would like your help with health care and space exploration and planetary defense. Does that sound fair to you" Tana asked?

"It sounded fair to us when Brian Garrett said the same words of brotherhood to us on your little blue planet. We will never turn on you or betray you to your enemies. It is not in our nature to fail at our responsibilities, and you are in some small way our charges out here in the great void of space" Tad stated.

He smiled and walked off to get to work on his planned improvements around the ship. How likeable these Tiguns were, friendly and very dutiful. They never seem to be around until you need them, then they are simply right there just as you have the need. It was kind of disturbing if you thought about it. These Tiguns were all geniuses, all of them. The ships guns were amazing and deadly, the Tiguns were a dangerous enemy even though they tried to deny it. If they ever decide to turn to the dark side, it would be a very bad thing for another race to cross them. Tana turned to continue on to her OPS meeting.

Ruby sat on the desk next to Jana as she wrote a report on a British sergeant who fell down the stairs and fractured his spine and left lower leg at the Tibia. It was hard for Jana to write with Ruby sitting on the desk. Ruby was small and slight but her beauty was second to only Tana. Victoria and Lee were gorgeous but Ruby was just so personable it made her stand out. Ruby was also very sexual and she was forward about it as well. She had a sexy way of paying you the attention you deserved; she made you seem to be the only person in the world. Jana had to admit, she did not want to be anywhere near Ruby in the beginning when Jay left, but she was wrong, dead wrong. Ruby came and got her that first night and practically carried her to her own quarters. Jana was scared at first but Ruby had a huge bathtub brought in for them. Ruby stripped and showered Jana and then they both got in the tub, where Ruby held and caressed Jana's body gently and they talked about Jay and the world, medicine and love. Jana had to remember to breathe at times because Ruby was so good at making her feel comfortable and the heat between them was rising. It is hard to deny yourself pleasure when it is so freely offered. While they were still in the tub, Ruby turned Jana's head and kissed her softly on the lips while fondling her breasts. In case you did not know vampires smell great and their kiss is like crack to an addict. So when Ruby began to push up on Jana, the human could not resist. Jana turned around and pulled Ruby up into her lap and they kissed for who knows how long, but Ruby's educated hands never stopped exploring Jana's firm body. Ruby picked Jana up and put her in the shower up against the wall without ever taking her mouth from Jana's. The shower was on and off and they never let go of each other. Only when Jana's back touched the bed did Ruby let her go.

"I don't think I should over do it the first night, I might ruin you for Jay" Ruby giggled playfully.

Ruby tucked Jana into the bed next to her and held her gently all night in her arms. The second night was more like being with Jay, Ruby positively molested Jana. When Jana came to her quarter to call it a day, Ruby was naked on the bed waiting for her. After Jana washed her body and shaved her leg and private parts she dried off and went to lay down to take a nap. Ruby grabbed her and tossed her on her back and kissed her passionately. Jana was dizzy from the effect of the kissing. Ruby slowly kissed her way down Jana's trembling body, each breast was fondled and suckled properly, Jana's nipples were so rigid they felt like they would explode. Ruby did not speak she continued down until her warm lips were between Jana's tone legs. Ruby teased and tickled Jana's tender parts until the poor human girl was over come with pleasure and let it all go in a rush of warmth. Too Jana and Ruby's surprise Jana returned the favor and tasted every part of Ruby's firm lean body, Ruby came well and often under Jana's attentions. So went the second night together. Jana finally understood what Will meant about the seductive abilities of a vampire girl. Ruby made her head swim when they were together.

"You know it is hard for me to concentrate when you're sitting half naked on the desk beside me, with your hard sexy legs touching my arm" Jana said with a smile.

"Do you want me to leave you and go away then" Ruby asked seriously.

"No, stay I am nearly done. We can go find Lee and Mya for lunch when I am done" Jana answered.

Ruby leaned over and kissed Jana on the lips.

"Okay, we should do that" Ruby said.

Jana finished her reports and she took Ruby by her hand and led her to the food court, where they saw Lee with Pepper in her arms. Raz and Aria were sitting in their wee tot hauler that Bing and Tad built for them; they were holding chubby little hands as they always did. The way the babies looked at you made it seem that they could read your mind. Perhaps?

"Hey Lee how are you today baby" Ruby said as she kissed Lee on the lips, then turn and kissed Pepper and the other two babies as well. Ruby loved everyone in the family with all her heart.

Lee stood up and walked over and kissed Jana on the lips. A few short days ago that would have shocked her, but after a few nights in Ruby's arms, Jana enjoy the feeling of Lee's lips on her own, but thought nothing more than that about it. Mya was not around to join them for the meal. Too bad Jana thought.

Midway through the lunch Tana and Mya walked up looking a little distressed. Tana kissed Pepper on top of her little head and plopped down next to her daughter. Mya hugged Ruby and Jana, then sat next to the babies and began tickling them. Mya really adored the wee biters. They loved her as well; she was their second momma as far as they knew.

"What is the matter mother, what happened to make you look like that? Is Chad and Sect okay" Lee asked?

Chad and Sect left for the planet yesterday as soon as Bing gave them a heads up on where to lead Will to rescue the captured dark ones.

"No, everyone is fine as far as we know. Tad and Tigre told me that he thinks there is at the least two starships on the other side of the planet. They are no match for this ship but they could keep us from retrieving our mates. If Victoria was not still on the ship I would be very edgy and lonely with Will gone. We all need to be ready to defend this ship. We might be boarding and destroying those starships, therefore I am going to keep clan Elite on board for just that purpose. I told Will my plan and he was not happy, but he agreed to my demands" Tana explained.

"No wonder you're in a shitty mood Tana. We are all behind you, you can't leave the ship defenseless, Will knows this as well, so you made the right call and you know it" Victoria said, as she walked up and embraced Tana.

A tiny voice cleared their throat to get everyone's attention. Every head turned to look at the glowing green eyes of the babies glaring off into the void, like they did when they saw something farther away in their minds. Aria was gripping Raz's hand so tight that the blood was unable to flow and both their hands were turning purple.

"Grom owy, monster hurt" Aria's faint tiny baby voice whispered.

"Monster come here" Raz added.

"What, babies? What about Grom? When is the ship coming here Razzy" Mya asked?

Almost on cue the ship shuttered and the Tiguns went into action. The city ship had orange flashing alert lights, they were flashing now. Tana was a blur as she went to speed heading for the bridge. Lee looked at Mya, Mya merely nodded and Lee was a blur of speed as well. Erik appeared at Mya's side, he snapped up Pepper and they both went to speed toward the safety bunker Tad built the children in case of attack or if the ship was breeched in anyway. Raz and Aria held out there chubby hands when Erik placed them inside, Erik was confused until Raz made a face and spoke.

"Give Peppa" Raz said snapping his tiny fingers.

(Laughter).

"Yes sir" Erik chuckled.

Mya put baby Pepper in her cousins hands; and the two small vampires took her gently and hugged her close between them. Although Raz and Aria had a small speaking vocabulary, they were very intelligent and strong. They were self aware, and aware of others as well, for instance they knew baby Pepper who was only three month younger than them was softer and delicate, so they held her and snuggled her as if they could break her at any time. They never bit her, even though nibbling was a favorite pastime for them. It was an odd scene to watch two babies looking after a third as if they were responsible for her welfare, which of-course is exactly how they felt. Pepper belonged to them, and they belonged to her. Raz protected the other babies; his strength was more in keep with a weak adult rather than a tiny baby. Aria did not display her strength but was observed to move at a rate of speed impossible for a human to match of any age and she had perfect balance and reflexes. Pepper was strangely focused for an all natural human baby, her eyes watched you and she seemed to remember everything and she was aware of who was who and where she was. When she was with Raz and Aria you could see the change in her, she relaxed and was fully happy. It made everyone wonder if the babies were more special than they knew.

"Goodbye babies I love you" Mya said.

"Check you later, you little monsters" Erik said with a small smile.

"Ga'bye, Mya and E-rik" Aria said.

(On the Bridge)

Tana came to a stop next to Tigre. Bing and Tad were working furiously on something off to the side. Tad's little body was shaking with the effort of his task. It was not a hard physical task, rather it was the insane speed at which the task was being done that was the strain. Bing who was usually a complete chatterbox and a smart ass was completely silent as he bent his back and brain to the task.

"NOW" Tad yelled over his shoulder!

The main guns ripped into the starship off to port and it nearly rolled under the impact of the volley. Tad's face turned to look at the main viewer, it was hardened and cold. Tana was shocked to see the same face on all the Tigun crew, It was pure hate.

"Give them another round Bing" Tad said in a gruff tone.

Another set of hidden guns on the city ship erupted in unison into the Korv battleship, it rocked again with the impact, this time it began to vent atmosphere. The Tiguns cannons had punch a hole right thru their shielding. The Korv turned away from the Tigun city ship and fled.

"They have found a way to nearly break our shields?" Bing said.

"No, they were not even close. I checked the shield report, they only slammed into our shields with a greater force than they ever had, it was a blunt impact, there was no chance that it would even flex out shield, little alone beat them" Tigre said. "Great job on the pulsar modifications; by the way".

"I was wondering about that method of modification, I was not sure how much more power it would give us, I guess it was significant or the Korv would not have fled after only two volleys" Bing said.

Tana looked at the Tiguns; they seemed at ease with what just happened. We were just attacked by other ship and they acted like this was nothing new. Maybe they had been fighting the Korv for so long that they didn't give it much thought anymore. They were utterly unafraid of being attacked again.

"They are going to come back with more ships next time. This is their breeding planet, they have to defend it or be wiped out" Victoria said from beside Tana.

"Perhaps, you are correct. We are more than a match for them however" Bing said.

The ladies must have been thinking the same thing because they began to speak in one voice.

"What if the shell the planet and kill our families and mates, or keep us from retrieving them. This ship might be able to handle the battle; but what about our shuttles" Tana and Vicky asked in one swift tone?

The Tiguns looked at each other as if this did not occur to them, which was impossible. Tana was not in the mood for smugness, she wanted a straight answer.

"We thought to destroy them first and then go retrieve the soldiers; however; if they decide to strafe the planet surface that could be problematic indeed. It would kill their own people, I can't see them doing that" Tigre answered.

"Really, what if this is not the only breeding planet and they decide to sacrifice those on the planet and nuke the whole damn thing, what then smart ass" Victoria asked in a nasty tone.

The former black queen was suddenly vibrating with anger. It was a viable plan from her point of view to blow up the planet to kill us. She was not use to being helpless; she was a true blood warrior and needed to fight when challenged. The situation was not such that this enemy could be fought or could it?

"Tana, give me a shuttle, have Bing and Tad outfit it with enough tech to get us into that crippled Korv vessel and let us take them from the inside and turn that ship against the other one, before more Korv ships come to help them" Victoria said in a rush?

Tana sat on the edge of the console and regarded her mate for a moment. Victoria could see her weighing the loss of her against the benefit of her plan. Lee would make the choice for both of them.

"Can you outfit a shuttle with stealth tech and a shield that could take a direct shot from their cannons" Lee asked?

Tigre and Bing looked at Tad. The Tiny Tigun sat on his custom seat and turned his thoughts inward. He sat still for a moment and he face screwed up in deep contemplation. He looked up and direct at Lee.

"Yes I can make those improvements, but I want Bing to place the four star wraith cannons on the shuttle in quad directional pattern with redirect option. I will need the chamber of a number three pulsar cannon as a power source, and will be going on the mission to make sure none of you are killed because our science failed you" Tad said.

"No, you're my brother and are too important to the main ship to risk" Tigre answered.

Tad acted like he did not hear Tigre speak. He was making calculations and giving orders over the com in a swift succession. Tigre got excited and shook Tad hard to get him to pay attention.

"I said you may not go" Tigre yelled at him from an inch away!

In one deft move Tad swept and flipped Tigre on to his back. He had him so at his mercy that Bing gasped. The Tiguns were not a physical race, they did not learn or practice any form of physical combat. Yet, Tad who was tiny even by the Tigun scale which was fifty percent the size of a human scale; had just very professionally taken his larger sibling down.

"I am not asking your permission brother, my rank is equal if not superior to your own, and I will not be mistreated. I know you are worried for my well being, but these fine people are risking all for us as well as themselves. We did not go to them just to save them from invasion; we went to them because they would fight no matter the cost to defend their planet and possibly our own if we can strike an agreement. That all will have to wait, right now I am going to help lady Victoria and Tana take down our enemy, if they fail then it will not be because I failed them" Tad said in a final tone to brook no argument.

"Where did you learn to fight" Bing asked?

"Sect, Chad and Erik have been kind enough to teach me some simple combat training. I am no match for them or a Korv but against one of our people I am capable enough" Tad explained.

Three hours later Tad had the Shuttle in good repair and outfitted with the extra goodies he wanted to install. It looked more like a gun ship than a simple transport, Erik approved. Victoria spent the time in Tana's embrace because this was for all purposes a suicide mission, they both knew it. Victoria kissed all three babies goodbye and Mya, Ruby, Lee as well. Victoria looked every bit the dark queen as she put her armor on and grab a set of short knives that Tana had never seen before. Victoria strapped them to her thighs. Victoria produced a small cross bow that she cradled in her arm.

"I am not a stranger to war and battle my love, I will return to you if I can, but I will do no less than Will would if he were in my place. My clan is called Elite for a reason Tana, and it is a well earned name. I am the only equal you have with a blade as far as women go, even Will and Navar would smart if they tried your sword arm. I will not waste my life and loose the love I have found easily Little Tana. If I do not return, know that I have never loved anyone like I love you and Will" Victoria said in a husky voice that held the promise of tears.

The regal Victoria turned her back and walked down the causeway with tears raining down her fine featured face. The Elite guard fell in step with her and there was no sound, not even foot steps.

(On the Black planet)

Gwen led the band into the foot hills where trees grew at odd intervals but in a steady way as if the pattern was man made. She moved marginally farther ahead than she would have normally but she saw something move and she wanted to get a look at it before she dropped back to report to Jay what lay ahead. Gwen could smell a strange scent, it was elusive, but she was sure she knew it. Kadi came out of the trees to her right and reach out and took her hand. They continued to walk holding hands in silence. Kadi could smell it as well and sniffed the air every so often to make sure it was still there. The beautiful female vampires pulled up and waited for the main body to catch up to them.

"What is that smell Kadi, can you make it out. It is driving me mad, I am sure I know it but I can't pull it out for some reason" Gwen said as she breathed deeply?

Kadi put her arm around her smaller mate and pulled her gently into her other arm. Gwen leaned back into Kadi. How strange it was though Gwen to love not one but three people and two babies as well in such a short period of time. How strange it all is, she was a human doctor in the Aussie air force, only three months ago. Now she was a super human immortal vampire. She used to be so painfully shy, that she did not even have a boyfriend, now she had a husband and two wives and a baby, and she was not shy about anything, if anything she was very forward and playful now. It was easy to think it was all as it should be with Kadi's muscular body pressed against her. Gwen wanted to find Navar so bad her heart threatened to burst from her chest at times. Kadi who was once a confirmed girls only gal, probably loved their husband even more than she did, if it were possible, which Gwen doubted, her love for him was intoxicating, like a drug or air. Without him she could not live. Further, when she thought that Mya was lost, her heart nearly broke and killed her from despair, Kadi felt the same way, especially since it was Mya that brought Kadi to their bed and their hearts.

"Penny for your thoughts Gwen" Kadi said?

"Oh I was just thinking how strange life is, I was so shy, but now I am a little horn-dog, I was seriously hetero, now I could not imagine being without you and Mya in our bed. I love you, you know" Gwen answered.

"I know. I love you too. We have to find our boy soon; I am getting jumpy without his calming touch. I never knew what a man could do to me if I just let them in" Kadi said.

"Navar is not just any man; he is special just like Will is. Ask Mya sometime, she has had human and Vampire lovers, she will tell you how much more exceptional Navar is to everyone else" Gwen said.

"She has, but since Navar is my only male lover it is hard to say. I love him no matter and don't want to experience any other man. I know Navar is your only lover as well, except us girls, so I guess we lucked out the first roll of the dice" Kadi laughed.

The wind changed and they could smell the rangers running up to their position, Jay was practically walking just to stay behind them. The rangers were a superb group, they were wiped out and not one of them mentioned it in any shape way or form. They just sucked it up and marched on. You could see the respect on Jay's face at the effort the human's were making; they did not want to be an anchor to the knights. Jay stopped and smelled the air, he pulled his sword and his eyes moved from side to side as he sniffed the air.

"Damn I wish the brothers were here, Aaron could tell me what that scent is and Ian could track it instantly" Jay said.

"You look like you're ready to fight" Gwen said?

"That scent was all over the battle scene back there, where we helped the dark ones after they were ambushed. We won't be waiting long to find them the scent it is getting stronger and it is coming to us now instead of away. Be ready ladies" Jay said grimly.

Jay ordered Gamon and the rangers to circle up and rest back to back. He did not have to ask twice, four of the tough rangers fell asleep the moment they settled to the ground. They were all exhausted. Gamon was the exception; he seemed to be fresh and alert. Jay was curious about how that was possible, no human could go at the pace they had been without being totally spent. Jay was about to take a closer look at Gamon when the trees erupted.

"Look out we are under attack" Kadi yelled.

A single Korv came out of the trees impossibly fast and attacked the rangers before they could even get up. Kadi snapped her short sword into the path of the Korv. The abnormal sized Korv slowed and would have stopped but Gwen cut one of it right arms off and pressed the attack. Kadi took the lower left off in the next breath. A huge beast shot out of the trees and knocked Kadi down, it had its teeth near her throat when Jay grabbed it by the back leg and body slammed it into the ground. Jay was about to run in through with his monster sword when the Korv back handed him away from the beast.

"Die monster" Gwen screamed.

The tiny red headed vampire was a streak of fire as her blade went right up the chest of the Korv. Kadi went down the back. But they both jumped back when their sword hit something hard and did not penetrate the Korv's insides. The skin fell away slowly to show the angry face of the being inside.

The giant beast lunged at Jay and was grabbed out of the air by the Korv.

"No, they are not your enemy" The Korv said in English.

The hide fell all the way off and Kadi was moving before it hit the ground. She was in the arms of the person she had just been fighting. Gwen was caught off guard. When Kadi began to cry, Gwen thought she was hurt, but when Jay sheathed his sword Gwen realized what had happened.

"Come here Gwen" A familiar voice called.

"OH MY GOD" Gwen yelled as she tackled both Kadi and the other person to the ground.

The rangers gathered round but Jay made sure they did not get to close. The Giant predator sat back on his haunches and watched the show with some interest. Jay was cautious of the huge tiger-wolf, be also curious. It was the biggest animal he had ever seen, and there was intelligence in it's dark eyes.

"What the hell is the matter with the blood suckers, why are they so upset about killing a Korv suddenly" A ranger asked.

The girls finally got off of the supine figure on the ground. When he stood up they understood fully why the vampire babes went wild. There standing between them was the crimson eyed prince of the vampires, Navar. He had moved around on the surface by wearing a Korv hide and he gained a monster companion to boot.

"So father sent you to find me. My heart is glad. We should find some water and bathe and them sup together and compare notes" Navar said as he held his mates close to him.

"Was that an order or what? Who is in charge now" A ranger asked?

"He is the crown prince, his word is law, his orders our duty, we follow Navar now" Jay answered.

"Great".

Navar turned and ruffled the fur on the base of the guardian's neck; and it looked into his eyes. They nodded at each other, and then Navar spoke out loud.

"Water my powerful friend, take me there" Navar said.

The giant monster predator got up and walked over to Jay and looked at him hard, and then smelled him thoroughly. The guardian jumped passed him and made for the low lands off to the east.

"On your feet, follow that monster" Gamon roared as he sprinted off after it.

Navar hung back; he held Kadi and Gwen back as well. He kissed and fondled each of them in a most private way. They were much faster than the others; so catching up would be child's play for them. Kadi had oyster tears on her vibrant face, she could barely let go of Navar to give Gwen enough room to snuggled up to him.

"When I am washed I want to greet you as my adored mates. I want news of our babies and Mya" Navar said softly as he kissed them vigorously.

They caught up in less then a minute, Jay was not surprised but the rangers were. The guardian led them straight to a river eddy where they could rest, bathe and sleep in safety. The giant beast sat looking out into the wilds with it's massive back to the humans.

"He is standing vigil for us, don't waste his efforts worrying about him, the Korv are his enemy as well as ours, as long as you don't shoot at him or attack him you won't be killed. Respect his space. If he begins to growl be ready to fight" Navar explained.

Navar removed his weapons and clothing, placed them on a rock and slipped into the water nude. Kadi and Gwen did the same thing; it was hard on the human rangers to see such gorgeous naked bodies prancing around like that. Gamon was down to his underwear when a female ranger stopped him.

"Sir, what are you doing" She asked?

"I am going to wash and change my clothing, and so are all of you. This is no time to be shy people, we eat shoot, kill and sleep together, why not bathe together. All of you are in good shape, show off what you got" Gamon answered her.

The female ranger stripped off her clothing and reached out and took Gamon's hand. He looked at her and was startled. Her body was just as fine as Kadi's and she was looking at him with unmistakable desire. Gamon fed that desire by picking her up and walking into the river, before they began to enjoy each other's bodies the girl spoke.

"If I might die at anytime, Gamon, I want it to be with the memory that I had your arms around me and your body in mine. I have tried to let you know how I felt about you, but you seemed to not see me or hear what I was trying to tell you. So just this once; love me like you mean it, just a man and a woman nothing more" Lory said.

"Lory I have been foolish, you're just what I have always needed, a kind, beautiful, intelligent woman to love. I will make it up to you...starting now" Gamon said as he pressed his lips to her breast.

The rest of the rangers jumped into the water and washed. Some of them pair off and made love, some of them were in threes and fours. Two just redressed and stood guard next to the guardian.

Gamon rolled a blanket out and made love with all of his person to Lory. He was not forceful, but physically attentive to how her body reacted to his. He realized when their lips were pressed together and their tongues were lightly brushing that Lory was what he wanted more than his next breath. Her touch and taste set him on fire. Her goddess like body was flexible and strong and she gave back more pleasure then she took. Lory whispered in Gamon's ear that she loved him and he knew his heart had found a home in her hands, so he whispered back to her as he rolled her on her back and entered her body.

"If we live through this war, I am going to ask Kadi to turn both us, so I never have to be without your love" Gamy replied.

Lory moaned and giggled at the same, she was enjoying Gamon's show of affection and show of erection as well. When they had both spent themselves on each other, they lay there holding close to each other and were startled when Navar's face was over theirs.

"Come with me you two" Navar said.

They got up and followed the still nude prince to a pool on the edge of the eddy. Navar slipped in and reach out and lifted both humans into the water. They looked at the three lovely vampires and were surprised to see Gwen suckling Kadi's breast. Navar smiled at them.

"I heard your declaration of love and commitment, I will grant you entry into our Garrett clan as long as you swear loyalty to us. You should know the penalty of betrayal in death. I can't turn you yet, it takes days for the vampires kiss to change you fully, however, if you take some of our blood, it will make you superhuman and less likely to be killed until you can be turned. Do you except" Navar said smiling?

"Yes, we accept" Lory answered for both of them.

"Kadi do it" Navar said.

Kadi pulled out Navar's dagger and cut her breast above the nipple, she came over and sat on Gamon's laps and put her breast in his mouth. Lory looked amused not mad. Gamon's eyes changed to super light blue as the blood took hold of him. Kadi seemed to be enjoying this, but she stopped Gamon.

"My blood no longer flows Gamy, so you're just sucking on me now for the fun of it" Kadi said.

"What about me, what do I have to suck to get the job done" Lory asked looking at Navar's equipment?

"I had Kadi help Gamon out because I know he always liked her. I don't want to embarrass you so how would you like to receive your blood sample" Navar asked?

"If Gamon can have his from her breast them I want mine from your manhood, I will suck the blood from there" Lory said firmly

"Gamon are you okay with that" Kadi asked?

"I can't complain after all I enjoyed my blood sample" Gamon chuckled.

Navar stood and leaned against a rock; he pulled Lory close to him and then made a small cut on the end of his tool. Lory set right on it, she sucked all the blood off and pleasure Navar in the process, her eyes were closed and she went to town. Unlike Kadi; Navar never stopped her, until he came. Lory only smiled at him slyly. Her eyes were even paler than Gamon's.

"He is a pure source, so his blood is more powerful than ours" Gwen explained.

Gamon was not listening he pulled Lory on to his lap and the love fest began again. Navar was making up for lost time with Gwen who was on his lap, Kadi was kissing Gwen while Gwen rode Navar. The small valley where they bivouacked was experiencing a great deal of good karma and love for a few hours. Vampires believe that if you're sexually satisfied then you can focus on work, war, or any task at your best.

"Jay, this is Will. Find my son now and join me, Grom has been captured by the Korv and we must rescue him" Will said over the com.

"Hey brother, Navar is with us, where are you currently" Jay asked?

"We are Southeast of you, down in the forest area" Will answered. "Tell my son to pull up his pants and let those vixens be".

(Laughter over the com)

"That is a good guess Will" Jay answered with a chuckle.

"That was not a guess, I know him and them well enough to know they were probably naked before they even finished with hello" Will said.

Jay filled Navar in, but he refused to leave until he had properly loved his hungry mates. Gamon and Lory were enjoying being near the Garrett's. Lory had her breast fondled and sucked by both Gwen and Kadi, and they kissed her while Gamon took her from behind. Gamon never touched the girls and Navar never touched Lory, although Lory looked like she wanted to give Navar a tumble. Navar noticed and decide that if his wives wanted to have Lory join them in the future he would couple with her, but only if his mates wanted to, he had no desire for anyone but his three goddesses.

(On the stealth shuttle).

Erik had taken charge of the mission because Victoria was heart sick at the thought of never seeing Will and Tana again. Erik brought twenty marines with him to guard the shuttle when they vampires ransacked the ship. All the humans were armed with two P90 rifles and enough ammo to start world war three. Erik trained them in dirty hand to hand Killing techniques as well, so the Korv would be at a disadvantage in the close corridors if a fight broke out.

The stealth shuttle landed and opened up in the Korv starship with no shots fired. It was almost too easy. Erik and the elite guard flew into the Korv ship and explored the halls and hatches, they found no Korv. Erik returned and ordered the marines to defensive position around the ship and down the corridors. Victoria was alert and dangerous looking as soon as Erik said it was time to hunt. Victoria pulled her cross bow out and loaded it with special arrows, she walked down the line of her clan, she gave a silent nod and they went to speed. The marines hunkered down and waited for the inevitable fire fight that would come and the horrible deaths they imagined were in store for them. Nevertheless, not a single one looked scared, they were at peace with their choice and so they embraced their destinies.

The sounds of Korv chatter over the ship com were hard to decipher the origins from. They were speaking of torture and weapons. Victoria and Erik shadowed the walls on opposite side of the halls, so if they had to fight it would be from two fronts. They had fought this way for two hundred years. Erik was a quiet combatant, he would be on you blades flying before you knew to defend your self.

"The weird thing wont tell Derko what he wants to know, how foolish" Laughed a Korv guard.

Erik stopped everyone with a sharp gesture from his hand. He looked into the corridor, and then slipped in alone. There were only a few strangled gurgles but nothing more. Erik returned dripping blood, not his. He led the way passed five headless Korv, into a side pathway. There was a hum of machinery and voices.

Victoria led to the hatchway, where she dropped down and peered through the slightly a jar door. Strapped to a science table was a dark one and he was being dissected. The dark one was alive, but barely. Victoria could not see them because the Korv scientist was in the way. A huge military officer was speaking.

"Why does the weak little creature not scream or show pain, and how is it still living after all we have done to it. Does it have no pain center in it brain. Why does it not speak or beg or something, did you break it before we could learn from it how to defeat it's people" Derko screamed in frustration!

The Korv moved to the other side of the room and Victoria was shocked to see Grom on the table, his weak head was covered in blood, and he sniffed once feebly, his face turned and looked right at Victoria. He mouthed the words leave me and run. Victoria mouthed the word never.

Victoria touched Erik's arm three times on his right arm, and twice on the left. That meant there were three Korv on the right side of the door, and two off to the left. Erik Understood, on the count of three they went in fast and hard. Victoria's ten arrow crossbow dropped one Korv on the right and one on the left in less than one second, Erik behead the other two on the right almost instantly. The remaining Korv on the left was Derko and he went through a hidden door and set off the alarm. The once clear corridors were filled with Korv sentinels in moments. Erik made a gesture and the elite guard went to work killing the Korv.

"Let's get Grom off that damn table and to the shuttle pronto" Victoria said in a grim tone.

"Leave...me...run...save...yourself" Grom managed.

"Never, you're family Grom and we will not leave you to these lizards" Erik snarled as he ripped the table restraint to shreds.

There were screams of pain and death in the hall. There was the sound of blasts as well, her knights used no guns.

"Muther fuker" Came the voice of a marine.

A chain gun ripped off five hundred rounds down the hall.

"Move your blood sucking asses, or stay here and die" The Gunny yelled as his chain gun burped another volley into the Korv.

Victoria grabbed a blanket like roll of cloth and wrapped it hastily around Grom's broke body and the cradled him in her arms and went for the door. Erik was at the hatch looking out at the melee in progress. The Korv were using some kind of powerful rifle that shot bolts of pure energy concentrated into violent projectiles. The bolts were punching holes in the elite guard. Vampires are tough but can't last forever against that kind of fire power.

"I will draw their fire Victoria and you run for it with Grom, get back to the shuttle and give the hell out of here. I will deal with the Korv and take the ship down. The marines brought C4 with them for just that purpose" Erik said with a little smile.

"No you take..." Victoria started to say.

"DAMN IT, don't argue with me. Look, I love you and I always have. You are bonded to Will and Tana the most powerful of all of us; I can never compete with that. Let me save you and Grom and perform my office till the very end" Erik said holding out his hand for Victoria's crossbow.

The brave vampire knight known by many as Erik the fair, or Erik the silent, took the crossbow in his left hand and pulled his short sword from the small of his back with his right and opened the hatchway. The Korv were arrogant, they did not entertain any possible defeat, that one factoid would prove a fatal error. Erik ran across the corridor, up the wall across the roof and down the other side all while sending deadly crossbow bolts into the eyes of the unsuspecting Korv. When the Crossbow was spent of arrows, Erik simply tossed it behind him where Victoria was waiting to retrieve it and pulled his other blade. Erik was among the fastest fighters who ever lived; he could make cuts even against Valor who helped to train him, which is really saying something. Erik went to speed. (The term going to speed means, he went from human fast to a blur, such violent acceleration that the eye can not track the movements. Only immortals can do this without coming apart).

The Korv had their sights on Erik and were about to riddle him with bolts from their dangerous weapons when he disappeared. They paused to look around. That was the last thing they ever did before their heads were removed form their shoulders and blood sprayed the walls. Out of the thirty odd Korv sentinels who were jammed into the corridor trying desperately to kill Erik and the Marines, only one lived and he ran for it, early on in the battle.

"Go now Victoria, the way is clear temporarily" Erik shouted.

The marines opened like the Red sea as Victoria ran into them, they closed like a bear trap after she went by, chain guns at the ready. Erik backed away from the dead Korv watching for ambush. There was none. However, there was a new battle starting up near the shuttle. Erik turned and ran up the wall and along it like a spider and came down agilely in the front of the marine company still running.

"Damn, I am so glad everyday that they are on our side" The Gunny said gruffly as they made to follow Erik.

The scene near the shuttle bay was a massacre. There were marines in pieces all over the place; several knights were torn to pieces as well. Victoria sent half of her thigh blades flying into the throats of the Korv attackers, killing every single one of them. It made little difference, there seemed to be row after row of Korv coming in to take the dead sentinels places. Erik came to Victoria's side, a bolt hit him squarely in the body, and Erik just ignored it.

"Gunny take them down" Erik ordered!

"With pleasure chief" Larsen said.

The sound of four chain guns spinning up dominated the area. The first belch of the guns sent the first four rows of the Korv to the Promised Land. The marines cut down everything in front of the chain guns, when one of the marines was shot down a vampire knight jerk him on to his feet, supported his weight and told him to continue while the vampire carried him. The Elite guard and the marines work in perfect harmony like than all the way the shuttle. The Korv had more powerful weapons, but when four mini guns are send thousands of rounds down the corridor, there is only one way to live...don't be in front of that. The Korv retreated, but to where Erik couldn't say.

"Oh my God it is you finally. Can we get the hell out of here now" A marine asked?

"No, we can not. We must disable the ship or steer it into the other ship and destroy both of them" Tad answered.

"Where do we place the C4 Tad to make the entire ship blow" Gunny asked?

The tiny Tigun held up a computer stylus and showed where they were currently and where the C4 needed to be to do the job. It was suicide; the heart of the ship was crawling with Sentinels. Erik studied it for a few moments and then spoke.

"I will go alone, get on the shuttle and prepare to leave" Erik announced.

"Like Hell son. I am going with you" Gunny answered.

Erik hit the Gunny in the jaw so fast only Victoria saw him move. Larsen crumbled to the floor of the bay. None of the marines moved, they all knew Erik just save the gunnies life.

"Brave fool" Erik said.

Tad and the marine helped Erik load a back pack with explosives. Erik put on some of the marines body armor for a little more padding against attack. Victoria looked ill. Erik did not look at her; he bent himself to the task ahead. Erik was ready and was about to leave, when Victoria grabbed him and turned him to face her.

Before she could speak he had his arms around her holding her tight. He brought his face forward, Victoria thought he would kiss her, but he did not. He face slid cheek to cheek with hers.

"I am already dead, I was shot earlier and my inside are ruined, so don't mourn me. You have a life and love waiting for you Victoria back on the city ship, I have only you. Tell Mya I love her and my friends I went to my reward with my sword in my hand" Erik said as hot tears ran from his eyes onto Victoria's face.

VAMPIRE WARS

Erik kissed Victoria on the cheek and went to speed before she could hold him there. That was the last time anyone would see Erik.

"Get on the shuttle, we are leaving" Victoria demanded in a gasping voice!

The shuttle took off cloaked and they went around the starship shooting them up. Tad thought this would keep them busy so Erik could get to his destination alive. Victoria knew Erik would get there no matter what. But she took great pleasure shelling the bridge of the Korv ship to nothingness, and watching the Korv floating into space.

Erik was constantly fighting all the way to the center hub of the ship. When the ship started rocking, Erik knew Tad was trying his guns out on the Korv. It made Erik smile. Erik's armor was gone, his blood supply depleted and his life running out all over the place, he was already dead when he burst through the wall into the reactor room, he killed the two technicians and set the C4 up. The second to last duty Erik did was he sat down and pulled a candy bar from his marine vest and began to eat it. A few Korv came in and watched Erik chew with a bloody smile. The timer went off and the Korv ship imploded in a huge nova-like explosion. If not for the shields that Tad built the shuttle would have been atomized.

"So passes Erik the Fair, the best of us all, my best friend, a true hero" Victoria whispered as tear fell uninhibited from her violet eyes.

(On the Black planet below)

The dark sky was suddenly brilliant as if the sun came up. A thunderous sound shook the atmosphere. Will looked up and so did everyone else. Will could see Jay and Ogre make quick calculation against the heavens to ascertain if it was the city ship that had been blown up. Navar had his com to his mouth already.

"Tigre are you there" Navar asked?

"Affirmative" Tigre answered instantly.

"What the hell is going on up there, are you all ok or what" Navar asked?

"It is a long story, we are all just fine, and your families are safe prince" Bing answered this time.

The Tiguns explained everything that had happened, the mission Victoria undertook, the Korv ships in orbit and the explosion of one of them a few minutes ago. Bing also gave Navar directions to a huge underground installation off to the south. It was the Tiguns opinion that it was the main facility.

"Son, let's stomp the lizards into the grave and get off this planet and go home" Will said.

He was seconded by a chorus of human and vampire voices.

"We need to find my father and my brothers before it is too late" Sect said.

VAMPIRE WARS

SHANE

CHAPTER 13: FINISH THE JOB

When the shuttle dock on the city ship and the hatch opened, there were cheers of victory. When Victoria carried Grom out of the shuttle in her arms; Jana was there waiting to see if there was anyone in need of medical attention. There were more than a few in need of medical help. However, Grom's needs were the most grave so Jana took Grom right to surgery and yelled for blood, lots and lots of blood. Victoria handed Grom over without ado. Grom grabbed her hand feebly but firmly to get Victoria's attention.

"He...will...not...be...forgotten" Grom choked out.

"No, he will not" Victoria said.

The once dark queen walked to the shared quarters that Tana, Will and her occupied. She shed her arms and armor and went and stood naked under the water in the shower. Tana found her curled up in the shower crying. Victoria's violet eyes were rimmed with red and her lip was bleeding from her biting it. Tana pulled her to her feet and carried her to their big bed. She dried Victoria's long black hair and body, and then she put her lover to bed and curled up next to her and held her tight.

"Are you not needed elsewhere" Vicky asked in a rough voice from crying?

"Lee is in command at present and can managed just fine, you need me more than she does, I am heart sick at Erik's loss, Lee will tell Mya if you want" Tana said.

"No, I will do it, he was my best friend and second in command, I could not leave this to another" Victoria said as she buried her face in Tana's chest and cried softly again.

In the med-lab Grom had IV tubes in his arms legs and everywhere Jana could put them, all were pumping in blood. Jana picked bone fragments out of the dark clan lord's chest; the Korv had beaten him with something heavy to soften him up for interrogation. It did not work of-course, Grom was an assassin master, and there is nothing that could make him talk if he did not want to. Still, Jana was appalled at the amount of damage the tiny vampire took.

"I am going to set your bones Grom, it is going to hurt like a mother, and since your body rejects any kind of pain medication I can't help it. Are you ready" Jana asked.

The small broken vampire shook his head minutely.

(Crack, snap, crack).

All of Grom's bones were lined up again in the proper way. It was a good thing that vampires and humans had the same physiology because Grom was pretty messed up. It seemed to Jana that the dark lord should be healing faster than he was, point of fact he did not seem to be healing much at all. Jana decided to ask Ruby about it.

"Ruby I need you to come to the med lab" Jana said into her com.

"What do you need baby" Ruby said from behind Jana?

Jana could not get over the insane speed that vampires could move at. She would address it later. She grabbed Ruby's hand and walked her to Grom and pointed.

"What is this" Ruby asked in horror, actually stepping back and away.

"What is the matter" Jana asked panicked by Ruby's reaction?

Ruby never answered, she turned in a blur and was gone. Less than a minute later Tana and Mya were standing by the bed, Victoria was right behind them. They all looked at Grom with an odd expression.

"We need Aaron" Mya said.

"No, we do not. Tana give me your arm and your dagger please. Grom open your mouth huny" Victoria said.

Tana moved close to the bed, she handed her blade to Victoria. Grom's eyes were like glass, when Victoria cut Tana's arm below her elbow and let the blood drip into Grom's mouth. The dark lord's eyes cleared and he reach out for Tana's arm, but Victoria grabbed his arm and held it. The exotic violet eyes of her clan were glowing as if back lit. Grom was straining to reach for Tana, Victoria would not budge.

"The dark ones are voracious eaters, if his mouth gets on to your arm we might have to kill him to get him off again. They are not good where pure blood is introduced and your blood my love is like pure heroine to Grom, a drug he can not resist" Victoria explained.

"My Pardon Lady Victoria and My queen Tana" Grom said as he relaxed on his back and let his arm rest across his chest.

"Your pardon plea is not needed, you are a hero and will be honored as such Grom. Tana's blood will beat the chemical they put in your body to kill you" Victoria said. "You will be stronger and faster than you were before; the Blood of Garrett is in you now, cousin".

"I will endeavor to live up to this gift" Grom said proudly.

Jana looked confused; she turned to ask Ruby what that meant when Grom's eyes changed. There was a new crimson ring around his blue eyes. That crimson of the Garrett blood. Grom sat up and bowed his head to Tana and then to Victoria.

"You both saved my worthless life, I will never forget your kindness to my wretched soul" Grom said.

Tana's goddess face contorted in anger. She slapped Grom across the face hard. It startled the room.

"You are as important to this mission and more than that, you're my family Grom, even before my blood touched your lips. I would not see you die or any of your brothers based on your looks. I do not understand the wrong that has been done to you in the past little brother, but it exists here not at all. I will not stand for it" Tana said with an authority she rarely used. But she was queen and her word was the law.

Later in the quarters of Navar and his family Victoria sat down with Mya and explained the passing of her brother Erik. Mya slapped Victoria so hard across the face that Victoria hit the far wall.

"You left him to die" Mya screamed!

Victoria cried not from the impact of the blow but from the loss of Erik brought back sharply to her, she felt just like Mya. She did leave him to die and even though that was his wish, she would always feel the guilt of it on her soul. Victoria wailed in grief and it startled Mya, she had always seen Victoria as the strongest woman she had ever know. Even Tana with all her power did not seem equal to the dark queen's menace. Yet, here leaning against the wall was a Victoria torn apart by grief. Mya went over and put her arms around Victoria and together they mourned Erik's loss.

"I am sorry Victoria; that was unjust of me. Erik was his own man, no doubt this is the death he would have always chosen for himself." Mya cried with Victoria in her arms.

(On the Black planet)

Tigre called Will on his com and told him that Grom was found and he was resting well back on the city ship. The news made the dark clan roar with cheers and Sect shed a tear of relief, he loved his father and could not bear to loose him.

"Hey Chad, this is Bing. The toys you wanted are ready to go, I will send a shuttle to your location and drop them off" Bing said.

"Good, we will be sending some of the wounded back" Chad answered, as he looked at Will.

Will only winked at Chad. Navar smiled and big Ogre patted him on the head. Chad was well liked and his judgment was respected by all. Will did not have problems with his men or women giving orders, he would speak up if his disagreed with the order, but for the most part Will had an excellent war band, and that included the humans.

Navar had his giant beast companion hunted for meat for the humans, and during the night it guarded him while he slept with his mates. However, when Chad brought down his bunker busters, Navar had the guardian find the hidden entrance to the main facility. It took the tiger-wolf very little time to find it. Will was impressed and told Steven to rip the hatch open with his brute strength, because Ogre loved to use his massive might as often as he could. Steven put his hand on Will's shoulder and Jay's as well and looked behind them out into a clearing to the southwest. There were deep burn marks.

"Shit" Will said.

    The Korv had evacuated the lab and likely the planet. That meant they had to go find them, that Earth was not their next stop. They all knew right there and then; they were never going home. The Korv are everywhere out in the galaxy, breeding and killing more civilizations. The city ship would be moving on, hunting for more worlds to liberate.

"Blow up the Korv based please" The guardian said in perfect English.

"What the hell" Ogre said.

    Everyone looked at the monster beast, it sat on it hind quarters in front of Navar looking very serious. Navar reached up and scratch the big tiger-wolf under the chin.

"How long" Navar asked?

"It took me some time to understand your spoken word, I looked into your mind and saw how and what to learn form you. I have seen that your race is really two but one at the same time. That you're loyal and true and that you will hunt the four arms and stop them from destroying worlds. I am not the only one of my kind, but the others are hidden to protect them from the four arms. They will roam the land again once your people leave" the Guardian explained.

(Laughter)

"We thought this planet was barren, your people were just clever enough to avoid detection. My compliments my friend, well done" Navar said. "One day I will like to return here and hunt openly with you in the freedom of the wilds".

"You will be welcome my strange little friend with the red eyes" the guardian answered.

Five days passed and the dark ones and Chad blew up the labs all over the southwest plains. Meanwhile, Jay and Tad search the planet and moons for Korv ships. There were none, the Korv escaped in to the stars, leaving the labs on the planet striped of supplies and subjects. Will and Jay were afraid that they still had a few live Dark ones as prisoners and they would study them to find a way to kill the vampires more efficiently. Sect agreed but told them not to worry, if the Korv took the dark ones, they would be better off killing them, if they did not, it is likely the death toll would teach them a powerful lesson in caution.

The reunion party that took place on the sixth day when all city ship personnel were back on the ship again was an amazing display of friendship and good will. The food was off the hook, every different national food was represented at the potluck. Booze was also plentiful, yet there did not seem to be any drunkenness. Brad Franklin who had been recovering from the beating on the planet made the first speech.

"Ladies and gentlemen; or should I say brothers and sisters; we came out here to find a menace and stop it; well that job is not done yet sadly. However, when we started we were afraid of our vampire brothers, silly now. Some of us have joined the clans and fought hard. Some of our family members have been lost in this war, they will be missed. Some like the knight Erik the Fair sacrificed himself to save us all. I would be lying if I said I did not shed a tear at the news of such a valiant heroes passing. He is a symbol of the unswerving commitment we all share. We may never be able to wipe out the Korv, but they will smart at the very mention of our names" Brad yelled.

(Cheers).

"I want to thanks all of the brave men and women who searched and died to save me from the merciless clutch of the Korv. We must never fall under their heel, it is better to be put to the blade than to live as their food source. I will not rest until the Korv fear to pee on any planet, for fear we will be there to lop off their tool" Grom said softly.

(Cheers).

   Will and Tana sat with Victoria in the front of the feast in the main court yard area. Will got up and kissed both of his mates and then walked up to the microphone.

"I am proud to serve with all of you. I will mourn and grieve for all those who were lost. I will never stop until the Korv are afraid to pee for fear of loosing their junk" Will chuckle and looked at Grom.

"You are all my family; and we have pulled together as one to send the mighty cowards packing with their tails between their legs, but we are not done, no. So I make this offer now with the blessing of all the clan lords and General Franklin as well. We want to be able to bring you home to Earth some day and it would be likely passed some of your human life times. Here is my offer, I will let any human who want to be embraced in to a vampire clan do so. You will no longer age or be touched by decease; your body will be fit and strong. However, it is a permanent decision, it cannot be undone, and it must be a personal choice. There is another thing, your clan placement will be random. A note; Clan dark ones were born the way there are, if they embrace you, you will not shrink to their size or have your looks change to mirror theirs. They are a powerful clan with a great deal to offer; it would be an honor to join their brave clan" Will said.

The entire Dark clan stood and bowed to Will. He bowed right back, they had taken heavy losses and Grom himself was nearly slain. They needed new blood to fill their ranks.

Tana who had been running the ship stood and proclaimed a week of holiday for everyone to catch up with their mates or heal their wounds or just rest from the ordeal they had to endure. There was an ocean of cheers for the queen, whose beauty was matched by her constant loving ways, and good heart.

Navar spent the first full day playing with his babies to the chagrin of his women. He made it up to them in the next five days, where even the immortal strength of all three of them was tested greatly. Navar had never been so intense a lover before. It was obvious to the girls he had always held back, not sure how much to give. The four of them tossed all cause out the window and loved with everything they had and then some. Navar made love with Mya more than the other two because she was not on the planet with them and had been alone the entire time. Gwen and Kadi were only happy to let Mya, whom they both loved have her fair share of ecstasy.

Will and Tana pinned Victoria to their bed like a slave girl, they even tied her up and raped her at her request. They played cops and robbers, Doctor and every silly game that they could think of to add sex to. In the end they just held each other close and were thankful they were together and alive. Their deep love became even more profound.

Jay turned Jana first thing and he held her the entire time until she woke up. Once she focused on Jay they broke the bed and bent the shower walls. They laughed so hard and loved like a hurricane.

Steven and Ruby locked the whole world out and made love none stop gently for the entire time they did not pull their body apart to eat or sleep. Ruby told Steven her love could stand no less, than his entire soul and being and she would have died if he did not come home to her. She cried which startled Ogre, because Ruby was tougher than he was. Somehow as impossible as it seemed he had found the love had had always yearned for in tiny mean little Ruby.

Telsa made Garth more than glad he had put Salen to death. The shy girl lost all her restraint when she got Garth alone in her quarters. She told him he may be the lord and ruler of clan Golden, but she was his ruler from here on out. He was so lost in love, that he almost missed her teasing. It did not stop him from laughing and tickling Telsa in spite of it. Garth was really lost as a lover, it had been forever since he had a woman in his bed, that last time was as a human, and he was awkward then. Telsa understood Garth better than he thought, because she took over and showed him what she wanted and he happily gave over his heart and soul to her and everything else he had. Telsa and Garth had found perfect bliss for the first time in their long lives, together.

Rip was the exception; he had no regular mate to spend his time with. He was not lonely though; most of the un-bound females in his clan loved him and were more than happy to be his lover. He made love to a different girl everyday for the entire seven days. In the vampire world this is just good practice, not slutty. If a vampire gets to wound up they are dangerous, so having a good lover or a few keeps the vampire calm and thoughtful.

CHAPTER 14: NEW LIFE.

In the weeks that followed the entire crew and population of the city ship got into a groove. The Tiguns were grilled for the rest of the Korv story, since they obviously left out some key things, such as the Korv were intelligent, no not intelligent, nearly equal to the Tiguns, and at the least the same as the humans. It was not Tigre but Bing who explained the entire history of the Korv and the measures the Tiguns had taken to survive the larger violent Korv. Navar took over the overall military duties; he went to the meetings and made the big decisions.

Will was tired mentally; he had seen his people murdered or fall in the line of duty. He should have done more to keep them safe. The burden of guilt was not common among vampires. Will was in no way a normal vampire. He was faster, stronger, more thoughtful, and more skilled. He was a great king, he loved all of his charges and felt honor bound to protect them. There was no longer a single person on the ship that did not follow Will because they chose to. He inspired loyalty and comradeship. Further, both of his lovers were the toast of the ship. His son and daughter and their mates were loved and respected as well. In-fact, the entire Clan Garrett was held up as the standard that everyone measures themselves by. This was not encouraged, the Garrett's were not stuck up or aloof, they were down to earth and friendly, Ogre was crude, Ruby was as well; but they were respected because they would be the first into battle and the last out to make sure everyone else was safe before they were. Therefore, the Garrett's are the standard, for bravery, valor, and friendship.

Will was brought out of his funk by a sudden urgent thought. He ran down the grand stairs and across the main courtyard area, roughly the size of Time Square, and on to the Tigun ready room area. Will burst in and saw Tad and Bing with their heads together over a diagram.

"Gentlemen, I have a need I think you might be able to fill" Will said.

"How can we be of serve King" Bing asked.

"I wish to speak to my Grand Sire back on Earth, it is urgent" Will said.

The two Tiguns began speaking in their native tongue and Will could not follow it, he heard Tigre mentioned, but that was all. They turned and pointed at the console behind Will several times and then stopped and stared at Will.

"WHY" Tad asked in an almost angry voice?

"What do you mean why? He is my family, and I wish him to know we survived. I wish to know the state of our home world, I want to know if the Tiguns have helped build defenses or if they turned on Brian when we left" Will said as the fire entered his eyes.

The Tiguns were shaking in fear. Will's lips barely moved and every Tigun on the ship suddenly had a vampire guard next to them. Will thought it was weird that there was never even an attempt at communicating with Brian back on Earth. The Tiguns never spoke of it and Will was busy leading his people and keeping the peace so he had not thought about it until now. Rip and Jay were Will's shadow instantly as his lips moved. Every vampire on the entire ship was alert and ready when they heard Will's call to battle.

"How did you do that Will" Bing asked?

"Can you patch me through to Brian right now Bing" Will asked, ignoring Bing's question completely?

"Yes, of-course I can. It is child's play, come with me" Bing said.

"Tad come along" Jay said, hold his hand out toward the door.

Will followed the Tigun up to the com center. Bing jumped into a chair and began working the dials. In a few short minute a voice came on the speaker, it spoke Tigun. Bing answered and then he said Brian's name.

"This is Brian Garrett, who the hell is bothering me in a time like this" Brian said angrily.

"Oh piss off you old woman" Will said.

There was dead silence, and then a riot of laughter.

"OH MY GOD WILL YOUR ALIVE" Brian shouted!

"Why yes, quite alive thank you and so are the bulk of my war band" Will said pleasantly.

"We had given you up for lost or dead. Son, it has been a year and not a peep. Anyway, the Damn Korv found Earth and we have our hands full down here" Brian said.

"Do you need us, we can be there in a month or so if we must" Will asked?

"NO. I mean please seek out the Korv and destroy them out there; we will deal with the trash on this planet on our own. Valor will be pleased you are well and has Victoria given you any trouble" Brian asked?

Will did not know how to answer that since he loved Victoria, she was his second wife, a bound mate. Will decided to fill in Brian about a lot of things quickly so he started with other things.

"Rip is great, has my back. Garth now leads clan Golden, since Salen was beheaded for her crimes. Grom and Sect are training my human soldiers in the finer arts of stealth and assassinations. Navar has three mates and two babies; Lee is married with a daughter. And…Victoria is mine and Tana's mate" Will explained.

"What"?

"Which part" Will asked?

"Salen is dead? How did it happen" Brain asked?

"She refused a direct order from Tana to go to battle and then she tried to kill Tana with a super poison. She would have sacrificed her clan in a fruitless fight with us, so Garth her second in command killed her to prevent a war. Garth is a better leader and his people are loyal and true" Will explained.

"Tell me about Victoria" Brian said concerned?

"She almost immediately came to us; we have been inseparable since that time. She is everything we could have ever wanted in a mate. Tana and I love her. Why do you seem to be upset" Will asked?

"We were once linked it was no good for either of us. She is tricky Will watch it. I would not trust her" Brian said.

"I would appear there is at least one thing I am completely superior to you in. People, and lovers, I am successful in both. Vicky has my love and my back. She has stood with us from the beginning; she has shown nothing but love for us. I am not sure what was between you…" Will said?

Victoria answered for Brian.

"He was an arrogant asshole, for all of his power he could not open up to love me or anyone for that matter. The great Brian Garrett is a coward, to afraid of being hurt to let anyone in. Tana and you are the love I have always wanted, I will go to my death before giving either of you up. I love you, but only tried to love Brian. He did not measure up as a lover or a man" Vicky explained angrily.

"Damn" Jay said.

Victoria wrapped her arm around Will's waist and put her head on his shoulder, since she was taller than he was. Will reached his arm around behind him and cupping Victoria firm butt with his hand. She smiled.

"Yes. I do have an issue with trust, mankind is not as forthright as they should be, and Victoria was once the dark queen, a butcher and evil to the core. Therefore I could never trust her" Brian told Will.

"That is why you fail Brian, because you choose to see the worst in a person, where I choose to see the best. I love Vicky and so does Tana without reservations of any kind. That is why we have won her heart and her love" Will scolded Brian. "I did not call you to talk about my sex life. I called because the security of our race is at stake and I want to make damn sure we survive" Will finished?

"That is the question of the hour is it not. Our wee Tigun allies have provided us with safety shielding for the great population in remote areas. Meanwhile the armed forces and Vampire knights have met and defeated the Korv at every turn. Will be careful with the Tiguns, they are not telling us everything" Brian advised.

Will told Brian everything he knew, starting with the origins of the Korv, and how the Tiguns were their cousins literally. Will moved onto the fact the Korv had genius level commanders and scientists. Brian listened without breathing a word to interrupt. Will knew more than he did. Brian guessed that the Tiguns told his grandson more than he got because they trusted and adored the Will. He was correct; the Tiguns under Will's command were loyal to him.

"Will find the Korv and break them in half, we will hold the planet forever if we must so you have a home to return to. If you decide to never return than you will be missed" Brian told Will.

"Pappa, I think if I returned it would cause trouble, the Earth does not need to kings, and the prince and princess are amazing as well. Victoria and Tana the truest of queens, would never bend a knee to anyone but me, none of my knights or clans will ever bend a knee to you again if we should return. I am not saying this because it is my will, and I am not challenging your authority. It is simply a fact, I am king by your blood and deeds, and I have earned my right to rule among the clans that have come with me. They will not alter their loyalty to me even on pain of death. I would gladly go back to a quiet life and let you rule, but Navar would not give up his mantle as prince and military leader to follow your rule. Therefore it is best for now, for us to stay out here and chase the Korv down" Will explained.

"You are a good king to understand your people so well and the politics of the job. I agree with you conclusion my boy. Good hunting, I have to go now, call again soon, I miss you my heir" Brian said and then he was gone.

Everyone looked at Will to see what he was going to do. He noticed and smiled widely. Victoria put her second arm around his waist and held him tight.

"I am blessed to have such close friends. We will likely be away from home for years, maybe generations but I am content to spend that time with you all" Will said as he leaned his head around and kissed Victoria on the lips.

"What I want to know if why you Tiguns are acting so suspicious suddenly" Jay asked.

"Aye mate, me too. If we are not able to trust ya, then we should know why; and now please" Rip added.

(Throat cleared from behind them).

"Come with me please" Tigre announced.

They all followed the tiny alien to a room that Will had never seen, which on a ship this size is not a huge surprise. There was a gigantic screen and seats set up.

"Please have a seat" Tigre offered.

Rip looked around and was surprised to see every ranking member of the mission. Navar and his three mates, Lee and Chad, Tana, Garth and Telsa, Brad, Grom and Sect. Gamon and Lory were there as well, though Rip did not know why.

Tigre took a deep breath and exhaled hard like he was scared. He turned to Tana and spoke directly to her.

"We have been exploring in the universe for more than fifty thousand years. Your race has not been able to make it beyond your moon yet. This is not a bad thing; it just means you are young and not yet ready to take your place in the universe with the older races. There are many races out here in the universe, some are war-like; and some are scholars, but almost all hate and fear the meat eating Korv. The Korv have never met their match in combat until now" Tigre said.

"You used us, they were never going to the earth, and you led them there, to get us to fight your war for you, didn't you? My guess is we are not the first race you plied against the Korv, but we are the first one with any form of success" Navar asked sagely?

The Tiguns looked at each other and the despair was clear on the tiny faces with large sad eyes. Bing seemed to be the only one not ashamed.

"Yes, we did that. You must understand, we have fought those four armed cretins, for thousands of years, and as you guessed not alone. The other powerful races together with our own decided to give your people a try at making war on the Korv. Your planet is riddled with constant war; therefore you should be expert in this field. We did not know about Homo superior vamparis, they, you are more than we could have hoped for. You made the Korv flee; that has never happened in the history of the universe. I wanted to tell you this earlier, but our high counsel forbids us from telling you" Bing explained.

"Why tell us now" Chad asked his little friend?

"Your have fought and won, and you have treated us as friends and comrades, not as only technical support, but as allies. We can no longer hide our agenda from you without making you our enemy. You are too powerful of an ally to loose over some idiotic ideology; we will disclose everything but the location of our home world. Not even the Korv know that, and never must they learn of it" Bing

"Honestly, as we reported the progress of the mission, the high counsel has grown to fear you. They believe if you ever beat the Korv and wipe them all out, you will be the new scourge of the universe, a feeling we do not share" Tad explained.

"What if you judged us to be unable to handle the Korv or a scourge as they say, were you just going to space us all. We already found the interlocks on our quarters and jammed them, so you can't space us. Yes we knew, from the beginning you would betray us when we were no longer useful" Victoria said.

The Tiguns spoke softly among themselves.

"Lory what did are they saying" Chad asked?

The Tiguns stopped dead in their tracks in shock.

"They said we are far more intelligent and dangerous than they had previously thought, it might be a good idea to use the master over ride to release the inner locks from the top and bottom instead of the sides" Lory said.

The look on the Tiguns face was priceless. The look on Navar and Will's face was not. The Tiguns were terrified.

"We are not amused" Will said in a gruff voice.

"We have learned all there is to know about the ship behind your back Tigre, we don't trust you, you lied to us from the get go and we knew it. We also knew you would bring the damned Korv down on our heads if we didn't play along. We no longer need you to operate the ship, therefore I want you to give me one reason I should not toss every GODDAMNED ONE OF YOU LYING LITTLE BASTARDS OUT THE AIR LOCK" Will shouted in anger?

Will's lips moved and there was no sound, but the Tiguns knew that every one of their people were now prisoners. Will was not the problem; Tana was. She was the reason Will was so mad. Anything that threatened her was a death sentence, and the Tiguns were a threat. They had never been outsmarted before, the Tiguns arrogance was their undoing. The question was now how long they would live. They were shocked when Will smiled at them and so did everyone else in the room.

"You are not to be killed. Contrary to your opinion of us, we don't kill for no reason, and being prepared to deal with a powerful race like us is only good sense. We do not fault you for trying to be ready, just in case it all went wrong for you. We however want your sacred vow to never turn on us, not ever. If you take the oath, then you are free to live as you see fit, if not, then you must leave the ship immediately. If you take the oath and then betray us, we will kill you without remorse just like we would the Korv. So it is for each of you to decide, stay or go. Allies or enemies" Tana explained.

"It will take time to decide this" Tigre said.

"No, that is bullshit Tigre. We all know that we want to be here and help them beat the Korv, never have we had such a host before as this, they are smart and fun, they respect us, they catch us plotting against them and still they give us a chance to live. I stay. They can have whatever oath they want from me, I am with them until we win or I am dead" Bing said in a huff.

"As am I" Tad added.

Tigre was at a loss, he was ordered by his superiors to make sure they could stop the humans if they got out of control, but his heart and mind knew what they had done was wrong and deceitful. The Vampire and human's had never attacked or treated the Tiguns with anything less than thanks and respect. Tigre made up his mind right then.

"I swear on the life giver that I will serve and protect the ship and it's entire company so long as I shall live" Tigre pledged.

"Sold" Will said. "Here is my oath my small friend. I swear on the lives of my entire family, that we will never attack or turn on the Tiguns in anyway so long as they do not attack us. We are allies until the Korv menace is eradicated or we are all dead. But our friendship need never to tested again, agreed" Will expanded?

"Whole heartedly Will" Tigre said as he shook Will's hand.

Will whispered and all the Tigun were asked to line up and give an oath of service, or board the shuttle for their home world. Not a single Tigun left the ship; every single one of them gave an oath willingly. They all said the same exact thing; they wanted to be part of the company who took down the Korv.

Hours later when that Tiguns were back to work and the crew went about their business, Gamon and Lory came to Will's common area (Court yard of sorts where only his clan gathered, it is private). Gamon asked to speak to Will. Evan called to Ian who was guarding the inner chamber door, to ask Aaron to inquire if Will would see a guest right now. The brothers took Will's family safety very seriously, too seriously for Will and Tana, but they were awfully good at it. Gamon was asked to come in. When the brothers presented Gamon and Lory to Will, they went back to guard the chamber doors.

"Gamon, Lory come sit, would you care for some green tea" Tana asked?

Lory looked embarrassed; because she was sure they all knew how her eyes go to be so light blue. Gamon on the other hand did not seem to mind the memory, he filed it under fair is fair. Anyway, Tana was smiling at them.

"Would you rather some blood" Tana asked and then giggled.

Lory's face turned purple with shame and Gamon snickered, because Lory decide how she wanted to get a blood jump start back on the planet, her method was quite erotic, but it had been her choice and there was no one to blame. Tana was suddenly sitting next to Lory and the human's never saw her move. Tana held Lory's face between her delicate hands and then kissed her on the lips softly but with zeal.

"Now calm yourself darling; we all have desires and if you turn and become one of us, you hunger and desires will be a thousand time more powerful than they are now. You may want many lovers, male and female, or only Gamon. He may want many lovers as well, but you will always be the core of the others love life, so try to enjoy the experience and never be embarrassed by it" Tana said.

"Now, what brings you two to our home" Will asked?

"We have a request King Will" Gamon said.

"No, no, just Will if you please, I am king, no need to point it out every five minutes. Please tell me what it is I can do for you" Will asked?

"I want to start by saying although we have been offered to join your mighty family as lower members of your house, we must decline temporarily. We want to ask Lady Victoria if we can have the honor of joining her clan. We are both good fighters and have special training, we would like to humbly offer ourselves to her" Gamon explained "It is to honor Erik's sacrifice".

Victoria was sleeping on the bed down the hall and heard the entire plea. She took a deep breath at the mention of Erik and got up and walked naked to the common area and sat on the table between Gamon and Lory. She reached down and ran her hands all over Lory's body.

"Stand child and strip" Vicky ordered.

Lory was embarrassed but she did as she was told, Victoria looked at her and then kissed her and her hands roamed her body.

Victoria looked at Gamon and motioned for him to strip also. Again Victoria felt all over his body as well. Gamon could not help but be turned on when she kissed him.

"What do you want more than anything right now, tell the truth" Vicky asked Gamon.

He simply looked at Lory and she at him. Victoria smiled.

"I accept both of you, you will take the place of my lost second in command, you will share the duties" Vicky announced.

"We don't know if we are fit to lead, we will be very new at this" Gamon replied?

"Do you question my judgment then" Vicky asked him?

"It is not that my lady, we just don't want to let you down or make a mistake that will cost our new family" Lory answered.

"I see, you're not afraid of command, only failure to measure up to my standards. I will help you along, as will the clan, and you will have Will's entire clan as well to support you" Victoria explained.

Then Victoria looked at Tana and Will. They winked at her and she smiled knowing they would do anything for her. How could Brian be so stupid and them so smart with the same blood running through their bodies. Victoria decided no matter what she could never let what Brian thought of her ever creep into their minds, she would fill their hearts with love in stead of suspicions.

"One additional thing; and it is something that only I know, but would disclose only to you four. Aaron and your brothers please either leave or do not listen to my words" Vicky said.

Aaron bowed and he and his two brothers left and sealed the chamber doors from the inside, so that no one could enter unless Will wished it. When the doors closed and sealed Victoria looked at Will and Tana.

"You know I am special, but you do not know why. I was once the black queen, with eyes to match. I was drunk with blood lust and blood. I killed and destroyed much in my time. I have changed, but I would have you know why I was like that. I am the first Vampire female who ever lived. Brian created me to be his companion and lover. He however was not pleased that I had a mind and will of my own and would not bend my knee to him. So he rejected me as broken and useless. It made me so mad that he scorned me because of my strength that I showed him what real strength was. Once along time, I was called the black queen and I ruled the know world, all who opposed me were destroyed or drank dry. My hatred of Brian made me both strong and weak at the same time. He came one day and stood before my throne and told me there could be no more. He was going to destroy my empire and me along with it. I saw what it was that made me worthwhile in that instant. I fought Brian to a stand still for three days, and then I tossed my blades at his feet and offered my life for my people's lives. This shocked him clearly. He granted my wish and then made me an offer. He asked me to assume the role of protector of all humanity; with himself and a few others, for this he would grant me back my life. I was tired of killing and power in general, so I agreed. But I have never bent my knee to that man and I never will. Brian's blood is in me as well, only my eyes are violet, the picture of my soul and spirit, where his are red like the fire burning in his soul and all of yours. This is the reason I can spar with Tana at full speed and not be killed, and the reason Brian could not beat me in combat. My clan and your Will are closer related than you ever knew. Now that you know my story, do you still want me" Victoria asked?

Will and Tana looked at each other, and then both walked forward and embraced Victoria firmly. She knew that their decision was love; not judgment. She was heart sick before she divulged her tale, but now her soul was finally free of the sadness she felt at keeper her secret for fear of loosing what she so desperately needed.

"Silly ass, we would never want to live without you. I love you" Tana said with little tears in her eyes. "How could you think anything else"?

"Truly, we love you my violet eyes goddess and we always will" Will added as he squeezed her.

That afternoon Victoria turned Gamon and Lory. She stayed with them the entire two days until they woke. They looked at her sitting between them, cradling their heads on her lovely legs and both of them sat up and kissed her with a passion neither ever knew they could muster. She thanked them for choosing her as their clan lord and then she took her leave so they could satisfy their overwhelming desires.

Brad Franklin was the only one of the human flag officers that wanted to be turned. All the other officers did not begrudge Brad his choice. Brad had cancer and had volunteered to take this mission because he was dying. When Baby Raz bit him six weeks ago, his pain and misery stopped suddenly, but it was beginning to return. If he received the kiss of the vampire he would live to do his duty until the mission was complete or they were all dead. The other officers thought he was correct in his decision to try to live. Therefore, Brad went to Will and asked to be embraced. Will called Rip and Garth to his office, well his corner of the common area where he had a big desk and a huge chair. Will rarely sat at the desk, but sometimes he liked to read or write, so he left the desk where it was in case he needed it. This was one of those times.

"Gentlemen I called you here to ask you if you would like to embrace Brad Franklin into your clans prospectively" Will asked.

"Oiy, Brad's a solid man and has the heart of a tiger, the Aussies would be honored to have you as part of our family Brad" Rip said.

"Telsa told me of Brad valor on the battle field, where he fought a giant Korv with a knife and an empty rifle, he had his ribs staved in and he still fought on. He is the kind of man I want to add to my clan Golden" Garth said.

"I too find Brad worthy, but I want one of you to acquire him as a new member, so I think a coin toss to decide it. That is unless Brad has a preference" Will asked?

"I am very fond of Telsa, she saved my life. But friendship alone should not decide this. I would be pleased to be part of either family. I have a question however that must be asked" Brad said.

"What is your question" Garth asked for the assembled group?

"I follow Will already as the absolute leader of the mission, but I am responsible as the general of the military to my soldiers, so if one of you embraces me, am I under your rule as well" Brad asked?

(Laughter).

"Brad, you will be your own man no matter what, your duties and rank will not disappear when your changed. You will be part of one of our families and subject to family ties, but you will have free will to do what your mind and heart tell you to do. Only Will, Tana and their children have the right to make any of us do a thing against our will" Rip explained.

"And I will not unless it is for the greater good give any such order ever. What makes us stronger than the Korv or even our brothers back on Earth is that we live as a family and friends, with a common goal to rule us. I look to each person to give all they can and no more. If you're doing your best for the mission and your clan, then you rule yourself Brad. Right boys" Will said.

VAMPIRE WARS

Both Rip and Garth shook their blond heads in agreement. Will tossed the coin and Rip called tails, and so it was that tails won the day and Brad became a member of clan Branagan, better known as clan Aussie, Pale blue eyes and all. Brad was a single man and had no mate, he was surprised when he woke to find his body was finely muscled and his hair was red again. That was pretty stellar by his reckoning, but the two naked vampire girls who were looking after him blew his mind. They treated Brad to the best loving he had ever had and then they announced that they were chosen to be his companions, they would teach him the use of blades, all about healing, how to manage the thirst and how to know another vampire is your enemy. They also told him that they wanted to be with him, it was not an order but a privilege. Brad was pretty happy as you might think, but he was startled when they showed him his own reflection in the mirror. Brad was fifty-one years old and the man in the mirror was maybe 25 if that. It was the face Brad wore as a young man and his body was stronger and his muscles more rigid than ever before. He was both happy and dismayed. It would be hard to assert his authority when he wore a face of a kid. Nonetheless, he was happier than he had been in a great long while. The omnipresent pain was gone, that was worth all of this. Brad decided that his new girlfriends should not go without his attention; so he poured his energy into his new favorite pastime, making love.

(Hours later in a war counsel).

Will sat at the head of the table, where all the leaders of the human military and the vampire clans were represented. The reason for this meeting was simple where do we go from here. Bing and Tad were there to lend their voice if asked, and Will would ask.

"Welcome everyone. We are here to discuss where to go from here. We need to continue to put the boot to the Korv but we need to know where they are to do that. The floor is open" Will said.

Brad stood and spoke first.

"Ladies and gents, despite my youthful appearance I am still the same man mentally. I think we should plot a course that extrapolates the most likely path the Korv would take, or have our Tiguns allies take us along the path of destruction the Korv have wrought" Brad suggested?

Most of the heads around the table saw the logic in this path of thinking and the course it should or would take.

"Nay, I believe we should think of it like this. The Korv are meat eaters, what is the closest planet with a meat source, for our hungry foes" Rip asked?

Bing and Tad pulled out a mini Tigun Stylus PC and went to town on it. They conferred and then Tad addressed the counsel.

"Basrtu, is the closest planet with a meat source as Rip says. There is a sizeable population of mid level intelligent beings, they will be slaughtered easily by the Korv" Tad said.

"Fine, I say we go there first and see if the cowards are there, then move on as necessary" Navar said.

"Objections" Will asked?

"Counter opinions, suggestions, and comments" Navar asked?

Not a single person had anything to add or offer, so Will changed the direction of the meeting.

"Good, Bing if you could set a course to Basrtu please? Now, I would like to talk about another issue. I have heard some scuttle butt about the clans stealing the militaries might away from them. This is not true. Any soldier, who is turned, will still be required to full fill their duties to the mission and their clan, as well as to their military command. If there is a dispute over the lines of jurisdiction, then we will handle it by committee if possible. If not I will decide the issue. We have never had a mission such as this, so new problems are bound to arise. I want those issues handled calmly and without blood shed, or ill feelings, since we are all we have out here in space" Will said.

"I have a question. When we none vampires die what are you going to do with us" A Colonel asked?

"Naval burial I should think" Garth answered. "Do you have another plan sir"?

"I was just curious" He said.

"We are vampires not Korv, we do not eat or recycle our people in anyway. Let your mind be at rest my friend, we will send you off like a king" Sect offered.

(Laughter).

"Okay, we needed that. Now let's get this tub moving and find the Korv and put the boot to them" Will finished.

There was a hail of agreements and then the meeting broke up for lunch and other tasks. The crew and war band as they took to calling themselves these days were all more calm and focused with a common goal once more. There was a feeling of anticipations in the air again, and it was a good one.

VAMPIRE WARS

CHAPTER 15: IMPOSSIBLE

In the months that followed the meeting that decide to continue on after the Korv, there was a renewed sense of zeal. Everyone seemed happy and focused.

There were less than fifty fully human personnel on the city ship. Most of the humans decided if they were going to live they better take every advantage they could and the kiss of the vampire was the fastest way to becoming better, stronger and faster. No amount of training could match or equal the upgrade to your body. The sex drive was easy for most, but hard for some others to deal with. The ships Pastor was one of those people. He came to Will and asked him if he could find a way to stop or slow down the adultery.

"Father James, we are different from you. Our view of adultery is different, our unions or bonds as we call it are no less strong and more committed actually since we don't die. There are a few married people on this ship and I have asked that they be left in peace to enjoy their own values. Has my order gone ignored then" Will said?

"No, not at all, they have not been bothered or touched in anyway" James answered.

"Then what is the issue that you feel I can help you with, James" Will asked?

"Will, your vampires are breaking the Ten Commandments" Pastor James stated.

"Really, we do not, lie, steal, and covet. We honor our God, mother and father, and so on. We only kill when we have to. However, our species needs to get out our vast energies through two forms of recreation, fighting and coupling. We can't get or give deceases and pregnancy is also not an issue" Will explained to the pastor.

James looked at him and thought for a moment and then conceded that Will was a good and just king. There was no rape or murder on the ship, and James had never heard of a single theft. It was said it you break the good neighbor rules Navar would kill you as an example. James did not hold with that, Navar was a gentleman like Will and James himself had baptized the wee babies of Navar and his mates. It was hard for James to try to adjust his thinking to the vampire community. He services were always full, vampires and humans attended. Will himself wore a cross around his neck.

"The best I think I could do James is ask that public nudity and sexual displays be frown upon. Since they are not breaking a law, and it is their right to couple, I can't interfere. I am sorry. You have an extremely hard job to do out here. I save lives, you save souls, so we are in this together. My job though dangerous is easier because it is mostly judgment and physical. You have to lead us and keep us on God's path; you are a blessing on this mission James, without you to remind us, we mighty become more savage and war like" Will said.

"I highly doubt you would ever let that happen, you are as good a leader as ever lived and you're a God fearing man" James said.

Will smiled.

"We are going to have a lot of dead in the coming years, so if you don't get embraced James your going to have to educate a chaplain for us once you pass on" Will said.

"I know, but who is there. It is not an easy thing to be a man of God, and not when we are at war and on a ship full of the most beautiful women and men you ever saw" James said.

"Why don't you settle down and find a mate, a mate that is only interested in your company James, and one that can give you a child" Will encourage?

"I will think about it" James promised.

"You're a young health man with a good mind and strong personality, you won't have to look far for a mate, you are a popular man among both the vampire ladies and human girls" Will said.

James smiled as he got up to leave the table he was sharing with Will, he Bowed which Will did not care for, but James felt it was Will's do and did not want to slight his friend.

Will spent the rest of the afternoon in weapons practice with the brothers. They worked like a machine when they fought together. They also did not hold back when they fought him like others did. All three brothers had served with Brian for many years and knew it was unlikely that they could even cut Will little alone kill him. Therefore they attacked like pack animals. Will loved it because they gave him no quarter. Will decide today to use the single two handed sword he was give by Brain to fight the trio, they could not get passed his guard, even with one less weapon.

"Let's try something different" Ian said.

The middle brother who was the most ruthless came directly at Will and Evan jabbed at Will from behind Ian's back as did Aaron. Will smiled when he felt two bites on his ribs from the attack, the brothers were not set in their ways, if they had to study you to beat you; they did and learn quickly. Will was also a quick learner. He jumped up and inverted upside down and stabbed Evan in the shoulder, and backhanded Aaron, as Ian turned he used his bracer to knock aside Will's sword and went to stab Will in the eyes. A brilliant move, and it would have injured or killed a lesser man, however Will was not a lesser man. Ian caught a forward kick in the gut that launched him into the wall. All three brothers were on their feet despite the injuries ready to attack again.

"Break. You boys are outstanding, I had to think about how to get around your guard and still if it were not for my enhanced blood abilities, you would have killed me" Will said with a big smile.

"If you carried your twins, we would never get near you" Evan said honestly.

"Perhaps but your bother pulled a card out of my deck of tricks and just about put my eye out, well done all of you. I appreciate the practice with you three, because I can't relax at all and still defend myself. If I were sparring with Navar and made a mistake his could do some serious damage, so I enjoy fighting with you" Will said.

"Our pleasure, you are our king" Aaron said.

"Yeah, about that? You are Brian's knights on loan to me, when we return to Earth one day how will you decide who to serve" Will asked.

He held up a hand before they could speak.

"All three of you had been the example of what a knight should be, I have no complaints. I could not have asked for three better men to guard my family" Will said.

As one all three brothers knelt in front of Will and laid their swords at his feet. Aaron and Ian looked at their youngest brother. Evan spoke for all three of them then.

"My sword and their swords will be drawn for you and your family forsaking all others, including good king Brian. He was a good master, but we were assets not people to him. You and your family treat us like friends and to some degree equals, though we are clear not. You are a fun king and you would never spend our lives like coins, you would give your life to prevent it; that is where you and Brian are different. Brian feels he is above all others; you don't, though you are above all others. In our estimation you are stronger than Brian is, in every way. We will never bend our knee to anyone but yourself, Tana and your off-spring" Evan said gravely.

All three brothers looked like they feared reprisal from Will for Evan's words. They were in no way ever going to recant them however. Their pledge of loyalty had been to Brian's house, never to the man himself, so they had broken no oath and they were free to choose their own master.

"Oh for God sake get off you knees. You're among the more powerful knights in all the clans; you don't bow to anyone unless it is an official function. We are here as friends, working on the improvement of our sword skills, not a lord and his lackeys" Will said with a grin. "By the way I accept your oath of service to my family, if I should fall please serve my wife or son or whoever takes my place".

"That is an easy promise to make master" Ian replied.

"I would tell you to stop that master shit, but I know you won't" Will snickered. "This seems like a good place to stop guys. I am going to go take a shower and hopefully Tana and Vicky are not busy" Will smiled.

The brother grinned as Will walked away. Will made it to his quarters; where Tana was organizing some schedules for the clan and there support troops. Will smiled at her and tossed his gear in the area where his armor went. It was magically cleaned in minutes by a Tiguns machine and it smelled like oranges when it was done. Will washed himself in the body wash that Tana liked. When he was done drying himself off he went over to where she was working on her stylus and lifted her on to his laps.

"Heeeeey Boy" Tana said.

Tana put the stylus on the bed side desk and sat up on Will's lap. His hand unbuttoned her leather vest and slid it off of her. Will leaned Tana back and massaged her breast gently with his hands, she closed her eyes, she loved it when he rubbed her the right way. Will's mouth was suddenly worrying her left breast, while his hand slid down and pulled her black silk thong off. Tana was so relaxed in Will's arms like she always was. Will had his power hands on her firm tan bottom; he laid her on her back and moved his mouth from her pert breast to her soft lips. They began to kiss in a slow burning passionate way. Tana lifted her hips and Will slid himself deep into her body, Tana sighed at the pleasant sensation. If she lived a thousand years she would never tire of the feel of Will's solid body against hers. They were totally consumed with their deep love. When round one was over; Will held Tana close to his chest and ran his hand down her nude back.

"I remember when you were to shy to wear a bikini at the beach, now you can walk naked through the ship and you are comfortable" Will said.

"I know, I am happy with myself and with you and Vicky as well, the two of you make me feel strong enough to not care what anyone else thinks" Tana said.

"You know the entire ship; male and female are in love with you except our own family. You are the hottest thing walking around these halls. And with Victoria walking with you, then it is a total tidal wave of lust that follows you. Most desire you, and all fear you little woman" Will said.

Tana did not answer she just crawled up and covered Will with her tiny body. He pulled the blanket over her and put his hands on her hips, she brought her lips back to his and looked into his crimson eyes. Tana said a dictionary with that one smoldering look. Tana closed her eyes; their body intertwined again and this time more vigorously than before. This was the first time they had been alone and making love since the first week on the city ship. They did not waste it talking. After a while they stopped; not because of exhaustion, but from longing for Victoria. Tana reached for her wrist com.

"Victoria come home now" Tana said.

Will smiled at her in an odd way.

"What are you mad; did you want to be alone with just me? Did I do the wrong thing" Tana asked quickly?

"Not at all baby, it is that I was just thinking that at this point, we have been making love for a few hours and it was great, but I wanted Vicky to be here as well, then you called her" Will said with a kiss in her cheek.

There was a rush of air as the chamber opened and a dark haired woman came in. It was not Victoria, it was Mya. She came and sat on the bed and began crying, she laid her head on Tana's chest and tears ran down between Tana's breasts. Mya curled up to Tana and sobbed. Victoria walked in and was momentarily surprise to see one of Navar's mates on the bed with her mates. And the child was crying, did they force sex on her; no that was absurd. Victoria walked over to the bed and ran her hand down Mya's spine.

"What troubles you child" Victoria asked.

Mya sat up and her lovely face was covered in tears. She tried without any success to calm herself.

"I am sick or worse. I don't want to die and leave Navar, Kadi and Gwen" Mya wailed.

Tana sat up and wrapped her arms around Mya. When the others were away fighting Mya and Tana had developed and very close friendship, they had face everything, Salen, the stupid marine that tried to take Lee, everything as friends.

Now her friend was hurting and she just wanted to make the hurt go away. This was her son's wife and as such was not only a friend but her daughter as well.

"Tell me why you think your dying" Victoria asked her in earnest.

"My stomach is hurting and I threw up blood, and I can not eat enough, I am starving. My tummy is swelling and my breasts are growing. I am a vampire, these things don't happened" Mya said. "I think Salen is taking revenge from the grave"!

Mya began to wail again, but Victoria was not about the let her mind slip away. So she shook Mya to get her attention.

"Strip child and lay on the bed" Victoria ordered.

Mya like all vampire females wore precious little in the way of clothing, but she had it off and was on her back in a second. Victoria ran her hands over Mya's body; she fondled her breast in a pleasant way. She did the same thing to her private places. Then Vicky tasted her breast and her lips. She stood up and smiled.

"You are not going to die, nor are you ill, just blessed I should think" Victoria said with a girlish giggle.

Victoria scooped up Mya and whispered in her ear what was up with her and Mya was shocked and then so happy that she kissed Victoria passionately for many long minutes. She stopped looking completely abashed.

"Sorry Lady Victoria, I should not have been so forward without your leave" May said.

"Little one, if I was not bonded to Tana and Will I would give you all the leave you desire, however it is your own mates that you need to be with now baby" Victoria said as she patted Mya's bare butt.

"Thank you" Mya said as she went to speed with her clothes in her hand.

Victoria said "I have a wonderful secret that I thought was a legend that I want to tell you two".

Will and Tana waited as Victoria crawled naked into bed with them. Whatever explanation was intended died on her lips as Will and Tana wrapped themselves around her hard body. Their desire for each other took paramount over anything else, and they made love as a complete set happily.

(In Navar's family quarters)

Gwen and Kadi were sitting on the floor with the babies playing with some amazing toys. Raz reach over and touched Aria's little chubby hand and both babies looked and Mya and smiled, and then they giggled. Gwen did not understand, she believed they were just happy to see her. That was not the case for the clairvoyant babies.

"Where is Navar" Mya asked?

"He is inspecting the tower guns of the west side of the ship, he should be back anytime. He said that he would have Ogre and Ruby take over the other inspection for today, after the tower guns were fully functional" Gwen said.

"Go my two loves and wash your bodies and shave yourselves, so that your bodies are soft to the touch everywhere" Mya said excited.

Gwen scooped up Raz and Aria in one deft move and placed them in their custom play structure, the little ones laughed with joy because they were usually being taken out of the structure not put in. Kadi already had the water to the right temperature and the scented rose soap they both like and Navar said made their goodies taste like spring. Quietly they agreed with him, having pleasured each other often enough to know the taste of their lovers bodies.

"Come to me little red riding hood" Kadi said to her small red headed mate.

Mya watched them lathering up each other's hot bodies and smiled. Kadi sat on the shower shelf seat and let Gwen who was a surgeon shave her pubic area expertly. Gwen finished and rinsed Kadi thoroughly, but she smiled and tasted Kadi's soft parts just to make sure they were soap free. Kadi giggled. She stood up and lifted Gwen on to the seat, she spread Gwen's leg and shaved her equally carefully, when she was done she licked Gwen until the tiny red hair beauty was out of breath.

"Just so you know how much I love you Gwen" Kadi said with a teasing laugh.

"I know; I love all of you too" Gwen said. "What do you think is up with Mya, she is acting kind of strange, but what is normal around here"?

Navar walked in and Mya took his hand and led him to the closet and hung up his armor and put the clothes in the wash. Mya stripped and took Navar to the shower and washed him all over, her mouth never left his. When Mya was satisfied that they were clean and heated up both she led Navar out of the shower and dried him lovingly. Gwen and Kadi sat on the bed and watched, Gwen sat in front and Kadi was leaned up against her back cupping her breast and rolling her nipples softly. Mya grabbed Navar suddenly and hurled him on the bed behind Kadi. Before Navar's back touched the bed, Mya's body was pressed to his.

"We are going to make love like we just met little boy and you two bitches are going to play along" Mya said with a huge sexy smile and a twinkle in her eye, they had never seen before.

"Your wish is our command mistress" Kadi said with a giggle.

"At your service love" Gwen said in her Aussie accent.

"Good, tie up the prisoner" Mya said.

"Hey don't I get a say" Navar said?

"NO" all three girls said at once, and then they laughed.

When the prince was tied up in silk robe belts that he could snap easily, Mya began. She told Kadi to blindfold Navar. When Navar was blind, she told Gwen to put her fresh shaven muffin in his mouth. Gwen did just that and the prince happily pleasured her with his tongue. Gwen's soft moans only made Navar much more excited.

"Kadi pleased pleasure the boy orally" Mya ordered her.

Kadi was only too happy to gently suckle her man, but Kadi made sure she backed off If he got too hot. Navar was shaking with the effort to control himself and his desire. Mya took Gwen's place when she came; Gwen traded places with Kadi and Navar shook harder still. Kadi massaged Gwen while she pleasure Navar. Mya came, so she sat Kadi on her boy's mouth. Gwen let Mya taste Navar, and Gwen brought her mouth up to Mya's breast and sucked softly on it.

"Here baby, make love to our prince" Mya said to Kadi.

Instantly Kadi switched directions; slid her body over Navar's tool and was moving her hip back and forth in a gentle rhythm, like waves tickling the shore. Mya kissed Gwen while putting her breast in Navar's mouth to suckle. Kadi came, and Gwen took her place on top of Navar. Gwen was like a gymnast, she was wiry and super flexible, she moved her tiny butt around in an impossible series of movements that made Navar's teeth snap together and his jaw lock, his stomach locked up. Gwen went wild and rode her boy like a mad cow girl. She came and rolled off Navar.

"Up boy, you're on top now. You girls suck my breasts. You came cum only after you make me cum Navar, understand" Mya ordered.

Mya was laid on her back; each girl kissed her passionately on the lips and then went to work on her lovely chest. Navar, who was by the time, insane with passion, very carefully entered her body and he controlled himself. He held Mya's knees up just below her breast and bent to his pleasurable task. It took forty-five minutes for Mya to finally cum, less than a minute later Navar who stomped on the sexual gas came like a mad man. All three of the girls wrapped themselves around Navar expertly so they were all locked on him and each-other at the same time. It was like a key and a lock, or a fine watch.

"That was great Mya, I love ya love" Gwen said as she ran her hand down and across Mya's tight bottom.

"It was the best, but what brought this on" Kadi asked?

Mya laughed softly as she could barely hold it in.

"Come on my little lover, what is up with all of this" Navar asked?

Mya took a deep breath and let is out softly. Mya kissed both of her wives; so softly it almost made them cry, it was so tender. Mya turned and looked at Navar with a sparkle in her exotic eyes.

"A miracle my family" Mya whispered.

"What kind of miracle baby" Kadi asked?

Mya was positively vibrating when she said the short sentence that was her heart's desire.

"I AM PREGNANT"!

VAMPIRE WARS

CHARACTERS

1) **Brian Garrett: crimson eyed vampire, the oldest of all vampire lords, ruler of the vampire world, has special powers and can't be killed by any know means. He is also the essence of justice and rightfulness. Red hair, 170lbs, 5'8**

2) **Will Garrett: the ancestor of Good king Brian, new vampire lord, also a good guy. Red-brown hair, slight pointed ears like a elf 150lbs, 5'7, Wears Red armor, has a two and half handed sword but prefers two short swords with gold and red hilts**

3) **Tana Garrett: wife of Will, mother of Navar and Lee, 4'10 100lbs, black hair, red tint eyes pacific islander, gorgeous, deadly, red female brief armor, and long curved daggers**

4) **Navar Garrett: Son of Will and Tana, quiet, rye, fast, loyal to only his parent, He is respected by both human and Vampire knights for his valor. 5'10 170 dark hair red hints, deep red eyes like water at midnight when a blood moon is up. 1.5 handed sword, two daggers**

5) **Lee Garrett: young daughter of Will and Tana, 5, 112lbs, wild sense of humor, pretty like her mother, can't have babies r/t abdominal wound, turned at 15, orange red eyes black hair. Carried a short sword and a dagger**

6) **Pepper Sorren Garrett: Lee and Chad's blond baby daughter.**

7) **Lady Victoria: Raven hair, white skin, 5'8 120lbs, violet eyes, clan leader of clan Elite, she is Will's friend and lover and Tana's as well. She is a fem fatal, but deadly to the extreme, her age is unknown, but her vengeance is well known. Black armor, and long sleek sword and dagger are her weapons**

8) **Chad Sorren : Human boyfriend of Lee Garrett, becomes her husband , Army ranger blond, blue eyes, 175lbs 6ft**

9) **MYA: Clan DeathKill Knight, Navar's lover and companion, black hair, blue eyes, Asian, she is Navar's mate, and she was remade in to the Garrett clan red eyes and all.**

10) **Gwen; Aussie, red hair green –orange eyes 5'2 105lbs, Raz's mom Navar mate Aussie AF Captain Doctor**

11) **Raz Garrett: Navar & Gwen son , red hair green eyes Born a vampire**

12) **Kadi: dark skin green eyes, short dark brown hair, Aria's mother, Navar's mate Army Special Forces LT,**

13) **Aria Garrett: dark skin green eyes with red , vampire baby of Kadi and Navar**

14) **Jay Har: Big black and full of life, Will's friend and his 1rst knight, Jay is not about to let anyone get to his friend and Lord, Jay's has amber eyes close to the clan lord's even Brian is not sure why. 3.5 hand sword and a dirk, not a good idea to fight Jay**

15) **Ruby: street fighter, 2ⁿᵈ vampire knight of Will's, she is 5'4, 115lbs, tan, long braided brown hair, bluer than blue eyes' red eyes after the embrace and a sweet person, until**

angry, Tana's friend. Medium length sleek sword as a weapon

16) Steven Ogre: scarred up giant, maximum security prisoner, 3rd knight Will created, Ogre is Hispanic. 7'5 452lbs, speaks little, loyal to Will and his knights, and Will's family, Ogre appointed himself bodyguard, His eyes are orange much like Lee. Four handed sword,

17) Aaron: oldest of the three Vampire knight brothers, red hair, pale blue eyes, 6'2 looking 5'11 120lbs 222lbs, quiet, loyal to Will, (all three brothers wear a sunrise on their armor and hilts of their blades in remembrance of their human mother) Heightened sense of smell and hearing. 2 handed sword and a dagger

18) Ian: 2nd brother of the three Vampire knights, red hair, pale blue eyes, 6' 195lbs, explosive temper, extreme loyalty to his brothers, Navar and Will. Special ability, omni-tracker, you can't hide from him. 2.5 handed sword

19) Evan: young brother of the three Vampire knight brothers, Loyal but disobedient to Will often, 5'10 185lbs, red-blond hair, lite blue-green eyes. Special ability to off balance or balance anything, he can find the weak spot in anything instantly. 2.5 hand sword

20) Valor: ageless Vampire lord, one of Brian's first Vampire knights, long black hair, near white pale blue eyes, elegant, 6' 185lbs, loyal to the Garrett clan. Will's friend and advisor.

21) Korv; lizard alien race, war mongers, carnivores, evil, vile. 7' or 8' tall, 600-800lbs, four arms, shark-like teeth, green skin, yellow eyes, Green brown armor, they carry lances

22) **Tiguns: small grey alien race, with big black eyes and vast technology, friendly to humanity, saved us from the Korv.**

23) **Isha Zu: Japanese ambassador, friend of Val and Brian.**

24) **Lady Salen Deathkill; clan leader**
Blue eyes, 5'7 105lbs, sword master, nympho, lover of Ogre and Will

24) **Erik: clan Elite Knight, Mya's brother, blond, blue eyes, super fast, deathly, loyal to only Mya and Lady Victoria**

25) **Garth: Salen's champion, 6'8 350 blond blue eyes. Broad sword**

26) **Rip Branagan: 6'5 250lbs, blue eyes, sandy blond hair, Will's advisor, and Clan Aussie leader. 3 handed sword and dirk**

27) **Jana Jones: black human girl, Doctor, 5'5 120lbs, USAF captain , Gwen's friend, Jays human lover. Later his mate and part of the Garrett clan**

28) **Brad Franklin; US army 4 star Gen, graying hair, 220 6', grey eyes, ranking officer of human military on the Tigun ship**
Gets turned by Rip

29) **Grom: Clan Dark ones leader, Hairless, 5'4 165lbs, super pale blue eyes, pointed ears like a bat, shark like teeth, very stealthy.**

30) Clan Dark ones: smaller than other clans size wise, stealthy, always in black, master assassins, ugly, paler blue eyes than any clan.

31) Sect: son of Grom or the dark ones, master killer, 4'5 120lbs, is called willow by his friends because he can bend in odd ways. Blue eyes young

32) Gamon Kirk (Gamy) captain Army Special Forces, Kadi's friend, brown hair, brown eyes, 5'10 180lbs, tough Victoria turns him into her new 2nd officer

33) Kurl: leader of the Korv on the black planet, four arms, 8' 650lbs, genius.

35) Telsa: female vampire clan Golden, Garth's mate, 5'4 105, deadly with throwing darts (Small points knives)

36) Bing: Tigun inventor, singer and all around smart ass, very close to Sect and Chad, and the babies

37) Tad: Tigun Mr. Fix it, smallest Tigun ever 2'6 47lbs quiet, very close to Bing and Raz, Aria.

38) Derko: Korv military 2nd in command, evil and ruthless, 7'8 650lbs, not smart, just mean.

39) Lory Simms: Brown hair, Carmel eyes, 5'5 115lbs, human, ranger, Gamon's lover.
She become Co-second in command for Clan Elite turned by Victoria

40) Gunny Larsen: human Marine Gunnery sergeant, 6'1 200lns, bald, scarred, loyal and tough as steel

41) Earth: planet home of the vampires and humans

42) Black Planet: Korv breeding planet.

43) BASRTU: next planet the Korv want to eat

ABOUT THE AUTHOR:

Shane was born Dec 21st, in Portland Oregon, to his mother Toffy Lee Wilson and Oscar Joel Wilson. He has an older sister Cookie Caroline Sinclair and a younger brother Curtis Casey Wilson.

Shane lives in Vancouver Washington with his Wife of over twenty years, Arlene; and he son Joston and his daughter Jessica Lee.

Shane races Quads and has won 14 over all championships. Joston has won two and Jessica has one title to her credit as well.

Shane has studied Martial art for nearly thirty years and has a 5th degree black belt in KAJUKENBO.

Shane loves to entertain people with his stories, so her beautiful wife bought him a laptop and told him to put them all to paper. It is Shane's goal to write a 100+ books and publish them all. At his current rate; he will reach his goal in under ten years time.

Shane offers this bit of advice:

"IF YOU THINK YOU CAN; THEN YOU ARE RIGHT. IF YOU THINK YOU CAN'T THEN YOU ARE ALSO RIGHT. THEREFORE, NEVER LET ANYTHING BEAT YOU!"

MY PERSON MANTRA IS:

I CAN BE BEAT, BECAUSE I WONT BE BEAT.

I MAY NOT ALWAYS WIN, BUT I NEVER LOOSE.

GOD BLESS YOU AND I LOVE YOU.